Turkish Delight

Tess Barnett

Cover Art by Lyndsay Simpson
www.lyndsaysimpson.com

His Princely Delicates
An Imprint of Corvid House Publishing
Fantasy and Science Fiction Gay Romance Novels

Pensacola, FL
http://www.hisprincelydelicates.com

ALSO BY TESS BARNETT

Tales of the Tuath Dé
Those Words I Dread
Because You Needed Me
To Keep You Near
It Ends With Us

Devil's Gamble

Domesticated: A Short Story Collection
In collaboration with Michelle Kay

Starbound

Left Undone

AS T.S. BARNETT

The Beast of Birmingham
Under the Devil's Wing
Into the Bear's Den
Down the Endless Road

The Left-Hand Path
Mentor
Runaway
Prodigy
Disciple
Apostate

A Soul's Worth

ACKNOWLEDGMENTS

Thanks to everyone who reads this really dumb idea of a book.
It was a lot of fun.

1

Everybody knew the house on Union Street. The story went that some kind of hermit lived there, or maybe a ghost. The lights would come on at night, but you could never see through the thick curtains in every window. Nobody ever went in, and nobody ever went out. It had been that way for as long as Jacob could remember.

And yet, here he was, driving the music store van on a delivery to that very address. He'd never even heard of Amy agreeing to make a delivery from the store before, but when a person orders six instruments at once and wants them delivered, you make it happen. Or you make Jacob make it happen, he guessed.

He pulled the van up the long driveway beyond the trees that hid the house from the street, parked behind a boxy silver Sentra that looked like its tires were about to melt into the pavement, and leaned over to the passenger window to get a look at the house. It definitely *looked* haunted. It was old, with black shingle siding up two stories and a wide covered porch with peeling columns. Even now, in the middle of the day, it was dead silent. Maybe Jacob would get lucky, and it really would be haunted.

But, more likely, it was some old hoarder, and the whole place would smell like cat pee.

He shoved open the van door and climbed out, grabbing the store tablet on his way, and climbed the creaky steps of the front porch. Even the wood surface of the deck had been painted black. It was like whoever lived here was *trying* to make the house seem haunted. Perfect for an old weirdo. Jacob reached out and pushed the doorbell button, but no sound came from inside. Of course it's broken. He lifted a fist and knocked instead. A few moments passed, and still no sign of life reached him, so he knocked again. Silence. Had whoever lived here finally made contact with humanity and then kicked the bucket before their delivery could arrive?

"Come on, man," Jacob muttered, and he banged on the door louder now.

The door moved as he was swinging for his last hit, so he faltered for a second as it swung fully open. A man was standing back from the doorway, one hand on the door knob and the other holding a book open near his face—and he was definitely not an old weirdo. He was young, Middle Eastern, and fit. Jacob could tell he was fit because he wasn't wearing a shirt—only a low-slung pair of cotton pajama pants that came very near to exposing the source of the thin trail of dark hair that crept up toward his belly button. He took a moment to give Jacob his attention, as though he wanted to finish reading his sentence before being interrupted. His warm black hair was a bit of a mess, and he looked out at Jacob with dark eyes and full lips without a trace of a smile.

Okay then. So a *hot* weirdo lived here.

"Uh. Good morning." Jacob remembered himself and raised the tablet to check the screen. "Are you Mr....Arzinjani? Sorry if I butchered that."

"It's fine," the man said evenly, soft and unperturbed. "Yes, I am." His eyes were on the tablet in Jacob's hands now instead of his face, which was a bit of a relief, if Jacob was honest.

"Cool. I've got your delivery from Amy's music?"

"Yes. Bring it in, please." He had an accent Jacob couldn't place—almost Eastern European, but weird. He backed away from the open door and disappeared beyond Jacob's line of sight.

He expected Jacob to just carry all this shit in himself. Okay then.

Jacob went back to the driveway and opened up the back of the van, dropping the tablet and taking up the handles of the guitar and violin cases. He carried them up to the house and hesitated just a second before crossing the threshold of his childhood haunted house. There were no lights on in the rooms beyond the entrance, and with their heavy curtains drawn, Jacob couldn't make out any details. The lights weren't even on in the living room, but at least the sunlight from the doorway made it possible to see.

He'd been half right about the inside—the guy definitely had some hoarder tendencies. The place didn't look dirty, but every flat surface was stacked with books—the coffee and end tables, the brick in front of the fireplace, the edges of the bottom steps leading upstairs. There were even a few piles on the floor, tucked up against the walls to leave walking space. Only the sofa near the center of the room wasn't completely covered, and even that had a couple of paperbacks wedged into the corner. The only sign that this was a place where someone lived and not a storage unit was a cell phone on the coffee table in between two stacks of books—an old Nokia. Jacob couldn't remember the last time he'd seen one of those.

He stood just inside the door for a second, awkwardly holding the instruments. "So just, uh...leave these here?"

The owner of the house was lurking by one of the far doorways, his eyes back on the book in his hand. "Yes, please," he answered without looking up.

Jacob stared at him for a few beats, then snorted softly and set the cases down in what little free space he could find in the living room. He made a few trips back and forth from the van, bringing in a mandolin, a sitar, a cello, and a lap harp, each piece settled carefully on the floor, and then he returned to the van one last time to take the tablet from where he'd left it in the back. By the time he made it back to the porch, the owner was in the doorway again with his hand on the knob.

"Well, I think that's it," Jacob said in his best retail voice. "Is everything accounted for?"

The man only briefly glanced over the cases, said, "Yes, thank you," and then shut the door in Jacob's face without even looking at him.

Jacob paused, frowning at the door. Then he knocked again.

When the door opened this time, the owner was staring at him, silent. It gave Jacob a bit of a chill. He held up the tablet with a slightly forced smile.

"I need you to sign," he said. "To say you received the order." He turned the signature screen toward the man and held the tablet out to him, and he waited, but the owner was just staring at the screen, not moving. "Sorry," Jacob tried, "I don't have a stylus or anything. You can just use your finger."

The man paused. "My finger." He glanced up at Jacob's face, then back at the tablet.

"Uh. Yeah, man." Jacob reached one hand around the tablet to draw an example scribble in the box, then erased it and offered the tablet again.

He frowned, hesitating, then set his book down on the small side table near the door and accepted the tablet. He touched the screen, and his eyebrows lifted slightly as though he was surprised it made a mark, even though Jacob had literally just showed him how to do it. Was this guy stupid?

Jacob watched with mounting disbelief as the man took approximately three thousand years to sign his name with the very tip of his index finger, carefully drawing each letter like he was signing a masterwork painting instead of a receipt. Jacob held in his sigh and rolled back on his heels while he waited, watching this hot weirdo take his time, but he paused when his gaze drifted to the open door. The long oval of etched glass in the center reflected the room beyond the entrance—but not the man standing right in front of it. Jacob blinked a couple of times, trying to focus on what kind of angle was playing a trick on him, but before he could decide, the man held the laboriously signed tablet back out to him.

"Thank you," Jacob said, hoping the relief wasn't too evident in his voice. "Have a good one."

The door was shut again by the time he made it to the edge of the porch.

Jacob climbed into the van, tossed the tablet onto the passenger seat, and immediately lifted his phone to his ear as he was pulling out of the driveway. Cordelia answered after a few rings.

"What is this call that should have been a text?" she asked in place of a greeting.

"Hey so shut up," he started. "You're not going to believe

where I just was."

"At your stupid job instead of here playing *Alien* where you should be?"

"Yeah okay but listen—you know the black haunted hermit house on Union Street?"

"Yeah."

"So guess where I just dropped off, like, way too many musical instruments."

She gasped. "Shut up."

"Oh yeah. I was inside. And guess who lives there."

"Jimmy Hoffa."

"Oh my god, shut up. The guy living there isn't some old doomsday prepper or whatever. He's young. And he's stupid hot."

"What? No way."

"I'm telling you," he said with a laugh.

"How young?"

"I dunno. Thirty, maybe?"

Cordelia scoffed. "No fucking way. Everybody talks about how nobody ever leaves that house. What, was he born in there, and he buried his parents under the floorboards?"

"I don't know, man; I'm just telling you what I saw. But get this. When I handed him my iPad, he looked at it like it was some kind of fucking alien transponder or something. Like he'd never seen one before."

The woman's paused, and then her voice was a bit quieter. "Oh my god, Jacob. Did you meet an actual ghost?"

Jacob stopped for a second, thinking about the missing reflection in the window. Then he scoffed. "If I did, I met one that can hold an iPad."

"What's this dude's name? If he ordered from the store, you know his name, right?"

"It's probably illegal for me to give out a customer's private information, Cords."

She snorted. "What the fuck ever. How private can it be if it's the same information I could get by going through his mailbox?"

"Also illegal," Jacob pointed out.

"Tell me."

He sighed. "Hold on." As he pulled up to a stop light, he held his phone up with his shoulder and reached across the seat for the tablet, then clicked it on and checked the order screen. "Emir Arzinjani."

"Ooh," Cordelia laughed, "a foreign and exotic ghost. I'll see what I can find out."

"Okay. Try not to get raided by the FBI."

"As if that's the worst thing they'll find in my search history. Later."

Jacob snorted as he hung up the phone. At least Cordelia would have a mystery to occupy her.

———

When Jacob got home, Cordelia was on the couch with her laptop, and she complained as soon as he walked in. She hadn't been able to find anything in the public records under the name he'd given her, which pissed her off. Jacob had to admit it was almost more suspicious to find absolutely nothing than to find very little, but Cordelia vowed to dig deeper.

He and Cordelia had lived together for almost two years now—ever since they started grad school together. They'd had some class overlap in undergrad, since he was studying Literature and she Screenwriting, and they'd moved out of the dorms after graduation. Cordelia's rich parents had offered to fund their rent as long as the students paid their utilities, so Jacob would have been stupid to say no. He paid his share from his job at the music store, and his parents helped out a little, while his actual tuition was financed by his ever-increasing student loans. But he wanted to go into academia—and that required a Master's, so here he was.

They ate dinner on the couch together and joked about the house and its occupant, taking turns making up progressively wilder stories about possible explanations for the weird hot hermit and why he might need so many musical instruments. Cordelia scolded him for not even trying to get a picture to show her. They were good together—neither was ever shy about reminding the other to pick up after themselves, they never argued about splitting dinner responsibilities, and they enjoyed the same hobbies. Well, mostly. Jacob could, perhaps, have done without the frequent sightings of animal bones that Cordelia seemed to find with suspicious regularity. He also wouldn't have chosen to keep Victorian death portraits framed on his bedroom walls—but Cordelia was Cordelia.

By the time Jacob went to work the next afternoon, he wasn't giving it much thought. He helped check in the kids and teenagers who came in for their music lessons and restocked smaller items, just like every day. He answered the phone while he was at the front counter, just like every day—but this time, he recognized the same accent and quiet voice from the day before.

"One of the guitar strings broke," the man said. "They must be replaced?"

"Oh, yeah. That'll happen. Usually people keep backups. We have them here at the shop; whichever string you need."

"I would like them delivered."

Jacob paused. "...Guitar strings?"

"Yes."

"*Just* guitar strings."

"Yes."

"Uh. 'Kay. We don't normally do that."

"You did it yesterday."

"Yeah, but I'm pretty sure that was a special case."

"I'll gladly pay any fees."

Jacob let his head fall back so his "ugh" didn't make it into the receiver. "Hold on, please," he said. "Let me ask my manager." He put the phone on hold and went to find the owner in the back of the store. "The guy from yesterday wants *guitar strings* delivered to his house now. You see what you started?"

Amy smirked and took the phone from him, then shooed him away. There was no way she would actually make him drive all the way there just for strings.

He didn't hear anything about it for the rest of the day, so he assumed she'd used her manager voice to get the guy to understand—but, close to closing, just as the sky was getting dark outside, the front door opened, and the hot weirdo entered. Somehow, he looked even weirder than the day before. He had on a light-colored pair of loose-fitting jeans held up with a snug belt, white hi-top sneakers, and a silky-looking green button-down that looked about two sizes too big for him—and it was tucked in.

"Oh my god," Jacob couldn't help whispering. What was he looking at right now?

The man glanced around a moment, then spotted Jacob at the counter and walked over. Jacob had to tilt his head up just a little to look him in the face as he drew close—and fuck, but the clothes didn't make those eyes any less bedroom-y. Jacob tried to just only see him from the neck up.

"Can you direct me to the guitar strings?"

"Yeah," Jacob managed. He gestured toward the far wall and then led him there. He helped him pick out the strings he needed and would need going forward, and he even helped find him some tab books to practice with, since he mentioned he was just learning. He took him back to the counter to check him out and, though he'd never admit it, took his time with the job so that he could sneak a few more looks at the man on the other side of the register—but the weirdo was just waiting, staring and silent, showing no intention of maintaining even a retail-level conversation. So, Jacob put his purchases in a bag and laid them on the counter, but he froze when the man took his wallet from his pocket. It was a canvas trifold, and Jacob heard the distinct rip of Velcro as it was torn open.

Velcro. Was Jacob being pranked? What fucking year was it, for this dude to show up in a silk shirt and Saved by the Bell shoes holding a Velcro wallet—and he even paid with cash.

Jacob tried not to stare as he handed back the man's change, but he glanced down as his fingers brushed the strange customer's hand. He was ice cold, but it must have been 75 degrees outside.

The man took his bag, thanked him politely, and was gone almost before Jacob could register what had happened.

What a fucking weirdo.

2

Later in the week, Jacob was relaxing on his sofa at home, leaning against the arm of the couch and reading *Culture and Imperialism* by Edward Said. It was on the reading list for his next course, so he wanted to get a jump on it while he had time over the summer. Cordelia was lying across the length of the couch with her feet in his lap and a controller in her hands, playing *No Man's Sky* with the volume low so she wouldn't disturb him. She was wearing a pair of black leggings and an oversized black t-shirt with the collar cut out, and she had her curly, dyed-black hair pulled out behind her to spill loose over the arm of the couch where she'd laid her head. Jacob didn't think he'd ever seen her wear anything that wasn't black or grey, and she always wore dark eye makeup and subtle red lipstick. She was the quintessential stylish goth girl, but it suited her. She always managed to make it seem like she wasn't trying very hard.

Before too long, he needed a break from the dense tome. The subject matter was interesting, but he knew he would have to read it again with notes open before the course began. He closed the book and leaned over Cordelia's legs to reach his beer on the coffee table, then sat back to watch her play.

"Hey," she said without taking her eyes off the screen, "so have you heard from hot hermit again?"

He chuckled. "No. Why?"

"Because I wanna know what his deal is, man! Don't you?"

She paused, then sat up to look at him. "We should go stake out the house."

"What do you mean, stake out the house?"

"I mean go check it out! He clearly comes out *sometimes*, since he showed up at the store. Maybe he does go out, just at, like, weird hours, so nobody ever sees him."

Jacob shook his head with a small laugh. "So what if he does?"

"So that's *weird*. How are you not more curious about this? Dude shows up looking like a *Fresh Prince* extra, he doesn't know how to use a tablet, you said he had a *Nokia*—is he a time traveler? Did he just come out of a coma? What's his deal?"

"Why do you care so much what his deal is?"

"Because I want to know what kind of person lives alone in a haunted house and has a fucking harp delivered there, Jacob. Come on. Plus, you said he was hot. You're really going to deprive me of that visual confirmation? I'm just supposed to *take your word* that the haunted house hermit weirdo is actually a babe?"

"Why the fuck would I lie about that?"

"Come on," she groaned.

Jacob shook his head and opened his book again, but she kicked it out of his hand and just glared back at him when he turned to her in disbelief.

"Come on. Stake out. Stake out. Stake out," she chanted, and finally he shoved her legs off of him.

"Fine."

"Yes! Stake out!"

Jacob drove, and Cordelia demanded they stop at the gas station for Red Bull and snacks, because—obviously—they needed these things for a stake out. He parked his car across the street from the old house, and they both leaned toward the window to get a look. The whole place was dark—not even a hint of lights through the gaps in the curtains. So they sat for a while, sipping their drinks and sharing a bag of Bugles while they waited for signs of life from inside.

Cordelia leaned her folded arms on the car door, her nose pressed lightly against the window.

"So is he out, or is he sleeping?"

"Neither would be weird, Cords; you know that, right?"

"Yeah, but they're both boring!" She sat back with a huff and reclined her seat so she could put her boots up on the dash.

They waited longer. Jacob looked past Cordelia and scanned the house. It looked creepier in the dark—like Jacob expected lightning to strike behind it at any moment, throwing it into stark silhouette. Maybe with a hanged person swinging from a tree in the yard. He'd always thought of it as the quintessential New England haunted house. But now, the more he looked at it, the more he thought it actually seemed exactly like the soft of place a solitary, soft-spoken bookworm might live. A faint smile touched his lips that was jolted off his face as Cordelia whipped her head toward him.

"We should take a picture."

"Of what? The house?"

"No, stupid. Of us *at* the house. Hashtag haunted."

"But it's very clearly *not* haunted, Cords. Just a weird book-hoarder lives there."

"The Ghost of Christmas 1990 lives there, okay? Come on—let's not make this a totally wasted trip."

"You're serious?"

"Be fun, Jacob. We won't hurt anything."

Jacob groaned, rolling his head on his shoulder to look at her. "Okay. But just a picture—then we go. This is someone's house, not a tourist attraction."

"I mean, I'd call it a local place of intrigue, at least. Let me have this."

"Yeah, yeah. Just go."

They both got out of the car, shutting the doors quietly behind them, and trotted lightly across the street. They stopped at the bottom of the steps, and Jacob sensed the same hesitation in his friend that he felt in his own chest. The porch light wasn't even on. Under the cloudy sky, it was hard to make out even the shape of the front door. Cordelia nudged his arm, and together they climbed the porch steps, slow and quiet, until they were close enough to the door to touch it. She unlocked her phone and held it up, adjusting her arm until she found the angle she wanted and then tugging Jacob in by his shirt so that they could both be in the photo.

The flash went off, and barely a second later, a voice spoke up behind them.

"What are you doing?"

They both screamed. Cordelia nearly dropped her phone in her rush to get off the porch, and Jacob half fell down the steps. The house's owner was sitting silently on an aging chair near the front window, staring at them from out of the dark like some kind of—ghost.

"Sorry!" Jacob called over his shoulder, already following Cordelia across the street at a jog. She repeated him as they fumbled back into the car, and they barely had their seat belts on before Jacob was hauling ass down the street away from the house. Cordelia's nervous laughter triggered his own, but he shook his head once he'd had a few breaths to calm down.

"Fuck, that was stupid," he said. "Why did we do that?"

Cordelia exhaled and picked up her phone. "I'll call it a success if I got a picture of the hot hermit." She flicked on her screen, and then, with a gasp, grabbed Jacob's arm so hard that the whole car swerved.

"What the fuck, Cordelia?"

"Fuck dude," she breathed. "Fuck!"

"What?"

"He's not in the picture."

"Fucking so? You almost killed us because of that?"

"No, shut up, listen—he *should* be in the picture and he's *not* in the picture. Look. Look look." She shoved her phone at him, and he held it up to look at the screen as he stopped at the next intersection. There were Jacob and Cordelia, and the side of the house, and the deck chair.

Empty.

"What...the fuck," Jacob said, and Cordelia took the phone back from him to zoom in on the background.

"What the fuck!" she echoed. "He was right there, right?"

Jacob frowned, not liking how his heart was racing. Ghosts weren't real. "I mean...I thought so," he tried, but Cordelia shook her head.

"He totally was. Fuck, Jacob! He really is a ghost!"

He shook his head again, a little more fervently this time.

12

"Cords, a ghost did not come into my store and buy guitar strings."

"Maybe he did, man! I don't know all the fucking ghost rules!"

"Jesus Christ," he scoffed, hoping he seemed more convinced than he felt.

Back at the apartment, Cordelia was stuck to his side, constantly checking the windows as though the restless undead might bash through at any moment.

"Cords, forget about it," he insisted, attempting to disengage his arm from her grip and shut his bedroom door. "We went to a guy's house at night and he startled us, that's all. We're lucky he didn't shoot us."

"Or—or. We went to a ghost's house."

Jacob sighed and shook his arm loose. "Listen. If you're so worried about it, why don't you do some research? You love research. I'm sure you can find something."

She nodded, but she was still wringing her hands. "Okay. You're right. Good idea."

"Good night, Cords."

"Yeah," she said after a brief pause. "Good night."

Jacob shut his door and dropped down onto his bed with a sigh. It's true—a couple of weird things haven't quite lined up about this guy. But weird things happen all the time. Just because Jacob doesn't know the explanation, that doesn't mean there isn't one. Mostly, he just felt like an ass. He was too old to be sneaking up to strangers' houses just because they were spooky.

What an idiot.

Jacob went to sleep feeling like an idiot, and he went to work feeling like an idiot. By the time he finished his shift in the afternoon, he'd made a decision.

He was going to have to apologize to the hot hermit.

3

Emir had started with the guitar—he imagined it would be the simplest. He broke three strings the first day before he learned how gentle he needed to be with them, but now he'd managed the first few chords in his book, so he spent his time practicing them again and again, listening to the sound the instrument made until he got it right.

He slept upstairs for most of the day, and after his evening bath, he dressed himself as much as he ever did when he didn't plan to leave the house. He had a nice pair of dark blue sleep shorts and a light silk robe he liked to wear. There was no point to putting on anything uncomfortable just to be at home. And he was almost always at home.

His recent trip to the store did concern him some, though. Things looked very different from how he remembered them. When that boy had delivered his instruments, he had something with a screen you could touch. He'd seen some screens like that on expensive PDAs, but they hadn't looked anything like that. How long had it been since he'd been out?

He'd lost track of time, somehow.

Emir put it out of his mind and settled in his small library sitting room upstairs with his guitar on his knee. He played at plucking the strings for a while, picking out a few slow, disjointed tunes, then set back to practicing his chords. A knock at the door made him pause just as he was beginning to be satisfied with his D chord.

He set down his guitar and moved to the stairs. He wasn't expecting anyone. By the time he reached the front door, he recognized the scent outside—the boy from the music store. Emir frowned faintly as he opened the door, and he stood back from the opening, as the sun was still out.

The boy wore dark jeans that are snug against his slender legs and rolled into a cuff at the ankle above brown suede boots, and a mottled lavender t-shirt with a single breast pocket. It fit him well. He stood with his fingers tucked into his jeans pockets, looking up at Emir with a faint grimace on his face. He isn't dressed like the young men Emir remembers at all.

"Yes?" he asked, and the boy rocked on his heels, seeming like he was struggling to maintain eye contact.

"Hey. Listen, I just wanted to say sorry for last night. My friend and I were just being stupid. We didn't mean anything by it. We were just fucking around—because of all the stories about this house, you know?"

Emir paused, his brow briefly lowering. Then he moved back from the door. "Come inside."

The boy hesitated. "Uh. Okay." He took a single step across the threshold and shut the door beside him, but then he lingered in the entryway, glancing uncertainly back at the door. "You're not about to murder me, right? You have to say so if you're going to murder me, or it's entrapment."

"No," Emir said simply. "Come." He led the way into the adjoining sitting room and moved a few stacks of books from the chairs so that there would be room for both of them to sit down, then gestured to one of the seats.

The boy stiffly sat, close to the edge of the cushion, his palms running over the knees of his jeans once or twice. He was a slightly gaunt boy, with sharp cheekbones, dark, messy hair, and deeply hooded brown eyes. Pleasant to look at.

Emir took his place in the adjacent chair and looked over at the boy, who seemed about to bolt for the door at the first sign of trouble. "Tell me what stories there are about my house."

He balked. "What, you don't know?"

Emir waited without answering, so the boy gave a small cough and adjusted his position on the chair.

"I mean, everybody in town wonders about this place, I think. Somebody clearly lives here, because lights are on and stuff sometimes, but nobody's ever seen anybody come out in, like, my whole life." He shrugged one shoulder. "Some people think it's haunted, but I always figured it was just some lonely old man waiting to die in here."

Emir's eyes narrowed faintly. "How old are you?"

"Uh. I'm twenty-five." He glanced over in the direction of the front door. "Look, I just came to apologize for fucking around on your porch, so—"

"And you've heard these stories all your life?"

"Pretty much, yeah."

Emir ran a hand over his mouth, frowning down at the floor. "Twenty-five."

"Listen, I'm not trying to get all up in your shit here; you clearly have a lot going on." The boy rose and edged toward the door like he didn't want to turn his back on his host. "So, sorry again, and uh, if you'd not tell my boss about any of this, that would be really cool of you." He hesitated just a moment more, than lifted his hand in an awkward half-wave. "So, uh. Bye." He bolted from the house, and Emir sat still in the quiet left behind after the door slammed shut.

Twenty-five. Had it really been that long?

He rose from the chair and nudged aside a stack of books on the living room coffee table so that he could pick up his phone, but when he pushed the power button, nothing happened. It was dead. He tore apart a couple of rooms looking for the charger, then gave up. He would have to buy another one.

He dressed himself and found his silver oval sunglasses in the nightstand drawer upstairs, then went out onto the street. He'd discovered when he tried to visit the music store that his car would no longer start, so he would have to walk to the mall, too. He didn't mind, though the trip through the city did remind him of how infrequently he stretched his legs. At least there was a Radio Shack at the mall, so he would be able to get plugged back in.

The mall isn't like he remembers it. The people shopping inside look different, too. He got a lot of odd looks as he walked, but he probably gave just as many out. So many people had unnatural hair colors. Women wore oversized sweaters or looked like they'd just come from the gym, and many of the men had large beards and pants that looked uncomfortably tight.

As he walked, Emir became more and more acutely aware of how much he must stand out. That wasn't good.

On top of everything, the space that was once the Radio Shack now seemed to have become a clothing store called Aéropostale. And there didn't seem to be another electronics store anywhere in the mall.

So many people he passed carried miniature versions of the thing the boy had presented him with at the door—smaller screens, but they were all touching them. What was everyone using them for?

He tried to find a newspaper stand and came up empty. How was a person supposed to know what year it was? Asking outright would certainly get him more attention than he wanted. Finally, he happened upon an abandoned magazine at one of the sitting areas at the end of one of the long corridors and found a date on the back cover near the barcode.

Emir slowly sank into the chair behind him. Twenty years. It really had been twenty years. He stared down at the magazine, hoping to will the numbers on the paper to change.

He lost track of time for twenty years.

That had never happened before. He'd gotten distracted, focused, absorbed in this or that, and lost months here and there in the past, but...twenty years.

Emir sat for a while and watched shoppers go by, seeing now more than ever the differences in the world he remembered and the one he was in. Clothing in the store windows came in styles he wouldn't have called fashionable. Even the cars in the parking lot on his way in had looked strange and unfamiliar.

He'd been left behind.

————

The following night, Emir waited outside the music store until they closed. He could see the boy through the front window occasionally, moving back and forth as he worked, but he kept his distance until the lights in the store began to shut off. Once the boy appeared by the door, pausing to lock it behind him, Emir moved into the yellow beam from the streetlight, and as the boy turned around, he started and let out a clipped yelp.

"I'm sorry," Emir said. "I didn't mean to startle you. I'd like to talk to you."

He took a half step backward. "Uh, look, the store's closed now, but if there's something you need, if you call in the morning—"

"No," Emir cut him off. "I would like to talk to you. Privately. Will you come?"

"Come, like...to your house?"

"Yes."

The boy frowned up at him with a distrustful cock of his head. "Why?"

"If I told you here, it wouldn't be talking privately, would it?"

"Yeah, but you're less likely to murder me in a parking lot than back at your house."

Emir gave a small tut and held in his sigh. "I am not going to murder you. Come. Please," he added.

He chewed the corner of his mouth with his hands on his hips, letting a few silent, pensive moments pass before he spoke. "Okay," he said quietly. "I'll go."

"Thank you. I'll meet you there shortly."

It wasn't difficult for Emir to make it back to the house before the boy did, but it did necessitate keeping out of sight until he arrived. Still, he made it to the inside of the front door a handful of seconds before the knock at the door. He opened it to let the boy in, then paused as he remembered that his guest might prefer some of the lights to be on. He flipped a few of the switches and walked toward the sitting room, but when he glanced back to make sure the boy was following, he found him lurking by the front door again.

Emir stopped and turned to face him fully. It wouldn't do for him to be nervous. "What's your name?" he asked, as gently as he was able.

"...Jacob."

"Jacob," he repeated softly. "I'm Emir. It's nice to meet you."

The boy still stared at him, even looking more confused than before.

"Now we aren't strangers," Emir explained. "You don't think I'd kill someone who wasn't a stranger, do you?"

Jacob let a faint, hesitant half smile show on his lips, and this time, when Emir walked into the next room, he followed. They sat for a few moments, Jacob rocking a little bit in his seat. He was uncomfortable.

"Do you enjoy working at the music store?" Emir asked, and Jacob gave a small shrug.

"Yeah, I guess."

"The books you recommended have been a great help. Thank you."

"Sure."

More silence went by, during which Emir watched his young guest glance furtively around the room, as if he might be scolded for taking in the wallpaper.

"So you came to my house because you heard it was haunted?" Emir tried again.

"...Yeah. My roommate is really into spooky stuff, and she wanted to take a picture, and I went along with it—" He shook his head and let out a small huff. "Look, I said I was sorry already yesterday. What do you want from me?"

"Your roommate," Emir gently pressed. "Not your girlfriend?"

Jacob pulled back slightly, his brow furrowed. "It's not any of your business, but no. She's just my friend."

Good. It made things easier if he was unattached. Emir leaned a bit closer to him. "And do you...like haunted things?"

"What the hell does that mean?"

"Haunted houses," Emir said. "Urban legends. Myths. ...Spooky things."

"I mean, yeah, I guess. Am I being interviewed, here? What's going on right now?"

"And you consider yourself—culturally aware? In tune with the zeitgeist of the modern era?"

"Dude," Jacob scoffed, giving a brief, humorless laugh, "you still aren't telling me what I'm doing here."

Emir looked into his dark, deep-set eyes. "I want to ask you for your help. And in return, I want to give you something likely beyond your imagining."

"...Dude," Jacob said again, this time disgust faintly curling his lip.

"If this is some kind of sex thing, I'm not about it."

"Not a sex thing," Emir assured him. "I find myself...disconnected. From the outside."

"Yeah, I got that impression," the boy said dryly.

Emir shifted in his seat to face him more fully, lacing his fingers near his knees. "I don't want to alarm you. But you are correct in thinking that no one has left this house for most of your life."

Jacob stared flatly at him, lips pressed into a skeptical line. "...Okay."

"*I* haven't left this house."

"For my whole life," Jacob asked, pointing a finger at his own chest.

Emir tilted his head. "Perhaps you think I look too young for that to be true?"

Jacob raised his hands in a shrug and let them fall back to his lap. "Not if you're a fucking ghost, I guess. My roommate thinks you're a ghost."

"I can promise you I'm not a ghost. But I am an immortal." Emir paused, waiting to gauge Jacob's reaction, but the boy was watching him right back, so he went on. "I know it stretches belief to hear, but...I'm a vampire."

Jacob's expression didn't change for a few seconds. Then he nodded, frowning slightly and looking down at his lap. "...Yeah," he said. "Yep. It sure does." He slapped his knees and stood. "So, I'm gonna go."

Emir looked up at him in confusion. This was not a response he had a ready answer for. "You don't believe me."

"Yeah, listen, this has been fun—"

As the boy turned to leave the room, Emir tried again.

"I'll pay you. Name your price."

Now Jacob stopped. He turned back to look at Emir, incredulity written on his face. "You'll pay me. To do what, exactly?"

"To teach me," Emir explained. "To bring me up to speed. I'm asking you to help me adjust—I haven't been a part of the world in twenty years. I need someone young. Someone who can get me...caught up."

Jacob snorted quietly. "You're really serious about this."

"I am," Emir answered with a nod. "What fee is agreeable to you?"

He folded his arms, considering a moment before answering. "How long do you want me to do this?"

"Until I'm satisfied. I can pay you by the week, or however you prefer. But I will expect you to be available to me. I won't interfere with your job, but beyond that, you must be at hand when I require you, either in person or by phone at the very least."

Jacob chewed his bottom lip, rocking back on his heels and glancing down at the floor before peeking back up at him. "This is a pretty intense gig you're asking for. Especially with no end date." He tilted his head. "I'll do it for 100k."

"One hundred thousand?" Emir repeated. "A lump sum?"

"Sure."

"Upon satisfaction," he pressed.

Jacob shrugged one shoulder and nodded his agreement.

"Done," Emir said, and he stood to offer his hand to the boy. For a few brief seconds, Jacob just gaped at him, but then he slowly, mechanically accepted the handshake, nodding a little too enthusiastically. "I'll need your phone number and your work schedule."

"Yeah, sure. Sure."

"But first." Emir released Jacob and walked by him to pick up his unresponsive cell phone, then handed it off to him. "I think this will need to be replaced. Please make this a priority. Tomorrow would be best."

"Uh. Yeah," Jacob agreed with a laugh. "Probably needs an update. You play Snake on this thing?"

"Not recently," he admitted.

Jacob looked up at him. "How am I supposed to get you a new phone? I can barely pay for my own bill."

"Ah. Of course. Wait." Emir left him behind and made his way to the bedroom upstairs. He took some cash from the small safe he kept in the closet and returned to the boy, placing the folded bills into his hand. "This is two thousand. Please put this toward any fees, the cost of the phone, and whatever other incidentals you may come across. You may keep the rest."

Jacob's mouth hung slightly open as he looked down at the money he held, and when he looked back up at Emir's face, his bitter skepticism had been replaced with hopeful disbelief. "Are you serious?"

"As a show of good faith," Emir said softly. "When will you be able to come tomorrow?"

"Uh, I...I get off at two, so I can go get the phone after that, and then come here."

"That will be fine. Please come as close to sunset as you can. Thank you, Jacob. I will see you tomorrow."

"Yeah. Yeah," Jacob repeated as Emir guided him toward the door. He stood on the front porch, seeming briefly stunned until Emir remembered to turn the front light on for him. Then he shoved the money into his pants pocket and looked back up.

Emir offered him a faint smile. "I look forward to working with you."

4

Jacob drove home from Emir's house in a haze, feeling like the money in his pocket weighed a thousand pounds. He walked into the apartment on autopilot and sat down at the kitchen table across from Cordelia, who was eating a bowl of noodles.

"Where've you been?" she asked once she swallowed. "I thought you got off at eight."

"Well," Jacob began, eyebrows lifting as he stared at the table. "Uh. I had a visit from the hot hermit."

Cordelia spit out the mouthful of noodles she'd just tried to chew. "For real?"

"He told me he's a vampire and he's going to pay me a hundred grand to help him 'get caught up to speed' on the modern world because he actually *hasn't* left the house in twenty years."

She lowered her face closer to the table and narrowed her eyes at him. "You're fucking with me."

Jacob dug into his pocket and dropped the folded cash in front of her. "He just fucking *handed* me two thousand dollars to go buy him a new phone tomorrow. To replace his fucking Nokia brick."

"Hold on. How are you talking about the money right now and not about how this guy told you he's a *vampire?*"

"Because he's obviously just a weirdo and not an actual vampire, Cords."

She smacked his arm. "Are you joking? Did you forget what

happened with the picture I took?"

"You mean the picture you took on a cloudy night under a porch roof in the middle of the night? Yeah, I can't imagine how anything weird would happen there. It was dark. I couldn't see shit, and neither could you."

"And he was *right there* and neither of us noticed him."

"Is being quiet a vampire trait I haven't heard of? Again—dark."

"*And* he told you he hasn't left the house in twenty years."

"He did."

"But he's young and hot."

"He is."

"So," she pressed, crossing her arms on the table and staring at him more pointedly now, "how is he only thirty and he's lived alone in that house for at least twenty years?"

He sighed through his nose as he stared at her. "Well, I might have asked him for a reasonable explanation, Cords, but *he told me he was immortal.*"

She scoffed at him and slumped back in her chair. "You met a vampire."

"I did not meet a vampire."

"You met a vampire," she said again, more forcefully. "And now you're his servant? You'd better watch yourself, Renfield."

Jacob shook his head and began to gather up the money again. "Look—I don't care if he's a goddamn unicorn if he's going to pay my student debt." He tilted his chin toward her bowl. "Did you leave any dinner?"

Cordelia didn't let him have a moment's peace until he retreated to his bedroom. He locked the door and sat down at his desk, but when he opened his book, he only managed to stare pointlessly at it until he smacked it shut again with a sigh.

Emir hadn't cast a reflection in the glass. He hadn't shown up in the photo. When they shook hands that afternoon, his skin had been so cold that Jacob worried he might stick to him like a tongue to a lamppost. But those were all just...weird things. Weren't they? Vampires weren't real, for one thing. That was enough to put a stop to the whole line of thinking right there. But also, Emir didn't look anything like a vampire. At least, not like what Jacob had been led to believe a vampire should look like. His eyes were a dark, inviting brown, not red or glowing. He had soft, honey-colored skin—he wasn't pale like a corpse.

He was just a weird loner with money to burn. And Jacob didn't mind taking money from a weird loner who wanted help learning how to use an iPhone.

———

All through the next day, Jacob kept glancing toward the front of the store, half expecting Emir to show up again and ask him what was taking so long, but he didn't. He had been telling the truth about not interfering with Jacob's job, at least.

When he finished his shift, he went into Best Buy and bought the newest, nicest phone he could find, and he folded up the activation paperwork to take to Emir. He waited at the bottom of the porch for a minute, staring at the closed door as the sun approached the horizon behind him. Time to get to work, he guessed.

It didn't take Emir very long to answer the door. He was actually dressed this time, which was just a negative all around, honestly— Jacob didn't get to see the other man's abs, and instead, he was forced to look at the truly ugly fat-striped, white collared button-down he'd chosen to wear.

He sat on the couch with Emir uncomfortably close beside him, looking over his shoulder while Jacob walked him through the phone's activation and setup. He tried to get the phone to recognize Emir's face so that he could unlock it that way, but it kept giving an error.

"Wait," Jacob finally said, and he leaned back a little to look Emir in the face. "It recognizes you with the camera."

"Oh. Well then I'm not surprised it doesn't work. I don't show up in photos."

Jacob stared at him. "Just gonna drop that into the conversation like it's a normal thing to say, huh?"

"It's the truth."

"Okay." Jacob subtly shook his head and returned his attention to the phone. "I'll set it up with your fingerprint instead. You have those, right?"

"Yes."

"Great." Jacob helped him to log his thumbprint, then handed the phone to him. "All done. Go nuts."

A light smile touched Emir's face, and he nodded as if impressed with the device. "Thank you, Jacob. And is your phone number in here?"

"Yeah. All good."

"This is a good start. But—why does a phone need such a large screen?"

"I mean, it's not just a phone," Jacob said with a small shrug. "You can text, you can go online, you can check your email...do you have an email address?"

Emir gestured across the room, where a transparent teal-backed, all in one iMac sat nestled safely unused among three stacks of books. "I've used America Online."

"Oh, wow. Okay. Yeah. Let's just ignore that. Do you *want* an email address?"

"I have no one to email," Emir answered simply, and Jacob paused. That was an immediate, kind of sad answer.

"Okay. Never mind then," he said. "You can always sign up for one if you decide to later. But just play around with it. You can download games, go on websites, take pictures, whatever. It's not that hard to just figure out, but I can help you with any specific problems that come up."

Emir nodded with his eyes on the screen, then looked back up at him. "Thank you, Jacob."

He tried to shrug it off. This guy really needed to stop saying his name—that accent was killer. Why did he have to be so hot *and* so weird? Hot or weird—that should be the rule. They sat in silence for a minute or two, Jacob feeling increasingly awkward while Emir flipped experimentally through various screens on his phone. He was too close. The air felt weird in the room—was it just him? Way too quiet.

"You know," Jacob began, hoping to break the ice a little, "my roommate says you really are a vampire."

"I am," he answered casually, without even looking up from his screen.

"Okay," Jacob said, his skepticism palpable. "But like. For real."

"I am being for real." Emir raised his head and faced him with a faint, slightly tired smile. "But I suppose I haven't given you much reason to believe it, have I?"

"I mean, step one," Jacob began, holding up one finger like he was ready to make a list, "you came to the music store during the day. So that kind of fucks the whole thing right there, doesn't it?"

He didn't like the amusement that formed in Emir's eyes.

"Does it?"

"That's sort of a vampire's whole thing, only coming out at night. The sun kills vampires. Everybody knows that. Unless you're Dracula. You're not Dracula."

Emir let his phone rest in his lap as he shook his head. "It doesn't kill so readily as other things. But I'm certainly not at my best."

"Wow." Jacob snorted and dropped his arm over the side of the couch. "You're really sticking to this, aren't you?"

"I told you the truth."

"So." He sat up a little straighter and leaned forward to look Emir dead in the eye. "You want me to believe that you are an honest-to-Vlad *vampire*—and you just *told* me?"

Emir's eyebrows lifted, and he tilted his head slightly. "What might you do about it?"

"Well. You're not worried about getting—staked, or whatever?"

He leaned a little closer, and his voice was a little lower the next time he spoke, sending a shiver up Jacob's spine. "Are you going to stake me, Jacob?"

His answer came out too quickly. "No. Because vampires aren't real," he added as a saving afterthought.

Emir seemed to consider him for a moment. Then he set his phone down on the arm of the couch and rose. "Come."

Jacob followed him into the kitchen at a distance, and he watched from the doorway as Emir began to open kitchen cabinets, both above and below the counters. Every one was full of books. There were a few worn-looking notebooks, some pens stuffed into plastic cups or mason jars, and a handful of binders here and there. Emir opened the pantry door, and it was full of brass instruments—a trumpet, a trombone leaned against the wall from the floor, and a case big enough to be a French horn stuffed under the lowest shelf.

There wasn't any food.

Jacob frowned. So Emir ate out a lot. So what? Except—he didn't eat out. He didn't go out at all. And if there had been regular food deliveries to this place, there wouldn't be so many stories about it being haunted or abandoned, right? So where was the food?

Finally, Emir opened the refrigerator and stood aside to show Jacob a shelf that wasn't empty—but instead of food, it was filled with a number of long rectangular bins, each one holding a neat row of thick plastic bags. They were marked with labels in different colors, with a letter on each—A, B, AB, or O.

Jacob stared at it for possibly a solid minute before he spoke. He looked up at Emir, who was waiting patiently beside the open door. "What the fuck is that?"

The corner of Emir's mouth twitched into an infuriating little smile. "What do you think it is?"

"Is that real blood?" Jacob demanded. "Why the fuck do you have real blood?"

Emir hesitated briefly, then tilted his head with his eyes narrowed in confusion. "I'm not sure you've been paying attention, Jacob."

Jacob took a step back from the kitchen doorway. "Okay—this isn't just being a fucking weird loner anymore, man. That is real fucking blood in your fridge—no. No it's not. That's fucking—Jell-O, or something."

Emir reached over the refrigerator door and took one of the bags from the front of the nearest bin, then he let the door fall shut as he twisted the cap loose on the long tube at the top of the bag. "Give me your hand, Jacob."

He clutched both hands protectively to his chest on instinct. "You're gonna put fucking blood in it!"

"So you do think it's blood."

"Well I fucking guess! Fuck!" Jacob shook his head and backed up another step. "Look man, you can keep your money. I'm not getting murdered in some fucking hoarder's house."

He turned and took long strides toward the front door, but before he made it two steps, he had to stop short—Emir was right in front of him, blocking his way to the door. Jacob swore again as he stumbled back a step, but when he looked up, Emir was just watching him, calm and composed.

"I told you I wasn't going to hurt you, Jacob. I've answered all of your questions truthfully from the very start."

He took a step closer, and Jacob backed up. How had he gotten here so fast? Jacob hadn't seen him move at all.

"Don't you want to know the real payment I was going to offer you?" Emir asked, voice low and soft, tingling Jacob's skin as he approached. "Aren't you curious?"

Jacob's back hit the wall, and he spread his hands against the wood as if he might find a secret escape lever. He swallowed hard and tried to force venom into his voice, but it was difficult with Emir standing so close to him. "Is it a fucking swift and painless death?"

"Much better," Emir murmured, and he moved so near that their bodies were almost touching. He reached up a hand, his thumb tracing Jacob's jaw to his chin and brushing over his bottom lip. His hand was cold, and he was giving off seriously dangerous vibes, but Jacob couldn't make himself move. He shivered without knowing if he was terrified or aroused. "I can give you a gift." Emir leaned down right next to his ear, and even the air brushing over Jacob's earlobe seemed cool. "A taste," he whispered, "of what you could have."

Jacob didn't dare move now. "What...does that mean?" His own voice sounded tremulous and pathetic, but he was frozen in place. His heart was beating at a sprint. Fuck, Emir was so close. This was too weird, and he was too fucking hot to be acting like this. Jacob's stomach tightened. It wasn't possible that this man was actually a *real* vampire, was it?

Emir gave a soft, pensive hum that shot straight to Jacob's gut. "Like a...test drive. And, when we're done, if you've behaved...such things can be made permanent."

Jacob's breath caught in his throat. Emir's hand was on his hip now, and he leaned back just enough to look down at him with those dark, tempting eyes. "You mean—" he started, then had to remember to breathe again. "You mean make me a—"

"If you like." Emir moved his free hand to his own mouth, and when he opened it, Jacob noticed for the first time the two pairs of sharp canines where normal human teeth should have been. Emir pricked the pad of his thumb with one white point and drew up a round well of blood, and then his fingertips were on Jacob's cheek, the bleeding thumb very near his mouth. He tilted his head and said in a voice so soft it was barely audible, "Do you want a taste, Jacob?"

Jacob couldn't force his gaze anywhere except Emir's eyes, his lips, his throat. He couldn't catch his breath. He couldn't think. He parted his lips and tilted his chin up just slightly, a shaky exhale falling out of him that became a quiet groan when Emir slid his thumb across his bottom lip, leaving a smear of blood there before pushing the cut fully into Jacob's mouth. The metallic taste was cold and hot all at once on Jacob's tongue, and his heart skipped, but he closed his lips around the other man's thumb, his eyes falling shut as he allowed the taste to coat his mouth. Before he was ready, it was gone, and he found himself licking his lips so he didn't lose a single drop.

Emir bent close to him again, his lips touching Jacob's ear as he whispered. "Would you like some more?"

He nodded perhaps too eagerly, a little anxiously, and then a gentle hand was at the back of his head. Emir reached up to his own neck and dug his thumbnail into the skin near his collarbone, making a thick line of dark red that began to slowly spill over. He tilted his head and urged Jacob closer with tender fingers in his hair, and the next thing Jacob knew, his mouth was open against the other man's skin, tongue lapping at him, fingers curled into his stupid ugly shirt. Blood spread over his tongue, and the first mouthful he swallowed burned like whiskey going down.

He wanted more.

His whole body warmed as he clung to the man against him, but Emir drew him away too soon, fingers tight in the back of his hair. Jacob stumbled, holding onto him to keep upright despite his faltering knees, and he looked up into Emir's face with lips still parted. Emir leaned down to him and licked a slow, careful line across his chin to the corner of his mouth, cleaning away the blood that had smeared there. His voice was gentle now.

"Very good."

He kept a hand on Jacob until he stopped swaying, then guided him toward the front door and opened it for him. When Jacob blinked blearily up at him, Emir smiled.

"Get some rest, Jacob. I'll see you tomorrow."

"Yeah," he answered hazily. "Yeah."

"Good night," Emir offered as Jacob stepped through the doorway.

"Good night," Jacob answered, but it felt almost like a question. He stood on the porch for a while after Emir shut the door, just trying to remember who he was.

He drove home in a stupor, stopping at every light to blink hard and rub at his eyes. They felt tender and strange, almost like they were swollen. By the time he made it back to the apartment, his legs felt like rubber—he stumbled through the door as dizzily as if he'd taken shots, and he had to support himself on the back and then the arm of the couch so he could make it all the way around it. He dropped down onto the cushions and sat as still as possible, his head back against the cushions.

After a few minutes, Cordelia appeared from the bathroom, wearing her pajamas and drying her hair. "Woah," she said as she came around the side of the couch. "You okay? You look wrecked."

Jacob didn't move, just stared up at the ceiling. "So."

"...So?"

"So he's a fucking vampire."

5

Jacob had a miserable night. Cordelia badgered him endlessly for answers and details, but he had pushed her off and begged her to let him rest. Even after she agreed to leave him be, she knocked half a dozen times. He had to threaten to throw up on her before she would leave him to his fitful sleep.

"This is wasted on you!" she called through his closed bedroom door before finally leaving him alone.

He spent hours tossing and turning, holding the pillow over his head. He felt feverish, alternating between kicking the blankets away from him and cocooning himself inside them. He had the constant sensation of falling even though he was lying still.

He could hear everything. He heard the neighbor's dishwasher running through the wall. A dog down the street. Cordelia's fucking vibrator. He could smell the dirty socks in his hamper even with his pillow pulled tight over his head. His heart hammered like his ribs might break.

What the fuck had he done?

When a person tries to feed you blood, you stop them. You don't open your mouth like a fucking good little boy, and you definitely don't lap it up off their goddamn chest like a—whoever the hell does a thing like that.

Jacob exhaled slowly beneath his pillow. He'd never been more turned on in his life.

In the morning, he tried to eat a bowl of cereal, but it repulsed him. He spit out the mouthful he did try to chew and threw away the rest of the bowl, then laid his head on the table resting on his folded arms. He felt sick—like waking up still drunk from the night before.

He stirred a little when Cordelia approached him and put a hand on his head. She moved his head just enough to get a good feel of his cheeks and forehead. "You're burning up," she said quietly, and she pulled up a chair to sit next to him. "What the hell happened yesterday?"

Jacob answered without picking his head up, though he did attempt to turn his eyes toward her. "It's real, Cords. I think. I think he's a fucking vampire."

Cordelia frowned at him, then reached for him again, turning his head back and forth a bit more violently now.

"Ow, what the fuck?"

"Did he bite you?"

"No!" Jacob smacked vaguely at her hands until she settled down again, but she didn't sound so comforting and gentle anymore.

"I fucking told you something was up with him! I told you," she insisted, so loudly that Jacob winced. She laid her head down on the table next to his so that she could look into his face. "So what happened?"

"I—I don't know," he admitted. "He had fucking...blood bags in his fridge, like from a hospital or something, and when I tried to leave, he was just like—*there* in front of me, and he was talking about giving me a gift, and—"

"Hold the fuck on," she interrupted. "Are you a vampire now?"

"No I'm not a fucking vampire now," he snapped back. "I told you he didn't bite me. But he had fucking—fucking fangs, Cords, I saw them."

"So he just...let you go?"

"Well he—" Jacob stopped and turned to press his face into the wood. "Fuck. I don't even want to tell you."

"You gotta," she insisted.

"Fuck," he swore again, grimacing into the table.

"Come on, man. You can't do this to me."

"Okay. So—" Jacob hesitated again, and he closed his arms a little tighter around his head. "So he didn't bite me, but he...I guess *I*...I drank blood."

"You drank *blood?*" Cordelia half shrieked and half gasped. "Whose blood?"

"His blood."

She shoved at his head until he moved it enough for her to see his face. "What the fuck, Jacob?"

"I know! I don't know!" He let his arms fall loose across the table, his loose fists thunking against the surface. "It was stupid. I can't go back there, Cords. No way. I'll have student debt until I die, but this is too much. I can't deal with this."

Cordelia went quiet for a moment. "What was it like?"

He stared at the table. "It was...weird. But...also good. Like...really, really good," he finished in a whisper.

Cordelia leaned back in her chair. "Man, I'm so fucking jealous."

"Jealous?" he shot back. "I feel like I'm gonna fuckin' die, Cords."

"A hot vampire fed you his *blood*," she said, as if that made her jealousy any more sensible.

Jacob frowned and didn't answer.

She gave another small huff, then paused and looked over at him with concern knitting her brow. "You don't think he'll show up here, do you? Like if you try to back out and say you won't help him anymore?"

"Oh my god," Jacob said in an extended groan, immediately pulling his arms back around himself.

"Okay, okay," she said over him. "This will be okay. You just...you go back to bed, and I'll see what I can figure out. Okay?"

"I have work, Cords."

She scowled at him over his elbow. "You're not going to fucking *work!*"

"Well I don't have a hot weirdo who's going to pay my bills anymore, so I have to!" He finally pushed upright and took a deep breath. "Fuck," he sighed, then shook his head, rubbed at his eyes, and huffed once more. "I'm okay. It's fine." He scooted back from the table and stood. "I'm okay. I need to get ready to go."

"Jacob, for real." She reached for him, but he backed away and offered her a reassuring nod.

"Yeah. For real. I'm fine." He felt her skeptical frown on his back as he left the room, but he ignored it. He didn't have a choice. He had to work.

He made it an hour before Amy caught him half laying over the counter by the register, saw the look on his face, touched his forehead, and sent him home.

He sat in the car for close to twenty minutes before he felt up to turning the key in the ignitions and driving home—and he honestly meant to go home. But when he parked and turned off the engine, he realized he was in Emir's driveway. He stared out at the house, frowning, and then got out of the car. He climbed the steps to the porch and banged on the door. It was the middle of the morning—any normal person should have been awake. But there was no answer. The car was still sat under the carport, just like always. He was at home. But no matter how hard Jacob knocked, it stayed silent in the house.

Jacob sat down in front of the door with his back leaned against it and his arms wrapped around his knees, stomach churning. He kept listening for any sound of movement, but nothing came. After a while, his head began to spin, so he laid down on the porch and curled up on his side. He shut his eyes, breathing through the clammy feeling under his shirt as sweat beaded on his brow and over his body, and he eventually fell asleep.

————

Jacob woke with a start as he lost the support of the door behind him and rolled backwards. He opened his eyes with his back on the sill of the door and blinked himself back to the waking world. It was dusk now, and Emir was standing over him with his hand on the door, dressed in nothing but pajama pants again. He smiled faintly.

"Good evening, Jacob." He bent down and lifted Jacob to his feet as easily as if he were a doll, then stepped back from the doorway and gestured inside. "Please come in."

Jacob did as he was told, wiping his damp palms on the pockets of his jeans while Emir shut the door. "What the fuck did you do to me?" he asked, wishing he sounded more pissed and less hoarse.

"I should have warned you," Emir said. "I apologize. Please sit."

Jacob fell onto the couch more gratefully than he would ever admit, and Emir briefly disappeared into the kitchen and returned with a mason jar full of room temperature water, which he handed off as he sat down. Jacob drank greedily from the glass and panted softly as he held it in his lap. "What's wrong with me?"

"It will pass. The first day is the worst, I'm told."

"The first day of *what?*" Jacob did his best to glare over at him. "Listen, it's—it's hard enough wrapping my brain around the fact that I'm sitting in an actual vampire's house right now, but I'm doing my fucking best, here, so can you please just be straight with me?"

Emir smiled faintly. "Of course. The usual term used for this sort of...state, I suppose, is to become a ghoul. But please don't let the name mislead you," he went on quickly. "You aren't in any danger of rotting, or dying, or anything like that."

"A...*ghoul?* A ghoul."

"As I said, the name is misleading. It's really more like...an apprentice?"

"An apprentice," Jacob echoed dryly. "An apprentice...vampire."

Emir nodded. "Well, I did say it was like a test drive. As you adjust, you will find that you are...well." He gave a small shrug. "Better. That's simplest."

Jacob scoffed into his next drink of water and set the empty glass on the table. "Better is not being able to sleep because I can hear fucking colors?"

The man—the vampire—let out a faint snort that made Jacob want to smack him, but he wilted pitifully under the soft smile on Emir's full lips. "Yes. As I said, you will adjust. If being paid in this way is something that you want to continue."

Jacob paused. "Are you...still going to give me the cash?"

Emir's eyebrows raised slightly. "We agreed on it, didn't we? I consider this a separate issue."

"So this is like...a bonus? It doesn't feel a lot like a bonus right now."

"This is beneficial to both of us," Emir explained. "You will reap the benefits of supernatural senses and strength, and I will have a...say an employee—more capable of helping me with whatever I may need."

Jacob frowned and hugged his own elbows. "And you said if I want it to...continue. What does that mean?"

"Well, you'll need to drink again," he said, far too casually for Jacob's taste. "Not daily, by any means—but the effects aren't continuous in perpetuity."

Jacob swallowed, his throat suddenly dry again despite the glass of water. "You mean drink...blood. Again."

"Yes. If you like." He sat forward on his seat and rested his elbows on his knees, looking Jacob sincerely in the face. "I don't want to force you. And you don't need to answer now. Give it another day, at least. Decide if the benefits are worthwhile to you." He stood and picked up the empty mason jar. "Tonight, I would like you to take me somewhere to buy new clothes. I did notice the way you looked at me when I came into the store. I stood out. I don't want to stand out."

Jacob scoffed before he could stop himself. "Good fucking luck."

Emir's brow knit faintly. "What do you mean?"

He wiped at his face with both hands, shaking his head. Idiot. "Nothing. Okay. Sure. Let's buy clothes." He sat and sighed while Emir excused himself to go upstairs and dress, but then he paused. He got up and went into the kitchen as swiftly and quietly as he could, and he hesitated with his hand on the fridge door before pulling it sharply open. The bags of blood still sat in their neat little bins like carefully sorted leftovers. Fuck. He was hoping he'd imagined it.

Emir returned in jeans and an at least somewhat normal-looking button down shirt, but it was still pretty ugly. Still—it couldn't change his face. Jacob's eyes went to the undone button at Emir's collar, and his whole body flushed hot. Stop thinking about licking his goddamn chest. Maybe Jacob was the real weirdo.

Jacob drove, since Emir claimed his car was useless. It was exceptionally strange having a hot confirmed vampire in his passenger seat, but Jacob did his best to keep his eyes on the road ahead of him. After a minute or two of silence, he forced a cough.

"So uh, what kind of clothes are we buying? Suits? Don't vampires wear suits?"

"It's not my preference," Emir answered, not taking his teasing bait. "Just average, casual clothes. It's best not to draw attention to myself."

Now Jacob did glance over at him. "You mean by, like, staying inside for so long that the whole town starts to think your house is haunted?"

Emir stared back at him. "Yes," he said flatly. "Like that."

Jacob couldn't help the smile on his face as he turned back to the road. "Got it."

"It wasn't purposeful, you know."

"What?"

"Staying inside. I simply...got distracted."

Jacob laughed. "For *twenty years*?"

Emir shifted in his seat, frowning as if he was mildly offended. "Time doesn't mean as much to me as it does to a human. I...lose track of it. I suppose I tend to focus on one thing for too long."

"Like buying six different musical instruments to learn?"

"I—had finished with the brass, so I decided to try strings next. That's all."

"Hold up," Jacob stopped him, turning to glance at him again and fighting more laughter. "You learned how to play the trumpet? And the trombone?"

"I wouldn't give myself too much credit, but I learned to be proficient, yes."

"But you're only awake at night."

"For the most part."

"So you were...you were practicing the *trumpet* in the middle of the night. Learning how to play...the *trumpet*."

"Yes?"

"Fuck," he snorted, hiding his smile behind his hand. "Your neighbors must have *hated* you. No wonder everybody thought there was a ghost." He stopped to laugh again. "Just this fucking...random-ass *honking* all through the night, like—" Jacob imitated the sound of a wailing, out of tune trumpet, and he had to stop from wheezing.

"I really don't see what's so funny," Emir said, though he looked pointedly out the window.

Jacob got himself together and exhaled a final long breath shortly before he pulled into the mall parking lot. He walked Emir over to the Men's Warehouse and released him into the store, trusting that he would be able to find clothes that he liked—but, as it turned out, the vampire's truly atrocious wardrobe wasn't entirely the fault of the 1990's. He was terrible at dressing himself. The few outfits he did have an opinion on and tried to put together would have made him stand out just as much as his baggy silk shirts.

"You could choose for me," he suggested, and Jacob shrugged.

"I just wear jeans and t-shirts, man. If you want better than that, I have no idea."

Emir frowned at him. "I thought you were culturally aware."

"Yeah, but I never said I was *fashionable*, man. Hold on. Cordelia, my roommate—she'll know how to dress a vampire, probably." He took his phone from his pocket and sent a quick text to Cordelia. She responded immediately and promised to be on her way, so Jacob and Emir waited outside of the store.

Emir wanted to get another look around the mall, so they wandered until they found the food court. Jacob hadn't eaten all day, but he still didn't feel up to solid food, so Emir bought him an Orange Julius, and he sipped it slowly. The smell of the greasy food around him was too much to stay in for long, so they were soon wandering again.

"You know, that reminds me," Jacob said around the straw in his mouth. "Nobody really uses cash anymore."

Emir glanced down at him. "No?"

"Nah," he said, shaking his head. "Everything's debit or credit cards. Do you even have a bank? Or do you just keep a bunch of doubloons or whatever upstairs? Like in a chest?"

"I do have a bank," Emir answered mildly.

Jacob took another sip of his drink. "And they don't care that you've had the account for like...a thousand years. Same dude."

"No. The bank is owned by vampires, for vampires."

"Shut the fuck up," Jacob laughed. "Really?"

"Mhm. There's one in New York. I have the phone number written down somewhere at home. I'm sure I could have a card delivered if I requested one." He smiled and touched Jacob's back just beneath his shoulder blades, the movement so casual and intimate at the same time that Jacob's body tensed. "Thank you, Jacob. I might not have thought of that."

"Well, gotta...earn my pay, I guess," he muttered, turning his attention to chewing on his straw.

Cordelia showed up before things could get any more awkward

39

than that, thankfully. They met her outside the clothing store, and she approached a little hesitantly, glancing between the two of them and seeming to ask Jacob with her eyes if it was really safe to come near.

Emir offered her a small, polite smile. "You must be Cordelia. I recognize you from my front porch in the middle of the night."

She let out a nervous laugh and pushed her hair behind one ear. "Uh, yeah. Sorry."

"It's forgotten," he assured her in a warm voice. "I'm Emir. It's nice to meet you."

Cordelia perked up then, and a smile appeared on her face. "You too. I mean, it's my first time meeting an undead immortal, so that's fun. And you're definitely as hot as Jacob said."

Emir glanced over at Jacob just in time to see him gritting his teeth at Cordelia. "Did he?"

"Cords, shut the fuck up," Jacob hissed under his breath, and then went on at a higher volume. "Hey so anyway, about those clothes."

"Yeah, no problem," Cordelia said with a smirk in Jacob's direction before returning her attention to Emir. "Come on. Let's get you out of whatever pre-*Matrix* ensemble this is."

Back inside, Cordelia handily chose a number of items and half pushed Emir into the changing room. She asked him what felt like a hundred thousand vampire-related questions through the door, which he didn't seem very keen to answer in the middle of the store, but he promised to keep Jacob apprised of the answers to her requests.

The clothes Emir arrived in were thrown in the trash almost the second he locked the door of the changing room, at Cordelia's insistence. The next time Jacob saw the vampire, he came out of the back hall in a pair of black, slim-fit jeans, black leather boots, and a light, cream-colored Henley shirt with the buttons completely undone and the sleeves rolled up to his forearms. Just a hint of the black chest hair Jacob knew went all the way down his stomach was visible where the buttons were open. Just there was where Emir had cut himself, cradled Jacob's head with strong, cool fingers, and let him taste his skin.

Jacob held his hands behind his back and pinched the meat between his thumb and forefinger as punishment to his brain. Stop thinking about licking the vampire's chest. Stop thinking about the way the blood tasted, the firmness of his chest under your hands.

Stop it.

"The style of pants now is very...snug," Emir observed, shifting his weight subtly in his new boots.

"Yeah," Jacob agreed without thinking, his eyes on the lines of Emir's thighs. He caught himself when he saw Cordelia's smirk and coughed loudly, turning away from them on the pretense of carefully considering a pair of socks on a shelf.

Thankfully, Emir didn't seem to notice. He paid for the new clothes and handed the bags over to Jacob without even looking at him. Jacob stared at him, letting him just hold them out beside him for a few seconds before he took them.

"Thank you, Cordelia," Emir said once they were outside again. "I really do appreciate the help."

"No problem. Glad I could help."

"I'll see you at home, Cords."

She nodded, but didn't move. She was smiling up at Emir now. "I mean, if there's anything else, or if you need help with something back at the house, maybe—"

"Bye, Cords," Jacob cut in loudly, and she narrowed her eyes at him in irritation.

"Okay, okay, damn. Bye." She gave the two men a brief wave and left them behind to return to Jacob's car.

He tossed the bags into the back seat with only half as much disrespect as he wanted to and climbed back into the driver's seat. It was even harder to be this close to Emir now that he was dressed well, and harder to keep his attention elsewhere when the vampire was watching him.

"You already seem much recovered," Emir said quietly.

"...Yeah," Jacob admitted. "I feel...pretty good, I guess. Everything is still...kind of a lot. But I'm not about to throw up." He looked over at the other man. "Is it like this all the time for you? Everything's so loud, and there are a lot more gross smells around than I realized. That food court was killer."

"You get used to it." Emir picked at something under his nails and glanced sidelong at him. "There are good smells you never knew about, too."

Jacob snorted. "Like virgin blood?"

One of Emir's eyebrows arched just slightly, and the faintest of teasing smiles pulled one corner of his lips. "Do you have virgin blood, Jacob?"

Jacob gripped the wheel tighter and kept his gaze steadfastly forward with great difficulty. "No," he said with maybe a little too much defensiveness in his voice. "It—I was making a joke," he insisted. "Vampires make jokes, don't they?"

"Mm," Emir agreed softly, the low sound doing absolutely nothing to quiet Jacob's quickly knotting stomach. "Occasionally."

Jacob kept his mouth shut for the remainder of the ride. When he parked, Emir got out and returned to the house without even considering getting his own bags from the back seat. Jacob snatched them up, not-entirely-accidentally spilling one of the bags onto the driveway and even-less-accidentally stepping on one of the shirts on his way to pick up another. He stuffed everything back in and followed Emir inside. He was already waiting at the bottom of the stairs when Jacob shut the front door.

"Upstairs, please," Emir said as he turned to take the next step, but Jacob got to the foot of the staircase and hesitated.

"Hey, uh. Do you have a coffin up there?"

Emir paused just long enough to glance back at him. "Come."

Jacob frowned at his back, but followed. He peeked through open doors he passed in the upstairs hallway, half expecting to see a dungeon, or maybe a torture chamber. But Emir led him to what looked like a very normal bedroom. A four-poster bed sat against the wall with heavy wooden nightstands on either side of it, both piled with books. The bed itself was made but rumpled, as if someone had been lounging on it.

Emir opened a set of double doors in the wall and took a step back from the revealed closet, gesturing to the clothes hanging inside. "These will need to be disposed of," he said simply. "Then the new ones can be put away."

Jacob stood in the doorway and stared blankly at him. "...Okay?"

Emir paused, looking vaguely confused by Jacob's lack of action. "I don't care what you do with them," he explained. "I won't need them again."

"What *I* do with them?" Jacob finally snapped. "Why would I do anything with them? You said you just wanted me to help you get caught up with the times, not be a servant."

The vampire looked at him evenly. "That's what I'm paying you *money* for. If you want to be given anything supplementary, then I will ask you for supplementary assistance. I believe that's fair; don't you?"

Jacob's face grew hot, and he threw the bags on the floor. "I'm not putting away your clothes, man. I didn't ask you for—for what you did to me yesterday, and it's not happening again. You understand me?"

"It's your decision," Emir said.

"I'm going home," he spat, even angrier at the vampire's apparent indifference.

"Of course. What is your schedule tomorrow?" he asked, but Jacob was already on his way down the stairs.

"I'll text you," he called back bitterly. He slammed the front door on his way out, and then he slammed the car door, too. He turned the key like it had been the one to offend him, and he steamed the whole way home.

Jacob had agreed to help him—for money—but that didn't make him some kind of fucking butler. The job parameters had been very specific. This—this blood stuff was just confusing everything. Fuck this guy. Fucking poncy vampire bullshit.

The next time he stopped at a light, he laid his forehead on the top of the steering wheel and sighed deeply. But fuck, he really needed the money.

6

The next morning, Cordelia was still eyeballing Jacob like he might fall over dead at any second, but he felt great. His nausea was gone, he'd slept a while, and he was even able to eat some toast and honey for breakfast without feeling like he wanted to chuck it across the room. He sat on the couch and read for a while before work, and it was a breeze. His mind was clearer—he didn't have to read the same paragraph three times to be able to really dig into what the author was saying, like he usually did with his grad school reading.

He left the apartment in a good mood, and while he was at work, Amy asked him to move some of the new inventory. It was like it weighed nothing. Jacob moved drum sets, full size keyboards, and a string bass without even working up a sweat. He could still hear customers speaking quietly all the way across the store, but it wasn't quite so dizzying as before—he was at least able to tune it out like normal chatter. Was this what Emir meant by just being "better?"

He seemed to fly through the day, but around the time the store was closing, he started to get a weird feeling. He tried to close out the register and do the rest of his evening duties, but he was preoccupied. He couldn't focus. He ended up counting the money in the register eight times before he was sure he'd gotten it right. Where the hell had the clarity from this morning gone?

He couldn't shake the feeling that he ought to be somewhere else. Be doing something else. He got distracted checking on inventory; he couldn't stop himself until he'd counted every single guitar pick in the box to make sure all two hundred and fifty were there. He took so long to finish up that Amy came to check on in twice, and when he finally said good night to her, he went to the parking lot and sat in his car for some time, trying to figure out what it was he had apparently forgotten. It was like a buzzing at the back of his skull, irritating him and driving him to distraction.

He'd double- and triple-checked the store closing. There were no assignments due that he'd missed—it was summer. He was just at his job. Was it a birthday? No; mom and dad were both in October, and Cordelia was January. Nobody else mattered.

Damn. What the hell was it?

He started the car, more than a little irritated, and when he turned out of the parking lot to head back to his apartment, his stomach immediately complained. He winced, the ache was so sharp, and he shook his head.

He couldn't just go home. He needed to check in with Emir. He did say he would still do his job.

At the next light, Jacob shot off a quick text. *I assume you don't have a card yet. Do you have some cash I can have? I have some ideas for you.*

He dropped the phone in the seat beside him, but it vibrated immediately. He was calling back. Of course he was calling back. Why just text and exchange information efficiently, when you can usurp someone's entire attention? At least Jacob's stomach felt better as he lifted the phone to his ear.

"Good evening, Jacob. Of course, you can come and have anything you need. How much money?"

"So, this is gonna sound like I'm about to rob you," Jacob admitted, "but I'll need probably like, ten grand. Also I'll need to be at the house for a while during the day tomorrow."

"Why so much?"

"To bring you into the new millennium, man," he chuckled.

Emir's tone softened. "You're very enthusiastic, considering how we parted company yesterday."

"Yeah, well," Jacob grumbled. "I signed up for a job, so I'm gonna do it. You're still gonna pay me when we're done, right?"

"Of course. I always keep my word, Jacob."

Why did that tone in his voice make Jacob's heart rate go up?

"...Right. Anyway—I'm off tomorrow, so I want to have the guy come to your place and get you hooked up for the Internet and stuff. But they don't really do night work, you know? So I'll need to be there. Have access to the house. ...And I'll need to know your bank info to sign you up, or they won't come."

"Mm. I understand. Come to me tonight, and I'll give you what you need. You're finished with work?"

"Yeah. I'll come now."

"Good. I'll see you soon, Jacob."

Jacob let out a long breath as he ended the call. It was unfair that even his voice through the phone should tingle Jacob's skin like this. He wasn't a kid—he was just an idiot, he guessed.

He drove faster than he should have to Emir's house, and he took quick steps up the driveway to the porch. When Emir answered his knock, the relief in his gut was so intense it made him kind of angry. What the hell was his brain doing to him? And, of course, Emir is half naked again, his robe just hanging open.

The vampire lightly touched Jacob's shoulder as he let him by, and he jumped. Why doesn't he have more clothes on? What was the point of buying him all those new clothes if he was just going to wear the same pair of fucking PJs all the time? The pants were so low that Jacob could see the muscular v-shape at his waistband, and he hated it.

"Here," Emir said, forcing Jacob to realize he'd been staring in the direction of the vampire's junk. He held out an envelope and pressed it into Jacob's hand. "Ten thousand. Please keep good track of it. I've also included a note with my bank's wire information."

"Cool," Jacob answered with a nod, feeling the weight of the money in his palm. He kept his eyes lowered so he didn't have to look Emir in the face. "So uh...if I come by in the morning, you'll be...sleeping?"

"Yes. That's why I have one more thing for you. Come."

He went up the stairs, and Jacob followed with a curious frown. Emir led him past the bedroom door and to the end of the hall, to the only fully closed door. He put his hand on the knob and paused a moment before looking back at Jacob.

"This is the only room in the house I will ask you not to enter."

"Uh. Okay. Super not ominous."

Emir opened the door, and Jacob craned his neck to see around him until he stepped inside and out of the way. The room was fairly small, and almost empty—except that in the center of the floor, a low platform had been built in. And, on top of that sat a coffin—though Jacob thought it might be more accurate to call it a sarcophagus. It wasn't just a wooden rectangle, or even a cartoon coffin shape. It was made of stone, with a triangular prism for a lid, and the whole thing had been painted a deep teal color beneath a covering of gold-painted carved calligraphy. It looked like Arabic, maybe. It was definitely old; some of the paint had chipped away from the corners, but overall, it was in good shape.

Jacob desperately wanted to touch it, but he felt in his gut that he shouldn't. He'd never even thought to ask Emir how old he really was, or where he was from, or anything you might want to ask an immortal person. Maybe he should. But Emir seemed somber now, watching Jacob as if trying to gauge his reaction to this reveal.

"So you do have a coffin up here," Jacob said in as casual a voice as he could manage, and Emir visibly relaxed, but he still snorted softly.

"It isn't a coffin."

Jacob turned to face him and stared up at him with a disbelieving frown. "Do they put dead people in it?"

"Yes."

"Then it's a coffin!"

Emir just glanced back at the apparently-not-a-coffin before continuing. "Semantics aside—you need to know that this is where I must rest. I mustn't be disturbed—especially by a stranger in the house, do you understand?"

"Yeah. Don't worry, I'll keep him out. He shouldn't even need to come upstairs at all."

"Good. Then the last thing." He reached into the pocket of his robe and held up a key for Jacob to see, which he then held out in offering.

Jacob wavered for a second or two as he looked down at the key. Emir only waited, so he held his hand out, and Emir dropped the key into his palm. It felt heavier than it should.

"You're giving me a key to your house?" he asked, frowning up at the other man.

"I prefer that to leaving it unlocked. You can be here to let the worker in. Please prevent him from disrupting more of my things than is necessary."

"Sure," Jacob said a little softly. This felt like trust. What had Jacob done to make Emir trust him this much? When he looked up again, he found Emir's dark eyes trained on him, his head slightly tilted as though studying a specimen. He stepped closer, and Jacob tried to move back and couldn't make his legs work.

"Do you feel uncertain, Jacob?" Why was his voice so gentle? It would have been easier if he really was some kind of vicious bloodsucker. At least that would vibe with the image Jacob had forever connected with the word "vampire" in his head. He didn't need dissociation on top of unwelcome arousal.

"No," he managed. "It's just a cable guy. It's fine."

Emir reached out and closed the fingers of the hand Jacob realized he was still stupidly holding out in front of him. He was so cold. It should have been more uncomfortable. "Good," he said. "Please stay until I wake up tomorrow."

"Uh. Yeah." Jacob pulled his hand away from Emir's lingering touch to shove the key into his pocket. Emir's hand on his was too strange, and Jacob liked it too much. "I'll have new stuff to show you anyway, so."

Emir nodded, but Jacob hesitated to leave the room. He didn't want to go yet. He worried the envelope in his hand and flicked his gaze down to the floor before daring to risk another look into the vampire's eyes.

"If the cable guy is coming, the house could stand to be...you know. Cleaner."

Emir's eyebrows lifted slightly. "Cleaner?"

"You haven't noticed this place is dust city? It's on everything."

"I...suppose I haven't."

"Yeah, I guess that's not a shock. Do you have anything to clean *with*?"

"Possibly," the vampire answered, but it sounded more like a question.

Jacob went back downstairs, laid the envelope of money carefully on the little table near the front door as if he thought it might run away, and then went into the kitchen. Behind the propped up trombone in the pantry, he found a wooden broom and a feather duster. Who the fuck has a feather duster? Someone who hasn't been out of the house since the 90's, Jacob guessed.

It turned out that trying to clean even a single room of a house filled with dusty stuff you can't get rid of was actually the worst. Jacob coughed and sneezed so much that he ended up asking Emir for something he could cover his face with. He had to call out to the vampire four times before he looked up from the sitting room chair, where he sat with his guitar on his knee, strumming the same chord—badly—until Jacob yelled at him.

Armed with a bandana that smelled like moth balls, a feather duster, and a straw broom, Jacob cleared away what tumbleweed he could from the living room, filling an entire garbage bag with dust bunnies. When he finally felt like he'd made a dent, he went back to the doorway of the sitting room and pulled the bandana from his face.

"Hey," he tried, and again, Emir didn't look up from the open tab book on the chair beside him. "Hey!" Jacob said again, skipping straight to shouting this time, and Emir raised his head. "Can we maybe just get rid of some of these books? I can take them to be donated if you're done with them—make a little more room in here."

"No," Emir answered flatly. He was already looking back down at his book, so Jacob spoke quickly before he lost him again.

"Not *any*? There must be a thousand books in this house!"

The vampire paused, then frowned at the floor for a few seconds as if running through the entire catalogue in his head. He stood, laid the guitar in the chair, and walked by Jacob and up the stairs. Jacob waited, watching the ceiling above him as shuffling and movement drifted down from the upper floor. Emir was gone for so long that Jacob was about to go ahead and start on cleaning the kitchen when the vampire reappeared at the bottom of the stairs—holding precisely two paperbacks in his hand. He offered them to Jacob, who took them with frowning amazement.

"...This is it?"

"Yes. I really didn't enjoy those."

Jacob gestured broadly at the stacks and stacks of hardcovers, paperbacks, anthologies, and even textbooks that he'd just spent the last hour rearranging, cleaning off, and replacing. "You enjoyed *all of these?*"

Emir's head cocked to the side slightly, as if it was an unusual question. "Yes."

"But you read them already."

"Most, yes. I keep the ones I haven't gotten to yet upstairs."

"So why do you need to keep them all if you already read them?"

"I may want to read them again."

"All of them?"

"Perhaps."

"So—oh my god. Okay. Fine. I will take these *two books* and go donate them for you tomorrow."

"Thank you, Jacob." Emir brushed past him again and picked up his guitar, not seeming to notice the stare of disbelief on the boy's face.

Jacob shook his head and scoffed as he crossed the room to set the two unworthy paperbacks by the door with his envelope, then tucked his bandana back up over his nose and returned to work.

As miserable as the cleaning was, for every space that Jacob cleared of dust, he felt a swell of satisfaction. He was helping. This would make Emir's home more comfortable. He would be more comfortable. Happier. Jacob paused mid-sweep. Why, exactly, was he cleaning the house? This had nothing to do with the vampire's modernization. This was ghoul work. Fuck.

Jacob almost slammed the broom down onto the floor, but he stopped himself and settled for just twisting the handle as if he could wring Emir's neck—or maybe his own—by proxy. He needed to leave. He stuffed the broom and duster back into the pantry, left the bandana on the kitchen counter, and stalked back to the sitting room doorway.

"Hey," he called loudly, and Emir actually looked up at him straight away. "This is more than good enough for the cable guy. If you want it cleaner than this, hire a maid."

Emir leaned his elbow on the guitar and nodded. "Thank you. You worked hard this evening; I appreciate it."

The flush of heat that spread up Jacob's neck and cheeks should have been from fury—but it wasn't. He'd been praised—he was pleased. He licked his lips and suddenly found himself faltering now that he had the vampire's dark eyes on him.

"Is there...anything else you need?"

"Purely related to my being out-of-touch, yes?"

Jacob shut his mouth tight. What the hell was he doing? Why would he ask that? Hadn't he just the day before thrown a fit because Emir had treated him like a servant? And now here he was, having spent the night cleaning the vampire's house, all "tell me your desires, master." He scowled at the wall and gave a purposeful scoff. "Yeah. Obviously," he said with as much disdain as he could muster.

Emir's stupid beautiful lips ticked upward into a slight smile. "No. Thank you."

"Okay. Then I'm going home."

Emir didn't try to stop him; Jacob heard the click of the upstairs door on his way out and glared at his own dim shadow as he stalked back to the car. Fucking asshole.

Jacob stopped with his hand on the car door handle. He didn't want to go. But he couldn't just stay—why would he? Stay and do what? He'd just end up saying something stupid again. He forced his hand to open the door and drove back to the apartment, his stomach roiling the whole way.

Cordelia was distracted by a movie when he came in, so he shut himself in his bedroom after a brief greeting to avoid her curiosity. He called the cable company and arranged to have them send someone out the following day. He gave them Emir's name and address and bank account number and signed him up for the fastest Internet package they had. Once that was settled, he spent the rest of the evening signing the vampire up for every streaming service he could think of.

When Cordelia poked her head in to say good night, he mentioned that he would be helping Emir the following night—with normal modern-day things. But he didn't tell her about the key. That felt too much like a secret.

7

Jacob was up early the next morning to borrow the music store's van, an arrangement that was going to cost him probably a week's worth of unpaid overtime. It would be worth it—he hoped. If Emir rolled out of bed—coffin—whatever—and wasn't damned impressed, Jacob was going to be pissed.

Since the cable guy wasn't due until the afternoon, Jacob spent the morning shopping. He bought a brand new laptop, the biggest 4K television he could fit in the van, and a VR headset. He made it back to Emir's around the middle of the day and carried the laptop and headset with him up the porch steps, but once he was actually standing in front of the front door, key in hand, he hesitated.

Could he really just...unlock it? Walk in like he belongs there? This vampire's house?

Emir trusted him to come inside while he was asleep. Vulnerable. Stake-able.

Are you going to try to stake me, Jacob?

Jacob bit down on the inside of his cheek. Shut up, penis. Nobody fucking asked you.

He unlocked the door and swung it open. It was never loud inside the house, by any means, but it was eerily quiet now. It was weird to stand in the living room without Emir there. The house really did seem empty, now. He shook off the feeling and set about unpacking the laptop and VR equipment—the television was much too big to move on his own, so that was going to have to wait.

Instead, he spent his time moving stacks of books from the living room into the side rooms, piling the literary Jenga towers a little higher where he could. He patted some of the dust from the couch cushions and brushed off the coffee table in an attempt to make the room look a bit more like a living room and less like a fucking garage sale.

He took the now empty boxes outside to the garbage can and paused with the lid open. Did Emir even get garbage service? He must. His house would be overflowing with empty blood bags if not.

Jacob went back inside and stopped on his way past the kitchen doorway. A pile of food sat on the counter beside the fridge—a bag of potato chips, some apples, a loaf of crusty-looking bread, a jar of mixed nuts. Jacob moved closer and picked up the small slip of paper lying nearby, marked with slanted, loopy handwriting.

Please help yourself. There are some drinks and cheese in the fridge.

Jacob's face warmed uncomfortably. Emir had bought food for him. He opened the fridge, and it still had a whole bunch of blood in it—less than before, but still a lot. But now, the door shelves had been filled with a few different kinds of small soda bottles and a couple different juices. A small stack of cheeses sat right next to one of the pastel bins of blood bags, so that was probably going to stay right there forever.

He took one of the sodas, but despite running around all morning, he didn't actually feel hungry yet. He would still have to remember to thank Emir for the thought.

Jacob sat on the cleared-away couch and went through all the setup and updates to get the laptop up and running, periodically glancing over his shoulder at the stairs. Emir had asked him not to go in that room. But he was up there right now. Fast asleep inside what was absolutely a coffin no matter what he said. Was he lying on his back with his arms crossed over his chest? Did he rise out of it with a cape on? Why did he have a bed if he sleeps in there?

While the laptop ran its last round of updates, Jacob crept up the stairs. He lingered at the top, peering around the corner at the closed door at the end of the hall. He shouldn't go in. Emir specifically asked him not to go in. Emir trusted him in the house—he shouldn't ruin that, right?

But he wanted to go in. He walked with slow, careful steps down the hallway as if Emir might hear him coming, and he touched the knob with his fingertips. He let his hand close around the cool metal and put his ear close to the door. It was silent inside. Still as the grave.

Jacob snorted a little and covered his mouth to muffle the sound. He focused on the slit where the door met the frame and wet his lips, his grip tightening on the doorknob. Emir was in there. Jacob wanted to go in. His heart jumped at the thought of opening the door and simply laying eyes on the dark sarcophagus. He wanted to be where Emir was.

Wait. What?

Jacob frowned at the dark wood in front of him. He wanted to sit outside the coffin and wait for him, so that he would be there the minute Emir woke up.

Why the fuck did he want to do that?

He took his hand off the doorknob and stepped back, holding the offending hand tight against his chest like he couldn't trust it not to betray him again. Was this because of the blood? It had given him some perks, it was true, but was it also making him into a more docile servant?

A loud knock from downstairs startled him, and he pulled himself away and hurried back down the stairs. While the guy from the cable company did his work, Jacob followed him around—probably way too much. But he didn't want to risk him opening the fridge or going near the door upstairs. He tried to cover his helicoptering by making a show of moving books and globes and other messes out of the worker's way. Thankfully, he only gave the surroundings a few strange looks as they went and didn't ask any questions. Jacob guessed this probably wasn't the weirdest house he'd ever seen, anyway.

The cable guy had finished his work, and Jacob was making sure the laptop connected to the Internet by the time he heard a noise from upstairs. He perked up at the heavy, slow scraping of stone from above him. A brief pause passed, and then he heard the click and creak of an opening door. He sat still and tense on the sofa, straining to listen while he waited with his heart in his throat. If Emir was taking footsteps, Jacob couldn't hear them. He gripped the laptop on his knees a little tighter.

Stop it. Stop thinking about him. He doesn't need you. He'll be here in a minute. Why do you even want to go up there? Idiot.

Jacob didn't like this at all.

When Emir did appear around the corner and make his way downstairs, he was dressed in a dark brown linen robe that flowed down to his elbows and all the way to the floor. It was lined at the collar with reddish lace and kept closed by nothing but a single toggle at his hips. He clearly wasn't wearing anything underneath, and it was way, way more transparent than Jacob was comfortable with. He could definitely see the shadow of the other man's dick. He forced his gaze away and scowled at the floor instead. Just don't look.

"Hello, Jacob," Emir offered as he reached the foot of the staircase. "The worker has come and gone?"

"Uh, yeah," he answered, still keeping his eyes on anything but the man in front of him. "It's all good. I have stuff for you. But it would be really cool if you could put some actual clothes on."

"Oh."

Jacob dared a glance up at his face and curled his fingers around the laptop so tight he worried he might crack it. Was this asshole smirking?

"Of course," Emir went on with a nod, and Jacob had to hold in his sigh as the vampire turned around. Of course his ass was fucking nice.

Jacob waited while Emir was upstairs, but he came back down in a nice pair of jeans and a black V-neck shirt, which wasn't that much better, if Jacob was honest. He asked for Emir's help bringing the television inside, but when they went out and Jacob opened the back of the van, Emir picked up the box like it was nothing and carried it inside, only taking care not to bump it on anything as he went back through the door.

Right. Okay.

They got it out of the box, and once it was sitting on the floor and Jacob had peeled off all of the protective plastic, Emir stood staring at it in silence for some time.

"This is...a television?"

"Yeah," Jacob said with a laugh. "A fucking nice one. You're welcome."

Emir circled the television, running his hand over the back and top of the screen and then standing back to admire it again. "It's enormous."

Jacob tried to squash the swell of pride in his chest at seeing the vampire so obviously pleased. "Come on," he said. "Let's hang it up."

"It goes on the wall?"

Jacob shrugged. "I mean, it doesn't have to, but that's easiest.

Emir's smile put a knot in Jacob's chest, so Jacob didn't look at him for a while. Emir held the television up easily while Jacob stood on a chair to attach it to the bracket, screwed everything in properly, and attached the necessary cords. He watched with curious interest as Jacob picked up the remote and set up the Wi-Fi connection.

"The *television* connects to the Internet?"

"Yep. And I signed you up for some streaming services, so you can watch whatever you want. Just try not to get sucked into a twenty-year-long Netflix binge."

"I don't know what that is."

"It's for streaming." When Emir still stared at him expectantly, he continued. "Streaming is like cable, kind of, except there are no commercials, and you can choose what you want to watch whenever. It's not like it used to be where it's like, this show comes on at 8 p.m. on Saturdays, or whatever."

"Remarkable," Emir chuckled, and he looked up at the screen while Jacob set up his accounts for him. He was standing too close. Jacob could smell him—did he always smell so fucking good? Or was this just another "perk?"

Jacob showed him how to use the remote to get to the various apps, and he turned on the first show that popped up on Netflix for him as an example. Emir stared at the screen in silence with an odd look on his face, and it took a few seconds for Jacob to understand what it was—awe.

"It's like looking through a window," the vampire said softly. "It's so clear."

Jacob caught himself staring at the other man's staring and gave a cough as he turned purposely away from him. "Yeah, well, modern technology and everything, I guess. Anyway—here's that." He passed the remote off to Emir and picked up the laptop from the sofa, then patted the spot next to him to encourage the other man to sit and look. "I know I told you you can use the Internet on your phone; I don't know if you've been trying that at all—"

"A bit. I don't...really know what I'm looking at."

"Okay. I figured this would be easier for you, since you've at least used a regular computer before. Here." He opened up the browser and pointed to the search bar, which caused Emir to lean very close to him. He ignored it. "What do you want to know about?"

Emir frowned faintly at him. "What do you mean?"

"I mean, any subject you can think of. You can type whatever you want in here, and Google—that's the search engine—will tell you about it. Like, show you websites about what you want. There's this thing called Wikipedia, and it's like a free online encyclopedia. Literally anything you want to know more about, and I can almost guarantee there's a wiki page for it."

"For learning guitar?" Emir suggested, and Jacob scoffed.

"Dude. There are entire YouTube channels for teaching people to play the guitar. Look." He pulled up a few examples and hated how warm he felt as Emir smiled. He was pleased. Good. Wait—no. Who cares? Jacob was just doing his job. His job for money. He frowned at the screen and tried to pretend it didn't make his stomach flutter to have Emir's face so close to his. "So anyway, you can just play around with this. I'm sure you'll figure it out. But there's one more thing I wanted to show you."

Emir watched him curiously as he set the laptop aside on the coffee table and pulled the VR headset out of its case.

"Come put this on your face."

"...Pardon?"

Jacob helped him fit the headset over his eyes, biting the corner of his mouth hard in an attempt to block out the thrill in his chest from getting to touch the vampire's soft black curls. Emir tried out the couple of simple games Jacob showed him, and he even laughed softly once or twice, which was murder on Jacob's attempted composure. But he took the headset off before too long, shaking his head and rubbing at his eyes. It made him too dizzy.

They sat together for a while longer, Jacob helping to guide him through some sites as Emir searched on the laptop for various topics. He tried to catch the vampire up on the most important things he could think of while they talked—like that someone drove a car in space, and that now there existed a private company sending people into space, instead of just the government. He showed him YouTube and Wikipedia and Google Earth, and Emir seemed to thoroughly enjoy the fact that his laptop screen was touchable—he spun the digital globe, zoomed in, and zoomed out, all with a smile on his face that upset Jacob's stomach.

"Look," Jacob said as Emir was admiring the Andes mountains. "You can just keep going in, until you get to the streets. They drove trucks, like, all over the world taking pictures, so you can explore everywhere."

Emir zoomed in experimentally, then backed up, and he moved the map until he could focus on Istanbul. Then he zoomed far in, and the smile on his lips changed subtly as he scanned the breadth of the huge city. "Incredible."

Jacob tried to watch him without focusing on how nice the other man's full lips looked when he was smiling. "Something special about Istanbul?"

"I haven't been in some time. It's changed so much."

"Is that where you're from?"

"Mm, no." Emir backed the screen away from the city and scrolled East, and he had to zoom in a lot farther this time before a much smaller city appeared on the map. "Arzinjan. It's still not very impressive," he admitted with a soft chuckle.

"So you're Turkish? I wondered about the accent."

"It was part of Persia when I was alive, but I suppose, yes."

Jacob frowned. The phrase was jarring to hear—when I was alive. It was a strange reminder that the person sitting beside him wasn't actually human anymore, no matter how he seemed. "How...long ago was that?"

"1629."

"Holy shit," Jacob said, a little more loudly than he meant to.

Emir shrugged one shoulder. "I'm not old by any means for one of my kind. I met a woman once who was a member of the court of Ashurbanipal, and someone must have come before her, too."

He laughed. "That's nuts."

Emir turned a teasing eye on him. "You're familiar with the concept of vampires, yes?"

"Well *yeah*," Jacob scoffed, "but it's still weird to have someone right in front of me who says they're from the 17th century. You're old, man."

"To you, I must seem that way."

Jacob watched him for a moment as he returned his attention to the screen. Emir *didn't* actually seem that old. Jacob would have expected a real-life vampire to be stuffy—to talk in a weird, old-fashioned way, like in a Dracula movie. Or maybe to be over-the-top dramatic and depressed, like something from Anne Rice. Emir's English was good, and he smiled and had conversations. Emir was sort of aloof and polite, which Jacob guessed was on brand, but he at least seemed like a *person* who was a bit aloof—not a monster.

"Do you intend always to work at the music store?" Emir asked, turning his eyes to Jacob's face and making him retreat slightly under the gaze.

Why was he asking about Jacob? What could it possibly matter to him? Jacob took a second to find his voice. "Uh—no. I'm actually in grad school now. The store job is just to pay the bills."

Emir straightened slightly and shifted to face him as if showing he had his attention. "What are you in school for?"

"Literature. Specifically, I'm focusing on subaltern authors and postcolonial issues in Sub-Saharan Africa."

The vampire tilted his head. "I don't know that word, subaltern."

"Like, the lower classes," Jacob explained. "The othered groups. In this case, specifically the native people in a colonized country. I've done a lot of work on people like Chinua Achebe, Ama Ata Aidoo, Ngũgĩ wa Thiong'o."

Now Emir's eyebrows lifted in surprise. "Really."

Jacob frowned. "What's that face for."

"Forgive me—I wouldn't have expected to find an academic working retail."

"Man," Jacob snorted, "you really have been in here for a long time, huh? My whole generation is broke as shit. Also, fuck you—I don't seem academic enough for you?"

Emir wasn't looking at him anymore—his brow furrowed as he glanced toward one of the side rooms, and then he set the laptop down on the table. "You know, the name is familiar. Hold on."

"What?"

Emir didn't answer him. He was already on his way out of the room, and through the doorway, Jacob could hear stacks of books being moved around. After a minute, Emir appeared again, but he only passed through the living room and went into the small den near the stairs. Another minute or two of shuffling passed before he finally came back. He took his seat beside Jacob again and handed him a hardback book with an off-white dust jacket. Large black text filled the cover—JAMES NGUGI - A GRAIN OF WHEAT. An illustration of a single golden wheat plant was printed over the top of the lettering.

"I read it when it was released; it's not entirely to my taste, but it was interesting. Is it the same person you mentioned?"

Jacob held the book like he might break it. His mouth hung open as he gingerly opened the cover to look at the inside. "You got this...when it came out? Like, 1967, you bought this book."

"Mhm."

He turned a page and scanned the small lettering of the front matter. "This is a first edition."

"Would you like it?"

Jacob's eyes snapped up to Emir's placid face, and for way too long, he only gaped at him like a fish. "This is probably worth a lot of money," he finally got out.

Emir tilted his head slightly. "I have money. This is meaningful to you, isn't it? Because of your work?"

"I—yeah, but—"

"It's only going to sit and gather dust here. If you want it, it's yours."

Jacob hesitated, looking down at the book uncertainly and closing the cover as if it was made of tissue. He couldn't accept a gift like this. What would it mean to take something so valuable from him? Did it even matter, if Emir himself didn't consider it valuable? Emir *wanted* to give it to him—because it meant something to Jacob. For once, he didn't fight the warm feeling spreading through his chest.

"...Thanks," he said softly.

"Of course. Have you eaten? It's getting a bit late."

Jacob needed to get out of here. Emir was too close, and he was being too nice, and he was looking at Jacob with eyes that were too soft and appreciative, and he smelled too good. Jacob was going to do something stupid.

"Uh. I have plans with Cordelia," he lied in a rush, and without pause, his mouth went on talking without his consent. "That's not true. I don't have plans." He stopped, his body tensing, and he looked up at Emir, who was smirking very faintly.

"You don't need to lie to me, Jacob. If you'd like to leave, you aren't a prisoner."

Jacob faltered. "But I—what the fuck was that? I didn't mean to—"

"I'll rephrase," Emir cut in gently. "You *can't* lie to me."

"Why the fuck not?"

Even as he asked, he knew the answer. It was the same reason he wanted to go sit by this man's coffin-bed until he woke up. The same reason he got anxious as soon as he knew Emir was awake, and the same reason he didn't want to be anywhere but right here. It was the blood.

Jacob got to his feet and stepped back before Emir could answer, anger prickling the back of his neck. "Fuck you, man!" he spat. "You didn't tell me about all this! How do I get rid of whatever you did to me? Fucking ghoul bullshit!"

Emir watched him evenly. "The effects will fade in time. Don't worry."

"Good! Don't ask for me again until it does. I'm not dealing with this garbage. I'll come help you again once this shit is...out of my system, or whatever. Fuck." He stormed to the front door and threw it open, then stepped out, paused, and leaned his head back through the doorway. "Thank you for the book," he said, hoping he sounded appropriately angry, and then he slammed the door closed behind him.

———

Jacob spent the next couple of days actively forcing himself not to think about Emir, which worked about as well as not picturing a pink elephant. He went to work, he did his overtime for Amy, he read, he played games with Cordelia. She still had vampire questions for him, so he passed on what little he knew, but he absolutely refused to talk about Emir the person. She reminded him more than once that being a sexy vampire's thrall was absolutely wasted on him.

He didn't eat much. He rarely got hungry.

Emir didn't text him at all. Good.

After a full three days had passed, Jacob began trying to pop his ears occasionally while he was sitting at home. He felt like he was going deaf. He couldn't hear things outside as well as he could before, and it made him feel a little numb, like he was wrapped in muffling fleece.

He still wasn't hungry.

That evening, he was exceptionally antsy. He'd recognized after the second day that the feeling meant Emir had woken up for the night, but he refused to accept the pull he felt. Once, he caught himself on the steps outside the apartment with his car keys in hand, ready to drive over to the house, but he stopped and about-faced before he could follow through.

Instead of acknowledging his growing anxiety, tonight he sat at the kitchen table with his book and an open notebook beside him, writing down notes and passages he means to come back to. But he frequently stopped to re-read a paragraph, or checked the previous page. He tapped his pen rapidly against the paper and bounced his heel, his head heavy in his hand where his elbow rested on the table.

He was re-reading the same paragraph for the third time when he noticed Cordelia crouching across from him and staring at him with her chin and fingers on the table, and when he spotted her, he jumped so hard that his chair scooted back an inch or two.

"Do you need lives for the master, Renfield?" she asked in a low voice, and he scoffed at her.

"Fuck you. I'm just...not in a good mood."

"Yeah, because you're avoiding your ghoul duties."

He sighed and pointedly dropped his head back into his hand to focus on his book. "I shouldn't even have fucking said anything."

"Seriously," Cordelia pressed. "I'm worried about you. You don't look good. Maybe you should ask Emir if there's anything you can do to make this go away faster?"

"I don't want to ask him shit," Jacob grumbled without looking up.

She rose to stand by the table. "Okay," she said, but there was reluctance in her voice. "I'm gonna go grab something to eat; do you want me to bring you anything?"

"No thanks. I'll have something later."

"...Okay." She lingered by the table for a second, seeming as though she wanted to say more, but then she let him be.

Jacob stared down at his book, scowling at it. Fuck. Fuck this.

8

Emir had gotten very little guitar playing done for the past few days—the Internet was amazing. He'd watched an entire YouTube series on radiation, read at least a dozen Wikipedia pages on various subjects, and spent an exceptionally long time exploring Google Earth. He'd kept his phone nearby in case Jacob called or texted, but he hadn't. He guessed Jacob had been serious about letting the withdrawal run its course, and Emir intended to let him. It was his decision entirely.

Tonight, he sat on the sofa in soft sleep pants with a show called *Cosmos* playing on the television and a bag of blood in his hand. It was only room temperature now instead of chilled from the refrigerator, but it was still nowhere near as satisfying as fresh. But Emir had gotten used to it.

He heard a car approach and turned his eyes to the front window once the door slammed shut outside. A faint smile touched his lips as Jacob's familiar scent reached his nose just a few moments before a knock at the door. He paused the show, set his half-empty bag on the coffee table, and went to answer the door.

Jacob glared up at him with his hands in his pockets, as if he wasn't the one who'd just driven himself over.

"Good evening, Jacob," Emir offered, and the boy chewed his lower lip and turned his head.

"Hey. I...need to talk to you."

"Of course." He stepped aside to let Jacob in and followed him into the living room, where the boy had stopped to stare at the bag on the table.

"Didn't mean to interrupt your dinner," Jacob said. He was being snide on purpose, but Emir wouldn't take his bait.

"It's no problem. Please, sit."

They settled on the couch, Jacob sitting as far from him as possible. He was still frowning at the bag, but after a few more moments, he looked up at his host.

"Where do you even get those? Do you rob local hospitals or something?"

"Of course not. They're delivered."

Jacob paused. "...Delivered."

"Mhm. Monthly. From a company in Boston."

Jacob stared at him with narrowed eyes. "You're fucking with me."

"Why would I?"

"Fuck," he scoffed. "Vampire banks, fucking vampire Meals on Wheels." He glanced back at the bag. "At least it's better than...the alternative, I guess."

"For me as well," Emir agreed. "It's much easier and more convenient than having to hunt for myself, and it draws far less attention. I haven't killed a human in decades."

Jacob made an uncomfortable face. "Well that's...good?"

"Modern solutions for a modern age."

"Right."

Emir watched him without speaking, waiting for him to continue. He was fidgety. Tense. Not meeting Emir's gaze. When nothing further seemed to be coming, Emir said gently, "You wanted to talk to me about something, Jacob?"

"Yeah," he finally answered. "I—fuck." He wiped at his damp forehead with the back of his hand and then rubbed the sweat away onto the thighs of his jeans. "I can't...keep going like this?"

"Like what?"

"Like—I feel like I'm in this cloud, like everything's duller, and I feel...heavy, and stupid."

Emir did his best not to smile. "Forgive the way this sounds, but that probably means you're getting back to normal."

Jacob's shoulders hunched slightly, and he looked down at his hands in his lap. "I don't want to go back to normal," he said, more subdued than Emir had ever heard.

"That isn't what you said before," Emir answered evenly. "Think carefully—you know these gifts have strings that I can't cut."

"I don't care," the boy said firmly. "I want...more."

Emir sat up and leaned closer to him, reaching out to touch his jaw and the side of his neck, letting his thumb brush the boy's chin. "Look at me, Jacob."

He was hesitant, but he looked—though his brow was furrowed, and he chewed the corner of his bottom lip.

Somewhere deep in his chest, Emir wanted to devour him. The boy's heart was racing, and his pulse was strong under Emir's hand. He looked timid now, not like the young man who sniped and swore at him. It would be easy. Pin him down right where he was, taste him, feel his desperate hands grabbing, pulling at him. Helpless. Feel the heat of living blood warm him from the inside, and take each last fading heartbeat for his own.

But he liked Jacob. And he wasn't an animal.

"Be sure," he said softly.

Jacob's Adam's apple bobbed lightly as he swallowed. "I'm sure," he whispered. "I want more. ...Please."

He watched the boy for just a moment more, trying to judge his answer. Then he nodded. "Come." He settled back against the sofa with his arm laid across the back and gestured for Jacob to move closer. The boy seemed reluctant to get too near to him—his eyes traveled over Emir's bare chest and down to the waistband of his pants, but after a pause, he scooted in.

Emir drew him close and easily scratched a deep line into his skin at the base of his neck, letting a swell of blood seep over his collarbone. Jacob's gaze locked on it immediately, so Emir tilted his head just slightly, and all it took was Emir gently threading his fingers through the hair at the back of the boy's head for him to lean in and lave his tongue over Emir's skin, scooping up the spilled blood. His hand pressed into Emir's stomach as he steadied himself, and he closed his mouth over the wound with a faint sound of relief and satisfaction.

Emir let his eyes shut and wet his lips, turning his head slightly toward Jacob and letting his nose brush the boy's dark hair. His hand was hot against Emir's skin, and his every heartbeat drew forth another mouthful of blood. Jacob's fingertips trembled subtly against him, pressing tight into his flesh, and his breath was ragged and quick. If only he could have been so pliant and agreeable the rest of the time.

When enough blood had been shared, Emir pulled Jacob gently away from him by the hand in his hair. The boy's eyes were lidded as Emir looked down at him, his cheeks flushed, his parted, panting lips stained red. Emir drew almost close enough to touch those softly breathing lips with his own, but stopped himself.

If Jacob looked this way all the time, Emir's life would be immeasurably harder.

He watched the boy lick his lips, still settled close against Emir's body and seeming in no hurry to move his hand. Emir's hand, too, lingered in Jacob's hair, fingertips brushing over the skin just behind his ear. It took quite a few seconds for Jacob to look up into Emir's face, but when he was able to move, he fell back against the far arm of the couch again and covered his mouth with his hand.

"Fuck," he said, muffled by his own fingers.

Emir wiped at the blood still oozing onto his chest with his thumb and licked it away himself. The cut would heal on its own shortly, but he'd rather not leave stains on the sofa.

Jacob sighed, squeezing his eyes shut and taking a few more heavy breaths. He finally let his hand drop to the couch, and when he opened his eyes again and looked across the couch, it was with a gaze of such satisfaction that Emir almost reached over and grabbed him again.

"I'm such an idiot," he grumbled.

Emir couldn't help his faint smile. "Do you think so?"

The boy leaned his head back against the arm of the couch and gazed up at the ceiling. "You know," he began in a quiet voice, "I've never been a huge drinker." He shrugged. "Never smoked, never did any drugs except for weed a few times. Never wasted money gambling. I'm not a person who gets...hooked on things, you know?"

"But?"

"But I think if you let me, I'd do that until I died. Or you did." He lifted his head just enough to peer over at him. "That probably can't happen, right? Like my whole stomach would explode before you were even yes."

Emir chuckled. "Probably, yes."

Jacob slowly pushed himself upright, licking his lips again as if hoping there might still be a drop or two to be had there. "Can you...promise me something?"

"Perhaps."

"I know what you said about there being strings. I get it," he said. "And I know that doing this again means I'm going to feel...certain things. Toward you. I just want you to promise me you're not going to...you know. Take advantage." He frowned. "I'm going to keep helping you—I want to—but I don't want to be anybody's slave. So if you can't promise that, then I'll just, like...have Cordelia strap me to the bed for a month so I can't come see you until I'm over it."

Emir tilted his head curiously. "You're asking to accept my gifts and give me nothing in return? That hardly seems fair."

Jacob squirmed a little on the cushion, his eyes passing over the last bit of blood sliding over Emir's collarbone. "Well...what would you even want me to do? I don't mind some stuff, but I'm not gonna just 'yes master' around the place."

"Mm." Emir scooped up the final drip of blood and leaned over to offer it to Jacob on his finger, and the boy took it into his mouth without hesitation—eagerly, even. His eyes shut briefly as he swallowed the last of the dark fluid, and Emir pulled his finger slowly from Jacob's lips. "I wouldn't mind an *occasional* 'yes master,'" he teased in a low voice.

"Fuck off," Jacob sighed as he opened his eyes again.

"I promise not to ask you to do anything degrading," Emir assured him. "But I may ask for your help when it comes to things I might need from in town. Is that agreeable to you?"

"...Yeah. I can do that. But if this keeps on for a while, when I start classes again—"

Emir shook his head and held up a hand to interrupt him. "I wouldn't interfere with your education."

"...Okay. Okay," he said again. "Then...good." He paused awkwardly, shifting in his seat, and then he glanced at the paused television screen. "...So Neil deGrasse Tyson, huh?"

"He's very engaging. I do enjoy this sort of thing—I saw the first one back in the 80's." He offered the boy a small smile and gestured toward the television. "Would you like to stay?"

Jacob looked quickly back toward the front door, but then he turned to look Emir in the eyes again and seemed to settle. "...Sure."

They stayed on the couch together until well into the night. Jacob gave Emir a number of sidelong looks as he finished drinking from the blood bag, but he didn't say anything. Eventually, he started to yawn, and his eyes began to droop, so Emir stopped the show and reminded him that he probably had work in the morning.

Jacob hesitated at the front door as Emir bid him good night, and he wouldn't quite look him in the face, but after a moment, he returned the good night in a hurry and rushed back to his car as if he might be chased. He must have still been hazy from the blood.

––––

Over the next few days, Jacob came to the house a lot. He stopped knocking; now that he had a key, he grew more and more comfortable simply letting himself in. Emir didn't mind.

He asked about the car—whether Emir wanted a new one. He barely waited for the answer—by the time Emir had agreed that it was probably wise to replace it, Jacob was already looking up the number for a charity organization that would come and tow it away.

Buying a new one was a trip that necessitated going out during the day, which Emir wasn't thrilled about, but Jacob brought him a new pair of sunglasses and smiled at the way Emir looked at him. So that seemed worth it.

Emir didn't care much about cars, but the ones Jacob showed him were very impressive regardless. They all had touchscreens and plugs for smartphones, and they would direct you to wherever you needed to go with a map on the screen. He saw the appeal, but doubted he would use it much. He ended up buying a new version of the care he had before, which seemed to irritate Jacob for some reason, but it was a pleasant drive home.

The next day, Jacob informed him that he'd made up a list of the most important movies Emir had missed over the last twenty years, and that they were going to watch all of them. They spent a lot of time on the couch together through the rest of the week—Jacob snacking on the food and drinks Emir provided and slowly staring less and less when Emir happened to be drinking near him. They chatted about the movies they watched—some, like *Lord of the Rings*, Emir was interested in because he'd enjoyed the books. Others, like *Harry Potter* or *Pirates of the Caribbean*, he didn't care to see more than one of.

Jacob was vocally disappointed to find that Emir didn't particularly enjoy horror movies. He did quite like *Cabin in the Woods* because of the interesting hook, but after sitting through *Insidious*, *28 Days Later*, *The Descent*, and *Hereditary*, Emir was forced to ask his young friend if they could perhaps try a new genre now, please.

They went to the movie theatre together to see a new film on a gigantic screen Jacob said was called IMAX. Emir paid for his popcorn with his new debit card, which Jacob was almost mockingly proud of him for using. Emir didn't mind the teasing. The size of the screen was very impressive, and he enjoyed having Jacob beside him during the movie despite the crunching of the popcorn.

Sometimes, when they were at the house, and the movie they were watching didn't particularly hold Emir's interest, they got distracted. They talked about some of the things Jacob had been studying, and Emir listened intently while he talked about themes in the novels he read that stemmed from the effects of imperialism, the essays and critiques of people like Camus and someone named Ndĩgĩrĩgĩ. He became far more passionate when talking about his favorite books than Emir ever saw him. More than once, he seemed embarrassed by how animated and worked up he got, but watching him made Emir smile.

Jacob had done a lot for him already with regard to informing him on the things he'd missed, but he continued to find things to teach him. Once, he came over in the evening and caught Emir listening to a CD on his Discman and called him an idiot for not thinking to use the Internet for music. He showed him an app on his phone that allowed him to listen to any song he could think of. Emir didn't mind the name-calling—Jacob was smiling as he showed Emir how to save his favorite songs to his app's library. Jacob even brought him a new pair of headphones he hadn't asked Emir to pay for.

Emir wanted to do something for him. A gift. Something to show his appreciation. Something to show that he thought of the boy as more than just an employee or a servant. Emir enjoyed being around him. He couldn't recall the last time he'd felt that way. But Jacob wasn't tiring the way most people were. It was...different. But Emir liked it.

The following evening, Emir drove to Jacob's apartment just before dusk. He hadn't been there before, but he didn't have any trouble finding it. He would never have any trouble finding Jacob for as long as they were connected by blood.

He stood at the apartment door with two small paper gift bags in his hand—it would have been rude to arrive at someone's home with only a gift for one of the occupants. It wouldn't hurt for Jacob's best friend to like him, either.

When Jacob answered the door, he stared blankly up at Emir for a solid five seconds. "Hey," he finally got out. "Uh...was I supposed to meet you tonight?"

"No. I wanted to bring you something. Is Cordelia at home?"

Jacob turned his head just enough to peer skeptically at him. "Yeah."

"Good. I have something for her, also."

"...Okay." Jacob stepped back from the door and held it open, but Emir didn't move. Jacob raised his eyebrows at him in question.

"...May I come in?"

"Oh. Shit," Jacob said with a laugh, "is that one real? I have to invite you?"

Emir sighed lightly. "Yes. You have to invite me in."

"Do you hit an invisible wall or something if you try?"

"Or something. Yes. May I come in, Jacob?"

The boy was yelling over his shoulder now. "Cords, come here! The inviting them in thing is true!"

Cordelia appeared from around the hall corner, the curious look on her face expanding to surprise as she spotted Emir in the doorway. "Oh shit," she said, already on her way through the living room to look around Jacob's shoulder. "Really?"

"What happens if I say no?" Jacob asked, looking back up at Emir with childish amusement. "Is there a waiting period before you can

71

ask again? Like you go on cooldown?"

"Jacob, please."

'Okay, okay." He made a show of bowing and making a grand welcoming gesture with his arm. "You may come in."

Emir stepped inside then without giving Jacob the satisfaction of acknowledging him. He moved into the living room and waited until Jacob had shut the door before doing a quick check of the bags in his hands. "I've brought small gifts for both of you. As a thank you for your help."

Jacob hesitated a moment before taking the bag from him, but Cordelia accepted hers the moment he held it out to her.

"Oh wow, thank you! I didn't even do anything!"

"You helped with my wardrobe, and you've kept my secret. That is more than enough."

The girl pulled the bag open to look inside and reached in, retrieving a pair of intricately-woven silver earrings. Each was made of a pair of linked, filigree-decorated rings marked with bright blue stones and a star-shaped post. Cordelia gasped softly, laying them in her palm as if they were made of glass.

"Oh my god, look at these!" She raised her head to look Emir in the face. "Are they real? I mean, are they—you know, old?"

"Classy, Cords," Jacob grumbled, but Emir smiled faintly.

"They are antique, yes. Do you like them?"

"I love them! Thank you!" She held the jewelry to her chest and inched a step closer to him. "Can I hug you?"

Emir blinked at her, mildly taken aback by the request. "I...suppose so."

Cordelia stood on tiptoe and put her arms around his neck, forcing him to hunch down a little while he awkwardly patted her back once or twice. She gave him a good squeeze, then dropped back down onto her heels as she released him.

"I'm gonna go put them in right now."

Jacob still looked down at the bag in his hands as she hurried away into the hall, and when he glanced back up at Emir, it was with a frown as if he thought the gift might be poisonous. "You didn't have to get me anything," he muttered.

"I know," Emir assured him. "I wanted to."

Jacob watched him for one more brief second, then reached into the bag. He held its contents in his palm—a bracelet of delicate silver in the shape of a snake coiled once around itself, the filigree forming a beautiful pattern of scales. Its small mouth was slightly open, a small prong of silver forming a forked tongue, and two dark orange stones formed its eyes.

Emir watched the boy's face carefully, trying to judge if he had chosen well, but Jacob's expression remained unreadable.

"Wow," he said quietly. "This is...I mean, I'm not really a big jewelry person."

Emir straightened subtly and attempted to make sure his disappointment didn't show on his face. But when Jacob looked up at him, the boy softened.

"But I like this," he murmured.

"...I'm glad," Emir answered softly, not trying to hide his smile.

Cordelia returned with the earrings dangling against her neck, and she shook her hair dramatically back from her face as she approached to show them off.

"They look lovely on you," Emir said. "I'm glad to give them a good home."

"Do you hear that, Jacob?" the girl teased, leaning toward him and tilting her head to make sure he got a good look at her ears. "The vampire thinks I look lovely."

"Old age makes everyone's eyes bad, I guess."

"Oh fuck off," she laughed. She caught sight of the bracelet despite Jacob attempting to casually conceal it behind his back, and she forced him to put it on.

Emir attempted to excuse himself, not wanting to overstay his welcome, but Cordelia insisted that he stay and tell them about the historical inaccuracies in a video game she wanted to show him—it apparently took place in Constantinople. The three of them sat together on the sofa for a while, the pair of roommates making a few jokes about the game that Emir didn't understand. Cordelia listened like an eager student whenever Emir did have something to contribute about the city, but he had to remind her more than once that 1511 was slightly before his time. She didn't seem to care.

He caught Jacob more than once looking down at the bracelet on his wrist, touching it with hesitant fingers. Emir didn't draw attention to it—but it made him happy.

By the time he left the apartment, it was close to midnight. Cordelia waved goodbye to him as if they'd been friends for years. Jacob walked him to the door, an Emir paused once he was outside to look back at him. He was worrying his lower lip, so Emir waited until he was ready to speak.

"Thank you. For the present."

"Of course. Will I see you tomorrow night?"

"Yeah," he muttered without meeting Emir's eyes. His face grew a touch more pink, and Emir could hear his elevated heart rate as he leaned in slightly closer, continuing in a lower voice. "I was hoping...you could do me another favor."

Emir understood his meaning without the need for elaboration. "I'll be waiting," he promised.

9

Jacob was restless all the following day. He got to Emir's house so early that he ended up waiting in the car for half an hour to avoid coming off too eager. He spent a lot of the time looking at the bracelet on his wrist, tracing the filigree patterns with his fingers. Emir hadn't needed to give him a gift. He was already paying him money as well as literal blood. Why did he also give him a present?

Emir was waking up. Jacob was now very familiar with the tugging, anxious, longing feeling that always began in his gut when the vampire rose. He took a breath and waited another minute or so just to be sure he didn't seem too enthusiastic, then went to the door to knock. Emir was mostly undressed, as usual—he had on a pair of dark grey cotton lounge shorts Cordelia had chosen for him, and nothing else. Why did this man even need a closet full of new clothes if he never wore anything but pajamas?

"You're here nice and early, Jacob," the vampire said as he moved back from the door to make room for him to enter. "Something I can do for you?"

Jacob shut the door himself, since Emir was already on his way back to the living room. "This is where we are now?" he grumped. "You're teasing me?"

"Come," Emir said, a faint smirk on his lips. "I won't make you suffer any longer."

Jacob stood his ground at the edge of the room. "If you're gonna be a dick about this, I'll go back to the getting-strapped-down-for-a-month plan, okay?"

Emir took an easy seat on the couch and patted the spot next to him, looking up at Jacob with taunting dark eyes. "Come," he repeated softly.

Jacob took his place beside him, awkward and straight-backed. He watched Emir's face for signs of the contempt he was sure must be lurking inside and hoped the man couldn't sense his anticipation. His stomach was tight, his heart pounded, and he couldn't stop staring at the other man's lounging, casual figure—soft brown skin too cold to the touch, sparse black hair across his muscled chest and stomach, a firm, rounded jaw, and those full, faintly teasing lips. Every time Jacob saw him, it became harder to keep composed.

Just as before, Emir laid his arm across the back of the sofa and made a cut in his neck with his fingernail. But this time, when the vampire urged Jacob closer, he didn't even stop to think. He leaned one hand into the couch cushion and supported himself with the other on Emir's leg, eagerly leaning in to taste the spilling blood before it could drip too far down the other man's chest.

How had he gotten this way? The blood had haunted and disgusted him the first time, but he'd still been desperate for it—and increasingly so since then. It burned sweetly as it poured down his throat in hurried gulps, the copper taste coating his tongue and setting his body on fire. Emir's fingers in his hair didn't help; they were impossible to ignore, as was the firm flesh of his thigh under Jacob's hand.

He wanted more than this. His body moved on its own, and in the next moment, he was straddling Emir's lap, his hands on the other man's bare sides as he ran his tongue over the open skin at his collar, hoping to urge the blood to run a little faster. Emir's grip in his hair tightened, making Jacob's stomach jump, and then the vampire's hand was sliding up his back, leaving a cool trail on his skin before holding him down firmly against him by the shoulder.

Jacob shouldn't have been so turned on. It should have been gross. He shouldn't be *wanting* to drink another person's blood, and he shouldn't be hard from sitting in someone's lap while he does it. But Emir was gripping him so tightly, and his chest was moving just a little unevenly under Jacob's hands—was he turned on, too? Did vampires get turned on?

Emir pulled him away from him before he was ready, and for a brief moment, they just sat looking at each other, neither quite breathing properly. Jacob was lightheaded, and Emir gazed up at him with slightly parted lips. Without thinking, Jacob kissed him, his fingers squeezing into the vampire's sides. When he opened his mouth, Emir answered him, sending a thrill through Jacob's skin. He longed to taste him properly, and he slid his tongue over the other man's lips, flinching slightly as he caught the tip of one of Emir's too-sharp teeth. He didn't care, but the hint of blood only made Emir grab him harder. The vampire gripped him by his hair and forced his tongue into Jacob's mouth as if trying to taste all he could, and Jacob shuddered and let slip a faint moan—but then Emir jerked him back with such force that Jacob half gasped.

Jacob couldn't catch his breath, and Emir, too, seemed unsteady. He stared up at Jacob with eyes missing their whites; they'd gone entirely black, darker even than his normal brown. Jacob recoiled on instinct. What the fuck was that?

After a second, Emir gently but firmly pushed Jacob off of him and stood, leaving the room in a few long strides. The kitchen sink ran briefly, and when Emir reappeared in the doorway, he had a small towel in his hand and was wiping at the spot on his chest that had been stained with blood a moment ago. He didn't look at Jacob. Was he angry?

Jacob felt sick to his stomach, but he managed to speak before Emir did. "Sorry," he blurted out. "Shit. That was stupid. I don't know what came over me."

The other man was silent for a few tense seconds. "...It's all right," he said, but he sounded subdued.

Jacob wanted more than anything, in that moment, to shrivel up and die. What was he thinking? He got up from the couch, tugging on the hem of his shirt a little, and edged toward the door. "Sorry. I'm gonna go. Just—text me if you need anything."

He thought he heard Emir say his name on the way out the door, but he didn't stop. He rushed back to the car, started it up, and pulled out of the driveway without waiting—if he slowed down, all his idiocy was going to catch up with him. Stupid. Why had he kissed him? As far as Emir was concerned, he was just giving his slave his weekly dose of slave juice. This wasn't a relationship. Don't get carried away.

This was a transaction. That was it.

Idiot.

———

In the morning, Jacob spent a long time staring at his bedroom ceiling feeling stupid. He had almost talked himself into *not* crawling under his bed until he starved to death when a rapid series of knocks on his door made him jump.

"Jesus, what?" he called, and Cordelia flung his door open and rushed to sit on the edge of his bed as he sat up against the headboard.

"Have you seen the news this morning?"

"No, I just woke up," he lied.

"There was a murder last night."

Jacob froze. "...What?"

"Yeah." She scooted closer to him to show him the screen of her phone, open to a local news page. "They found some guy by the nature trail at Dorrs Pond." She frowned and leaned over to look him in the face. "Jacob, the...the article says the body had been drained of all its blood."

His heart dropped into his stomach. "...No way," he breathed.

Cordelia's voice fell to a whisper, as if they might be overheard. "You don't think it was Emir, do you? He wouldn't, right?"

"Oh shit." Jacob covered his mouth as a chill washed over him.

"Oh shit what?"

He hesitated, then slowly dropped his hand, unable to look her in the face. "Last night...I...I think this is my fault."

"What? Why? How could this possibly be your fault?"

Jacob's mouth had gone dry, but he swallowed and tried to go on anyway. "I...kissed him. And I—I cut my tongue, or something, and he was...off. I thought maybe it was just because I'd fucked up by doing it, like he didn't think of me that way, but maybe..." He shook his head with his face pressed between his hands in distress. "Augh, his eyes were all...*weird* after, and I didn't think about it until now! Did he taste the blood and...after I left, did he...?"

Cordelia punched him sharply in the bicep, and he winced and grabbed at the injury.

"What the fuck, Cords?"

"You *tongue-kissed* the hot vampire and just came home and didn't tell me about it?"

"*That's* your takeaway from this story?"

"So you really think he did this?" she pressed. "Because he got a taste of you and didn't get to finish eating you?"

"I don't fucking know! Fuck!" He laid down sideways on the mattress and pulled the pillow tight over his head.

"You've got to ask him."

"What?" he asked, muffled by the pillow. He lifted it just enough to stare out at her in disbelief. "Just show up and ask if he *murdered* someone last night?"

"Yeah, man! If he acts like an innocent blood bag hermit but he's actually out there killing night joggers or whatever the fuck, you might not want to keep Renfield-ing for him without some serious consideration."

"Can you please stop calling it that," Jacob groaned, and Cordelia peeled the pillow away from his face.

"Look," she sighed, "he's been nice to us, but he's still a *vampire*. Isn't that a vampire's whole thing, that they lure you in, they seem all charming, and then they eat you?"

He scowled up at her. "You're the one who was all in for me tongue-kissing him."

"Uh," she scoffed, "it seems like *you* were all in for tongue-kissing him, Mister Tongue-Kisser."

"Okay, let's just both stop saying tongue-kissing."

"Jacob, we let him into the house. We need to know if this was him or not. So we know if we need to buy...I don't know, garlic or whatever. A bunch of crucifixes. Did you even ask him about that stuff?"

No," he admitted, slowly slumping upward to lean against the headboard again.

"God! We're both stupid! We should have been using this time to figure out real vampire weaknesses!" She threw her phone at the mattress and crossed her arms. "But there's no way it was him, right?

Ugh," she groaned loudly. "No—this is how they get you. We have to stay on our guard. Just in case."

"That's easy for you to say. He's already turned me into a fucking *ghoul*, servant, whatever. I probably couldn't stake him even if I tried."

"Sorry, I'm having trouble feeling sorry for you, here. Didn't you just go over there to suck his blood for like, the third time last night?"

"Listen," he began, but Cordelia cut him off.

"Anyway—look. It's not like we can just go to the cops and tell them we think this was a vampire, right? And you and Emir are clearly a whole thing now. You need to just ask him. Be cool about it. Maybe he'll just admit it."

"Great," Jacob sighed. "That's definitely the best case scenario."

"The best case scenario is there's some serial killer out there draining people's blood, and our new vampire friend is innocent."

"Right. Right. I guess." He shook his head. "Never thought I'd have my fingers crossed for a serial killer." He gave another long sigh, and Cordelia touched his arm.

"It'll be okay," she said, and he nodded. "Even if it does turn out to be him, he's a *vampire*, right? We can't exactly act shocked. It would be like expecting your cat to be a vegetarian."

"I think this is more like expecting your cat to eat its cat food and not go hunting for other things to kill."

"And yet," she said with a shrug, "the world shows us that's also unreasonable. Killing things kill. Eaten things get eaten. It...just so happens that in this case, both the killing thing and the eaten thing look like humans. So it's harder to parse. But that doesn't make it any less natural."

Jacob turned his head and frowned at her in confusion. "I'm pretty sure a vampire is *literally* one of the most unnatural things I could think of."

Cordelia's expression softened. "I'm not sure it is. He exists, right? So he's a part of this world. Vampires are part of this world. Just like a cat, or a bear, or any other killing thing. There's nothing that actually exists that can be called unnatural—because it's all part of our natural world. So is death. That doesn't mean we have to like it, but we don't have to be frightened by it."

He watched her for a few moments in silence. "You're a weird one, Cords," he said, and she shrugged.

"Anyway, he likes you—and he seems to like me. So we're probably safe. That's normal, too, for vampires to like people. And you're half vampire already anyway, so...we'll be fine."

"Sure," he said, lifting his hands and letting them drop back to the blanket. "Great. Good pep talk, Cords. I feel heaps better."

She picked up her phone, gave his hair a soft tousle, and left, shutting the door gently behind her and leaving Jacob to mush the pillow back over his face and groan into it.

———

Jacob didn't care about seeming eager today. He was already at Emir's door by the time he felt the other man stir upstairs, and he forced himself to keep his hands still at his sides while Emir came into the living room in his stupid low sleep pants and his long robe. He needed to play it cool.

"You're here early tonight," Emir commented.

"I need to talk to you," Jacob said as forcefully and evenly as he could. "About last night."

Emir paused before he got any closer, then nodded as he faced Jacob properly, as if he was the one who had to steel himself for this conversation. "All right," he said.

"The cops found a body at Dorrs Pond. With all its blood missing."

Emir's eyes narrowed as he frowned. For a second, Jacob wondered if he was really about to be murdered this time, but when the vampire spoke, his voice was even and quiet. "A body?"

"Yeah. Was it you?" he asked before he could stop himself. Way to go, Jacob. Way to be cool about it.

His eyebrows went up. "You think I killed someone?"

"I mean..." Jacob shrugged. "You're a vampire."

"I told you I don't do that anymore."

"...Ever?"

"I can barely remember the last time. This wasn't me." Emir's lips pressed into a frown as he looked down at the floor, rubbing a hand over the back of his neck. "There must be someone else here. This isn't a major city—if there is another vampire here, they're...probably just passing through. But even if so, I can find them and hurry them along."

"Really?"

Emir stepped close to him, and Jacob tensed at even the gentle press of his hands on the smaller man's shoulders. "Please go home tonight," he said. "Keep yourself and Cordelia indoors. I'll find whoever did this."

"What if it's...not a vampire at all?" Jacob asked without much hope.

"Then I'll put a stop to it regardless, if I can."

Jacob frowned faintly up at him, trying to judge by the look in his eyes whether he was being honest or not. "...Okay," he finally said.

Emir guided him out of the house, so he went back home as he was told. He stayed up with Cordelia until almost dawn, waiting for some word from Emir, but nothing came. They finally both fell asleep on the sofa, leaned against each other, and when Cordelia stirred the next morning, they both rushed to be the first to check the news on their phones. Jacob's heart sank as he read the headline.

A body with no blood was found in the plaza outside the art museum.

10

As soon as Jacob's car was out of the driveway, Emir dressed himself and left the house, patting his pockets to be sure he had his things.

He had been the only vampire to have a noticeable presence in this city for over a hundred years. That was why he'd chosen it—hubs, capitals, metropolises...they all tended to be saturated with vampires. More vampires meant more dead bodies. More attention. More trouble. Even with services available like the one that kept Emir fed, there had always been and would always be vampires who refused to give up the thrill of the hunt and the satisfaction of the kill.

Vampires in groups always caused drama, too. And Emir had had his fill of other people.

But before he got ahead of himself, he needed to know if this had even been done by a vampire or not. It would be easy enough to confirm, but humans were just as capable of murder as any vampire.

His car gave him directions to the medical examiner's office, so he made the drive without difficulty. He spotted a security guard at the front desk through the glass front door—unsurprising. There weren't likely to be any doctors or attendants at night, at least. He knocked on the glass to get the guard's attention, and as soon as the man drew near enough for Emir to look into his eyes, he unlocked the door without hesitation and opened it wide.

Emir didn't bother speaking to him. He brushed by and carried on down the corridor in search of the morgue. He poked his head in a few doors before finding the walls of coolers, and he opened each drawer as he came to it, checking the tags strung to the black nylon bags. There were no bodies from today. Where would a murder victim be, if not the medical examiner?

He returned to the security desk, causing the guard to start as he came into view. He began to rise out of his chair, but sank back down as Emir caught his gaze again.

"Where is the man they found in the park today?" he asked, and the guard blinked hazily at him. Humans always looked a bit glazed while they were being coerced, but they always forgot just as quickly as soon as Emir was gone. No lasting damage.

"In the park?" the guard echoed.

"Yes. The murder victim."

"Oh, right," the man said, nodding without taking his eyes from Emir's. "He's gone already."

"Gone?"

"Yeah. Fast-tracked, all done. Jewish. Gotta be buried quick, you know? It's the rules, I guess." He shrugged. "Never heard of it before."

Emir sighed softly. Perfect. He left the guard and the building, then sat in the driver's seat of his car to think. Buried already. Was that poor luck, or purposeful victim choice? Either way, it didn't change anything—he still needed to see the body himself. But he couldn't go into a cemetery. It was sacred ground. His kind wasn't welcome.

What he needed was a ghoul.

He paused with his hand over the ignition button. He couldn't ask Jacob to dig up a body. He would likely refuse—and Emir wouldn't force him.

...Not him.

Better if Jacob stayed indoors, anyway. On the off chance it *wasn't* a vampire. He would have to find someone else. He pushed the button and began to back the car out of the parking lot. Mikaiel. Mikaiel would help him.

Emir drove to the outskirts of town, down streets that no longer looked familiar, until he found the house he recognized. He parked in the driveway and walked up to the front door, but he paused as he raised his hand to knock. This wasn't right. This home should have been open to him. He should have been welcome here. Had Mikaiel moved?

He let a light sigh escape him. It had been twenty years. But if the house had been sold, he could just feign a mistaken address. So he knocked.

After a long pause, a young man answered the door. He might have been in his mid- or late-twenties, and he wore jeans and a t-shirt that looked too large for his skinny frame. He pushed a pair of thick-framed glasses back up his nose as he took in the sight of his guest. He looked a bit of a mess—perhaps unaccustomed to visitors. "Uh, hey."

"Pardon me," Emir began. "I'm looking for Mikaiel Khavejian. He used to live here."

The boy shook his head. "You're about eight years too late. He died a while back."

"Oh," Emir said softly. "I'm sorry. I didn't know. Was he...ill?"

"Stomach cancer. By the time they caught it, he didn't have long. Were you a friend of his?"

"I like to think so." He paused, tilting his head to look at the boy. "So you're Taniel, then."

The young man frowned at him in confusion. "Taniel is my dad. I'm David. Sorry—who are you?"

A grandson. Emir really had been out of touch. For so long that Mikaiel had died, and he never knew. Why hadn't he reached out?

"Excuse me," he said. "My name is Emir Arzinjani, and—"

"Holy shit," David interrupted. "*You're* Mr. Arzinjani? Like—and in *the* Mr. Arzinjani Papik always talked about?"

Emir paused. "Did he?"

"You're the—" The young man dropped his voice and leaned forward to speak in a conspiratorial whisper. "You're the vampire, aren't you?"

Emir relaxed slightly, relieved he would have less to explain. "Yes. Now—"

"Holy shit," he said again. "Dude, Papik told me my whole life about how you were, like, the savior of this family."

"Oh," Emir said with a shake of his head, "I don't think that's—"

"He said you brought him with you from Constantinople during the genocide. You saved his life."

"I suppose, but—"

"He was *a hundred and fourteen years old* when he died, man! He said he was your—damn what was it—not a goblin, or a ghost."

"A ghoul, yes—"

David snapped his fingers and pointed at the man on his step. "A ghoul! And you bought this house! Man, I always hoped I'd get to meet you, but—"

"Excuse me," Emir cut in more forcefully. "I came because I need a favor."

"Oh. Shit," he said, and he crossed his arms. "Okay. Uh. A favor like what? You don't mean...a meal, right?"

"No," Emir sighed. "I need you to enter somewhere I cannot. A cemetery."

"Dude," he laughed, "no lie, I spend so much time in cemeteries anyway. I actually have this YouTube channel where me and my friend check out these haunted—"

"It sounds fascinating, but this is pressing. Will you come?"

"Will I come with the vampire to the cemetery in the middle of the night," David muttered, sputtering sarcastically. "Yes I'll come!"

"Do you have a shovel?"

That question gave him pause. "Uh. Hold on. A shovel?"

"Yes."

"What...kind of favor is this?"

"I need to see a body that was recently buried. But I can't go in myself."

"Dude," David said, his brow furrowed with concern now, "that's...super illegal."

"I understand. I wouldn't ask if it wasn't important. There may be another vampire in the city—one that isn't as discreet as I am. I need to be sure."

"Oh shit—I saw they found that body, and I wondered." He hesitated, glancing down at the ground and over his shoulder back into the house as though conflicted. "If I get arrested, you'll bail me out, right?"

"I will," Emir promised.

"...Okay," the boy said after a long pause. "Shit. Okay. Yeah. I'll come."

Emir returned to the car without waiting for him, and by the time he had the engine running, David had retrieved a shovel from the side yard and stowed it in the back. He buckled himself into the passenger seat and tapped his hands in a disjoined rhythm on his knees as they drove.

"So," he said after only a minute of blessed quiet, "this is for real, right? You're a vampire. For real for real. My Papik was like, your Igor?"

"Igor? No." Emir shook his head. "Mikaiel helped me. I employed him. When he no longer wished to be employed by me, the arrangement ended. That's all. I helped him get settled here as thanks for his help over the years."

"But you are for real a full-on vampire."

"Yes," Emir sighed. "Full-on."

"Fucking sick," David said in a laugh.

The Hebrew Cemetery wasn't far—thankfully. Emir parked near the gate, and they both climbed out, David looking supremely uncomfortable as he stood on the sidewalk with his shovel. He took a few sharp, quick breaths, as if to hype himself up, then emptied his lungs in a forceful sigh.

"Okay," he said. "Who am I looking for?"

"I don't know the name. But they would have been buried today—I'm sure you'll be able to tell which grave is new."

"Cool," he said with a nod. "Cool cool cool. Fresh-turned earth and whatnot. And then just...see if it's death by vampire?"

"I'd like to see the body myself, if possible. It would be ideal if you could bring it close to the fence."

"I'm...not super keen on dragging a dead body all over the place." He thought for a moment, leaning both hands on his shovel, then perked up again. "Okay. You have a cell phone?"

"I do."

David took his own phone from his pocket, added Emir's number to his contacts, and then told him to wait. When Emir answered the call, he was surprised to see David's face looking up at him from the screen.

"See, this way I can just show it to you, and...hold on. I can't see you. Is it turned the right way?"

"What?"

He moved next to Emir and tilted the phone in his hand, then paused. "You're not...in the shot."

"Oh, of course," Emir said. "It's a camera. I wouldn't."

David looked back up at him in confusion, but then he smiled. "Right! That's some classic vampire shit! Dope. Okay. I'll just talk to a random night sky; that's chill. Just watch your screen then, and I'll see what I can find."

Emir waited in the car so as to arouse less suspicion from passersby, and watched the boy's progress on the phone as the young man disappeared into the dark of the cemetery. The flashlight on David's phone lit his way, so mostly Emir saw flashes of feet in the grass and little else. Eventually, David found a grave piled with promisingly loose soil, and he set the phone down on top of the tombstone to illuminate his work. There wasn't much to see or hear beyond the sound of the shovel in the dirt, but after a while, a slightly different sound came through the phone's speaker.

"Oh. Oh god," David said, sounding ill.

"What?"

"I just—oh god. I was expecting to hit a coffin. I didn't—oh god. It's juicy."

Emir briefly shut his eyes, lips pressed into a thin line. "No," he said remarkably evenly, "there's no coffin. Have you damaged the body?"

"I uh—" He paused to swallow a gag. "I think I hit the legs? Fuck. I'm gonna puke."

"Do not vomit on the—"

It was too late. He was definitely vomiting. Emir sighed, waiting to give the boy a minute to stop heaving and catch his breath.

"David," he said once the sound of gagging had subsided. "You need to open the shroud."

"Shit." He gave a wet cough. "Okay. Hold on. This is super gross."

Emir heard the shovel hit the ground again, and then the screen finally moved. The camera focused on the white cloth covering the body, and David's hand appeared to pull at the fabric around what looked like the head.

"Show me the neck first," Emir directed.

David gave another gurgle as if he was fighting back another wave of vomit, but he continued, uncovering the corpse's head. Emir had to urge him again to turn the head so that he could see the dead man's neck properly. But there, on the left side of the neck, he spotted it— two ragged cuts near the jaw.

"There," he said. "That's it."

"That's it?"

"Yes. This *was* a vampire. Do you see any other marks? On the arms or the torso?"

"Are you serious, man? Okay. Okay." He scanned as much of the body as he could uncover with the phone's camera, making heaving sounds every time his hand touched the pale, loosening skin. "Fuck this is disgusting. I don't see anything."

"That's all right. Cover the body again and come back. I'll take you home."

"Okay. Okay, I'll...be there in a minute."

David ended the call, and Emir waited until he reappeared by the gate to get out of the car. The boy's jeans and hands were stained with dirt, and his ruddy face dripped sweat onto his damp shirt. Emir took the shovel from him and tossed it into the trunk, allowing him to slide wearily into the passenger's seat. While they drove, he stared straight ahead through the windshield, sitting very still as though any sudden movement might make him throw up again.

"Thank you, David," Emir offered. "You did very well."

"...Sure."

He was quiet on the drive back, at the very least. When Emir pulled into his driveway and parked, David sat silently for a few seconds before turning to look at him.

"Did...my grandfather have to do stuff like that?"

Emir paused, considering. "I...can't say I ever asked him to dig up a grave. But he did help me with a few unsavory things over the years, yes."

"No—" David held up a hand to stop him. "You know what? I don't really wanna know." He opened the door to get out, and Emir stopped him with a light touch to his elbow.

"You were a help to me, David," he said as the young man looked back over his shoulder. "You have my phone number. If you ever have a problem you think I can solve—use it."

He laughed, but it sounded a little hollow. "Committed a felony and threw up on a corpse, but at least I got a chit from a vampire out of it. Cool." He tilted his head toward the house. "I'm gonna...go try to forget tonight ever happened, if it's all the same to you."

"I understand."

David collected his shovel from the trunk and trudged up the driveway to the front door, dragging the shovel noisily behind him. Emir watched until the front door shut, and then he shook his head as he put the car into reverse. Mikaiel never threw up just because he had to handle a corpse.

Emir spent the rest of the night checking everywhere in town he could think of that a vampire might go hunting—everywhere he might have gone, if he were looking for prey. He went to a couple of bars, the park—anywhere humans went when they were lonely. But there was no sign of another vampire anywhere. He didn't smell anything strange in the bars or on the streets. He couldn't sense anyone who wasn't human. Another vampire had killed someone in *his* city—but where were they now? Maybe he'd be lucky, and they really were just passing through. Careless to leave the body so easily discovered, regardless.

Close to dawn, when he'd given up the search and was on his way back to the house, a familiar scent reached him through the open car window. He pulled off the road immediately and parked with two wheels on the sidewalk in his hurry to stop the car. He left the door open and walked quickly toward the source of the scent, breathing deeply and following the trail left to him.

But he was too late. In the center of the concrete plaza, a body lay crumpled underneath a steel sculpture, a pool of blood growing underneath a matching set of tears in the throat.

Damn.

11

Five nights went by. Jacob stayed in the apartment when he wasn't at work, like Emir asked him to, but it didn't make him feel much safer. Every evening, Emir texted him to ask if he was all right. He claimed he was still looking for whoever was responsible for the deaths, but the body count was rising. There had been a murder every night for almost a week now. The police had started asking people to stay inside their homes at night, until an arrest could be made.

Jacob answered Emir's texts, but he tried to be as brief as possible. He felt sick. Heavy in his chest. Was this all a game? Had Emir been lying to him in the weeks they'd known each other before this? Was he lying now? Why? Why not just eat Jacob and get it over with? It would almost be preferable to this constant worry.

Nights were much more miserable than days. During the day, he could distract himself with work. But as soon as the sun fell, he grew more anxious. He wanted to be near Emir. He paced the living room and swore at himself for being so stupid. Cordelia tried to do her part to keep him distracted with games, movie nights, and beer, but it wasn't very much help.

On the fifth night, Emir texted Jacob to ask if he could see him. Jacob held his phone close to his chest, turning his back as if heading into the bathroom as Cordelia looked over at him from the couch.

I'll come over, he answered. He hit send before he could stop himself. Fuck. He was acting like an addict. He almost handed his phone over to Cordelia for safe keeping, since he clearly couldn't be trusted, but then it vibrated in his hand. A message from Emir.

No. Stay there.

Fuck, that was even worse. He was going to come here.

Jacob should have told Cordelia. He should have asked her to help him bar the windows, or something. But he didn't. He had a long shower and told his caring, didn't-deserve-it roommate that he'd taken some NyQuil and was going to bed.

He waited up in his room, listening for the sound of footsteps on the stairs outside, but none came. There was no knock. He laid down in bed and focused all his efforts on hearing Emir coming—but he could only hear the stupid dog down the street.

Just as he started to feel himself drifting into sleep, a strange tingling washed over him, and his heart rate spiked. He turned over in bed and glanced at his window—cracked. A thick mist like dry ice was seeping through the gap, pouring over the sill and onto the floor. Jacob kicked and scrambled his way to the far side of his bed, almost falling off the edge, but then the window dropped shut with a small snap. Jacob blinked, and then Emir was in the room with him, standing near the foot of the bed.

"What the fuck?"

Emir shushed him gently with a finger to his lips. "I'm sorry," he said. "I didn't want to disturb Cordelia."

"Well you fucking disturbed me!" Jacob hissed. "You can't just turn into a fucking cloud and come in through someone's window!"

"Usually we call it mist," Emir murmured, and he frowned when Jacob mockingly repeated him.

"What the fuck ever."

Emir studied him with concern written on his face as he took a step closer. "Are you all right?"

"Yeah. Fine. I guess."

"You haven't been feeling like you've been followed? Noticed anything strange during the day?"

Jacob looked up at him in the dim moonlight from the window. He looked tired. Had he been resting enough? "No," he said. "Nothing. If I wasn't checking the news and getting constant murder updates, it would have been a regular, boring week."

Emir let a sigh fall from his lips as he sat down on the bed beside Jacob. He was frowning, his brow furrowed in irritation. "I don't know how they're keeping away from me—or why," he admitted. "What are they going here, and why are they being so blatant? It's idiotic," he spat, perhaps the first show of frustration Jacob had ever seen in him. He shook his head, his expression softening as he turned to look at him. "But you're all right? Feeling well?"

"Yeah, I'm...I'm okay." He didn't want to admit how hard it had been to be away from him. Emir was very close to him, and Jacob was hyper aware of the fact that the vampire was sitting on his bed. Within reach for the first time in days. He was wearing one of the Henley shirts Cordelia had picked out for him, the open buttons showing just enough of the skin of his chest to make Jacob lick his lips.

After a pause, Emir tilted his head slightly to catch Jacob's gaze. "Is there something you want, Jacob?"

Jacob should say no. He should, right? He should absolutely say no. The man in front of him was a killer—even if he wasn't now, he definitely had been before. Emir was looking at him so kindly now— but that was how vampires got you, wasn't it?

Emir had had a hundred chances to kill Jacob and hadn't done it. Was that just because he was still useful? Still a helpful servant? Or was there some other reason?

"I'm sorry," Emir said before Jacob could make up his mind. "I know I probably shouldn't have come here. Whoever this other person is, if I lead them here, and something happened..." He stopped. "But I wanted to see you," he said in a softer voice. "I was...worried."

Jacob didn't know what to do with that. If Emir was worried, then that meant it wasn't him. Right? Or was he just saying that? But— why would he lie? Emir had seemed, at least, to be pretty up front with everything Jacob had asked him so far—if he was lying about things, he was doing it so casually and easily that it would be impossible to distinguish from the truth anyway.

Especially because Jacob was dealing with fucking vampire shit, which shouldn't have been real to begin with. It didn't make any of this any easier.

Emir cleared his throat quietly, and he straightened a little on the bed, keeping his eyes on the carpet. "But mostly I came because I thought that you might be suffering after so long away from me, given your situation. But of course," he went on quickly, "it's your choice if you want to continue or not. If you would rather put an end to it and stay strapped down until it's out of your system, I understand. Especially given...recent events."

"I...don't know," Jacob answered. He sighed and rubbed his hands vigorously over his face before continuing. "Listen. I know you've said this isn't you killing people, but I keep thinking back to that night. When I...kissed you."

Now Emir looked at him. "...Oh?"

The words Jacob had been holding inside for a week spilled out of him. "I fucked up. I just...I got carried away, and I guess I thought you were feeling it too, but then you seemed like you were pissed at me, and then later I remembered that I'd gotten cut, and then someone died, and—fuck. I keep thinking this is all my fault."

"You think that I lost control because of you?"

"...Yeah."

The vampire's expression softened. "Jacob," he murmured, "do you think that it's me doing this?"

There was no point trying to lie. "Maybe," he admitted.

"...I see." Emir hesitated, then shifted to face him. "Jacob, do you know that when you kissed me the other night, it was the first time I'd had—any sort of that kind of contact with someone for...possibly a hundred years?"

Jacob stared at him.

"Well you know that I don't exactly get out much," the vampire went on before Jacob could fully express his incredulity. "Company generally exhausts me. But not yours." He stopped as he seemed to catch himself. "What I'm saying is that I was...a bit started. Pleasantly so," he added quickly. "But then, I also...got carried away."

Jacob looked down at his hands in his lap and then peeked back at the other man. "Because you wanted to eat me?"

Emir swallowed. "...A bit, yes."

Jacob shifted his weight, not liking at all how that idea and the intense look in Emir's dark eyes twisted up his stomach. Was that dread? Or something way, way worse? "Did you," he began uncertainly, "want to eat me...more, or...less than you wanted to kiss me?"

"Less," Emir answered quickly, his voice quiet.

Jacob's whole chest tightened. "...Okay. Good. That's...promising for my survival."

"I'm not going to hurt you. And I'm telling the truth. There is another vampire here. I'm going to find them."

He nodded, but he had his eyes on the blanket again. "Okay."

"Do you believe me?"

"I...want to," Jacob whispered. At least it wasn't a lie.

Emir reached out for him, fingers touching his hair and drifting lightly over his cheek and jaw. His voice sounded a little weaker now, and it made Jacob ache. "How do I make you trust me, Jacob?"

Jacob leaned into the caress without really meaning to and finally lifted his eyes to look into Emir's face. "I don't know anything about what vampires are like," he said, a faint touch of relief forming in his chest as he allowed the words out. "In the movies, they're always charming, and they draw you in, and then as soon as you're comfortable—"

He was cut off by Emir's mouth on his, capturing him in a soft kiss that Jacob couldn't help but whimper into. His hand gripped the vampire's wrist as fingers pushed deeper into his hair. Emir put a hand on his waist, squeezing him gently and opening his mouth to him, and Jacob struggled to breathe. He grabbed at Emir's shirt and twisted the cotton in his fingers to keep him close, but then Emir broke the kiss, touching his lips instead to Jacob's chin and over his cheek, his jaw, and down to his neck. Jacob's body tensed automatically with the vampire's mouth so close to his carotid, but Emir only kissed him lightly, gently, his tongue brushing Jacob's earlobe.

"I wouldn't hurt you," he whispered against Jacob's heated skin. His hand slid underneath Jacob's shirt, pressing into his side as he pressed a slow kiss just below the boy's ear. "You'll never be in danger from me, Jacob."

Jacob was getting hard embarrassingly quickly. He put his hands in Emir's hands and tried to catch his breath enough to speak as he pulled the other man up to look into his dark eyes. "I believe you," he said. They both waited a beat for the truth to spill out instead, but it didn't come. Jacob closed the gap between them and kissed him.

Emir pushed him back onto the bed, eagerly tasting him and pushing his hand fully under the boy's shirt. He was cold, and it should have been strange, but Jacob didn't care—he just wanted more of the vampire's hands on him. He wrapped his arms around Emir's shoulders as the other man settled over him with a knee between his thighs, not bothering to hide his muffled moan as Emir's thumb ran over his nipple.

Jacob hesitated to be too aggressive with his tongue after what happened the last time, but Emir was taking the lead anyway, leaving no part of Jacob's mouth unexplored. Jacob's whole body was on fire. He gripped Emir's shoulders and lifted his hips against him, surprised by the small jolt the movement made in the man above him. He was hard. Jacob didn't know vampires could get hard, but it was honestly the best news he'd heard all day.

Emir broke away to kiss his cheek again, leaving a cool line down Jacob's jaw and chin with his lips. His tongue ran over his Adam's apple, and Jacob gave a low, trembling groan and pulled at the back of Emir's shirt. He wanted more. More of Emir's hands on his skin, more of his mouth on him. More of everything. It had been too long.

He tugged Emir closer, kissing his lips and letting out a longing whimper as he moved to nuzzle and nip at the other man's neck. "More," he whispered. "I need more."

Emir sighed against his temple, his hand on Jacob's waist almost painfully tight, but then he pulled back slightly, and with a firm grip on the boy's jaw, turned his head to face him. He kissed him again— but this time, when Emir's tongue entered Jacob's mouth, he tasted blood. Jacob clutched at him in an attempt to control his trembling, but he couldn't help his moan as the first mouthful burned down his throat and into his chest. More.

He pulled himself up to press his body against the man above him, his heartbeat deafening in his ears. A slow drip of escaped blood ran from the corner of his mouth, and he whined softly at the loss. When Emir pulled back from him, he had a smear of red on his lower lip, and without hesitation, Jacob put a hand in the vampire's hair to pull him close again so that he could lick it away.

"Enough," Emir whispered against the boy's lips, and when Jacob tried to follow him again as he retreated, he gently pushed him back into the mattress. "Enough now."

Jacob lay panting on the bed as Emir sat up, and he wiped at the spilled blood on his own cheek and licked it from his fingers. He slowly pushed himself up into a seat with his back against the headboard and tried to breathe more evenly. Emir was watching him with an odd look on his face, but he didn't speak.

"Thanks," Jacob said in a quiet, teasing voice. "For not eating me."

Emir chuckled and lowered his eyes. "Of course. ...I'll go now," he said as he rose from the bed. "Please stay in the apartment as much as you can until I've figured this out."

Jacob scooted forward on the bed, resisting the urge to reach for his hand. He wanted to leave now? This hadn't been just another feeding, had it? "Can't I help?"

"No," Emir answered immediately. He moved to the window and pulled it open. "Please tell Cordelia to remain indoors also. She's at a greater risk than you are."

Before Jacob could argue further, Emir was out the window—but he didn't drop down. With a sudden, heavy fall of black smoke, he was gone, and Jacob scrambled forward on the bed just in time to see a massive black bat flapping away from the apartment.

Jacob stared in silence for almost a minute. When the fuck was Emir going to tell him he could turn into a goddamn bat?

12

Emir woke up the following evening ready to start his search again. Jacob believed he was innocent—he was more determined than ever to find this interloper now. Once he found them, he could either convince or force them to leave. Things would be back to normal.

Things with Jacob would be back to normal. Perhaps even better.

Emir couldn't remember the last time he'd cared to be around another person, let alone *wanted* to. But Jacob was different. Maybe Emir ought to tell him so—clearly.

He pushed aside the stone cover of his resting place and sat up, some of the dark earth inside falling from his shoulders, but then he stopped. Something was wrong. He pulled himself from the sarcophagus and left the room without bothering to shut the lid or dust off his robe.

Someone was in the house.

As he rounded the corner of the stairs, he stopped short. In the middle of the living room, a woman lay in a smear of blood, taking breath in weak gasps. Her legs were twisted at an unnatural angle, and a bloodstain grew on her shirt around the center of her torso. She wore black pants and a white button-down with a nametag on it. Julie.

Emir went to her immediately, kneeling beside her and turning her head gently toward him. He pushed the hair out of her face, and her eyes fought to focus on him. She was in rough shape.

She took another shallow breath, then spoke in a whispering, raspy voice. "Help me."

"Who did this to you?" Emir asked.

Blood began to pool at the edge of her mouth. "A man...grabbed me...outside the restaurant." Each hitching breath seemed like a battle, but she carried on. "I screamed, but no...nobody came."

"Did you know him?" Emir pressed gently. "Can you tell me what he looked like?"

The woman reached up for him, weakly clawing at the open robe near his chest. "He said...he said to tell you...he missed you."

Emir froze. He frowned, his brow furrowing. No. After all this time—

The woman hiccupped, but it became a cough, and she tried to grab him tighter, but her hands didn't have the strength. Tears fell from her eyes and dripped into the drying blood on the floor. This wasn't survivable. She had been lying here too long. Emir shushed her gently and slipped an arm under her shoulders to lift her up, even that little movement making her wince and cry.

"I'm sorry this happened, Julie."

He turned her chin with a light touch and bent over her, locking his teeth into the skin at the curve of her neck. Hot blood spilled over his tongue and pulsed into his mouth with each weak beat of her heart, and he couldn't help the soft sound of satisfaction in his throat as the blood warmed his chest. Her stifled cry of pain and alarm barely reached his ears—all he could feel was her pulse, pouring life and heat through his body. Her unsteady breath slowed and then stopped, and her fingers slipped loose from his robe. Her body grew heavier in his arms, and when her heart stopped giving, Emir broke away. He sat back on his heels with his eyes still shut, licking his lips to make sure he didn't lose a single precious drop and taking a slow, savoring breath.

It would be pointless to pretend it wasn't better than a bag.

After a few seconds, the warm haze over him faded, and he felt he was being watched. He looked toward the door—and if he'd had a beating heart of his own, it would have stopped.

Jacob was standing in the doorway.

13

Emir was sitting on his living room floor—with a dead body. A dead body that had very clearly *not* been dead before Emir put his fangs on it. He'd gripped the woman's shoulder, cradled her, and when he'd sat back with that calm, satisfied look on his face and a corpse in his arms—

Jacob felt sick.

When Emir finally turned to him, his mouth fell open, and he glanced guiltily down at the dead woman before laying her back on the floor and pushing to his feet.

"Jacob, please listen," he said. "I had no choice." He stepped closer, but Jacob moved back, so he went still.

"No choice?" Jacob echoed, barely able to find his voice. "Are you serious?"

"She was dying anyway. All I did was make it quick," he insisted, and Jacob's lip curled in disgust.

"You fucking lied to me!" he spat. "What the fuck was all that last night, you—all this time, you said it wasn't you, and I believed you just because—"

"I haven't been the one doing this," he said over the top of the boy's anger. "Please. This wasn't my intention."

"Even if you haven't been!" Jacob snapped. "There's a dead person in your living room right now! Who's dead because you fucking drank their blood!"

Emir visibly softened. "Jacob," he said, sounding sad and resigned in a way that shouldn't have made the boy's chest hurt the way it did. "You knew what I am. This was unfortunate, but now I know who has been killing these people."

"Who?" Jacob sneered. "You with a goatee on?"

"It's Titus."

"Who the fuck is Titus?"

"...The one who made me what I am."

Jacob paused, momentarily shocked out of his anger. "...Oh."

"I need to find him," Emir said. "He's not going to stop until I do. Please go home—you'll be safest at the apartment."

"But I came here to—"

"Jacob, please. Another time."

"What the hell is going on?"

Emir frowned. "He's playing games," he answered grimly.

When he approached, Jacob didn't retreat, but he did jerk his shoulder away from the vampire's reaching hand. If he let Emir touch him now, he might feel the warmth of the dead woman's blood in his skin—and that might make him throw up. Emir pulled his hand back without comment, but he had a frown on his lips.

"I promise I can explain everything soon," he said, guiding Jacob toward the front door without touching him. "But for right now, you need to—"

Jacob interrupted him by stopping short a step outside the front door, and Emir bumped lightly into his back as they came to a sharp halt.

A man was standing at the bottom of the yard, dressed neatly in navy slacks and a white button-down rolled up to his elbows, his hands casually in his pockets. He was olive-skinned, with a long, aquiline nose, his dark hair cropped short and a light, neatly trimmed beard covering his jaw. He looked across the yard at them with dark, staring eyes beneath a heavy brow. He was smiling, but there was nothing behind it—it didn't touch his eyes.

"Hello, Emir," he called. "Did you enjoy my gift?" His accent was strange—Jacob couldn't place it.

Emir stepped forward to stand next to Jacob, barely touching his arm with the back of his hand as he moved subtly in front of him.

"What are you doing here?"

"I finally find where you've been wasting away this past century, and that's the greeting I get?"

"I didn't ask you to come looking for me," Emir said a bit more forcefully. "Especially drawing this much unwanted attention."

"It's just a bit of fun." He tilted his head and locked eyes on Jacob, who tensed. "I didn't mean to interrupt a spat," he said with a smirk. "Who's this?"

"Just my ghoul," Emir answered immediately, not even sparing a glance in Jacob's direction. "What do you want, Titus?"

The other vampire shrugged as he approached the porch, taking the first step and pausing there to look up at Emir. "A man can't visit one of his oldest friends? I thought perhaps you might be lonely."

"I am not," Emir said flatly.

"Well, then I won't overstay my welcome," Titus continued without hesitation. "Are you going to offer me your hospitality, or not?"

Jacob peeked sidelong up at Emir. He looked conflicted—a little angry.

"...Of course," Emir said after a heavy pause.

Titus came up the porch then, smiling as he brushed very close to Emir on his way by. He went through the front door and into the house as casually as if he lived there.

Jacob opened his mouth to say something rude, but Emir gripped him by the elbow and leaned down close to his ear.

"Don't speak unless spoken to," he whispered, so quietly Jacob barely heard it. Then he followed the other man inside, so Jacob followed, shutting the door behind him with a skeptical glance toward the living room.

Titus had already made himself at home. He was settled on the couch, arm stretched across the back cushion and legs crossed— paying absolutely no attention to the corpse on the floor. He glanced around the room, taking in the stacks of books and the guitar leaned against the side table.

"I like what you've done with the place," he said dryly. "Used bookstore chic."

"Thank you," Emir answered through a tight jaw as he took a place at the far end of the sofa from the other vampire.

Jacob stood back by the wall, feeling awkward. He didn't particularly want to squeeze in between them on the sofa, but there was nowhere else to sit. What the fuck did Emir mean, anyway, don't speak unless spoken to? This was some more poncy vampire shit, wasn't it? Emir has to show off his obedient servant for this guy? Jacob stuffed his thumbs into his pockets and chewed his lip in irritation.

Titus looked like a dick. This was the person who had made Emir a vampire? Who had been killing people every night for a week? Emir said it wasn't a problem to have blood delivered—so this person had been killing because he wanted to. Because he enjoyed it.

That told Jacob all he needed to know.

"I'd ask what you've been up to," Titus went on, "but I see it's more of the same." His crossed leg lightly bounced as he nodded, a look of amusement on his face. "Books, and books, and books. You'll grow a hunchback, my friend."

"I'm not concerned," Emir said mildly.

A few beats of silence went by, and Titus leaned his head back to finally look over at the body. "You know, that will leave a stain on this...vintage wood. Ought to get rid of it sooner rather than later, no?"

"I'll take care of it."

"You?" Titus's eyes flicked up to Jacob. "Isn't that what ghouls are for?"

A chill went up Jacob's spine. Emir turned to look at him with a frown on his face. He seemed to hesitate for half a second, then tilted his head toward the corpse.

"Please," he said. "Make sure it isn't found."

"You—" Jacob forced his mouth shut under the intensity of Emir's stare.

"And clean up the floor."

Angry heat flushed Jacob's face, and his fingers tightened against his jeans pockets, but Emir just steadily held his gaze. After a couple of seconds, Jacob snorted and stalked toward the stairs.

Sure. Just take care of the body of the person Emir killed. Great. Just *dispose of a corpse*, no big deal. And don't open your stupid human mouth in front of the important undead blood-sucking monsters.

Jacob ripped the blanket off of Emir's bed and hauled it downstairs over his shoulder, letting it drag on the floor behind him. He glared at the back of Emir's head as he came back into the room, but he stopped when he reached the body on the floor.

It didn't look like it did in the movies. The woman's head had fallen to the side, her eyes open—but there was nothing inside. For the first time, Jacob understood what people meant when they said the light had gone out of someone's eyes. There was no mistaking this for a living person—even though, in many ways, she still looked totally normal.

Well. Except for the fucking bite mark on her neck.

Jacob knelt down on the floor and covered her up as carefully as he could, then began to wrap her in the duvet. Neither of the men on the couch even looked at him. Titus was smiling pleasantly, tilting his head at Emir.

"Still breaking this one in, hm? He looks a bit feisty."

"He's adjusting," Emir said, sounding sufficiently apologetic that Jacob was a little rougher with his next roll.

"You know, if you came with me, we could find you someone more suitable—we could go to Ibiza. Have you been? Incredible. A hundred beautiful men and women would line up round the corner for someone like you."

"No thank you."

Jacob tucked in the ends of the blanket, checking to make sure that no human parts were visible. Even dealing with a dead body was more appealing to him than listening to Titus's voice.

"Keys?" he said to Emir as he stood at the side of the couch, but the vampire didn't even look at him. He gestured toward the small table by the front door, so Jacob did his best to hold in his scowl as he fetched them.

He started to drag the body toward the door and almost fell over from how easily it moved. He looked down at it for a moment, considering, then tried to crouch down and scoop the wrapped woman up in his arms instead. She wasn't even heavy. It shouldn't have been this easy to carry a body. A perk of being a ghoul, he guessed, flicking off the porch light on his way out of the house with a bitter frown on his face.

He laid the woman in Emir's trunk and shut it, letting his hands lay against the car for a few moments. Even if she hadn't been physically heavy—it should have been harder for him to carry a body. Was this part of being a ghoul, too?

Jacob failed to stop himself from slamming the car door as he got into Emir's car and scooted up the driver's seat. This fucking vampire was not worth this. It wasn't Emir who would go to jail if Jacob got caught with a corpse. After all his friendly talk and "Oh, I appreciate you, Jacob," and "How do I make you trust me, Jacob," now as soon as another vampire showed up, Jacob was just another human. Only scarcely more useful than a blood bag.

Jacob drove away from the house, but the farther away he got, the deeper the realization sunk in that he had no idea what to do with a body. The easiest thing to do would be to leave it on the side of the street somewhere and hope it was rolled in with the past week's victims. But Jacob wasn't a vampire—he was much more likely to be spotted. And then he would definitely go to jail.

In the water. That was the best way. Then maybe it would at least take them a while to find her.

He took a deep breath and turned a corner to head out of town. He'd never driven so carefully, and so precisely at the speed limit, in his entire life. The last thing he needed was to draw attention to himself before he even got the body out of the car.

Jacob took the highway out of town and pulled off to head down the turnpike. Traffic was light, and by the time he came up to Deer Neck, he was the only car on the road. He pulled as far to the side of the bridge as he could and turned off the engine and lights. Far more quickly than he should have been comfortable with, he walked to the trunk, heaved the young woman out, and tipped her over the edge of the bridge, allowing the blanket to unroll and drop her into the water with a splash that seemed to reverberate in the quiet night. Then he shoved the blanket back in the trunk and threw it shut.

He drove the long way back around town to get back to Emir's house, slightly less nervous about having a wadded up blanket in the trunk. There was blood on it, of course—but at least it wasn't visible at a glance. Doing the dry cleaning would be Emir's problem.

By the time Jacob arrived back at the house and dropped the keys on the table just inside, Titus and Emir were sitting much closer to each other on the sofa. Titus still had his arm stretched across the back, but now he was able to touch the other man—his fingertips brushed the back of Emir's neck, and his thumb stroked the skin just behind his ear.

Emir didn't look at Jacob as he came back into the room—and he wasn't sure if that made him more or less angry than if he'd tried to look contrite.

Right. His job wasn't done, after all. He still had to clean the floor.

With a scowl on his lips, Jacob stalked into the kitchen and banged around in some cabinets until he found some cleaning supplies. They all had peeling, faded labels, and the only sponge he could find in a small bucket was warped and shriveled, but it would have to do—and if it fucked up Emir's floor, Jacob could honestly say he didn't give half a shit.

Jacob scrubbed at the bloodstain with all the spite he had—which was considerable—and kept his scowl toward the floor.

"Why don't you come out with me tomorrow night?" Titus said, his voice far too low and intimate for Jacob's liking.

"I don't like to go out," Emir said simply. But he wasn't even trying to pull away from the other man's touch.

"Come on," Titus purred, leaning in close enough that Jacob swore he saw his nose brush Emir's cheek out of the corner of his eye. "I'll make it worth your while. Haven't you been lonely?"

"No. I like it here."

"Then consider it entertaining your guest," Titus tried again with a quiet chuckle. "Or perhaps you'd rather stay in together?"

Jacob slammed the sponge back into the bucket and picked it up as noisily as he could, bashing it against the kitchen doorway and letting it drop heavily into the sink. He poured the water out from high enough that it splashed onto the counter and the floor, then left the soapy bucket and sponge sideways in the sink. He walked out and stood in front of the sofa with his hands tight at his sides, staring at Emir until the vampire finally turned his eyes on him.

"Thank you, Jacob," he said mildly. "You may go."

Jacob opened his mouth, ready to tell Emir exactly which bodily orifices he could stuff his thank you into, but Titus's gaze on him made him pause. For the first time, Jacob felt as if he was being watched by a predator. Emir had never seemed like that—even in his haze after their kiss, when his eyes had changed to that frightening shark black, Emir had never seemed...carnivorous. But this man did.

Instead of arguing, Jacob pressed his lips together, turned on his heel, and left the house. He'd been such an idiot to get involved with all this. And he was an even bigger idiot for imagining that he meant something to the vampire in the haunted house.

14

Titus stayed until almost morning, sitting on Emir's couch or perusing some of his stacks of books. He even picked up Emir's guitar and plucked at it while he chatted about the places he'd been, which gave Emir a previously unknown-to-him sort of anxiety. Titus promised to return the following night, and, though Emir had made it plain that he by no means wished to see the other man again, he appeared on the doorstep just the same.

They'd been apart for over a hundred years now. Back when they'd lived together, Titus had been indefatigable—he'd wanted to go out every single night, whether it was to a tavern, or sometimes a brothel, which was even more excruciating. Emir had trailed along behind like the faithful companion he'd been made to think he had to be. But Titus had refused to travel with him to Switzerland so that Emir could visit the newly-opened Amerbach Cabinet—public art and sculpture collections were few and far between in those days. Titus didn't seem to care. He'd even stayed behind when they'd traveled to Rome, and Emir had wanted to visit the Capitoline and Vatican museums. He wouldn't hear of rising before sunset.

The trip Emir took on his own to Switzerland had, perhaps, been the beginning of the end for them. His first taste of freedom. He'd thought he'd managed to free himself for good by crossing an ocean— and yet, here Titus stood in his living room, watching Emir with a derisive frown as he drank from one of his refrigerator bags and stared resolutely at the book in his hand.

"This is really all you do?" Titus asked, dropping himself onto the sofa with his legs hung over the arm so that he could look up into Emir's face upside-down. "This is absolutely dreary, my friend. Look at you. What a waste."

"A waste of what?" Emir asked without looking up.

"Of immortality! You could have whatever you wanted in the world, but you sit here reading instead."

"This *is* what I want," Emir pointed out, and Titus blew a brief, mocking raspberry up at him.

"We should at least find something more entertaining to occupy ourselves with, if you won't come out," he teased, reaching a hand over his head to slip his fingers up the other man's thigh.

Emir dropped his heavy book sharply onto Titus's hand and frowned down at him. "No thank you," he said simply.

Titus sat up to face him and gave a small snort. "This is how little you want to do with me? If I linger, will you uproot and disappear again, as before?"

Emir returned his eyes to his book, forcing his face to remain neutral. He wouldn't uproot his life now—not when it would surely mean leaving Jacob behind. "This is my home," he said, offering no further explanation.

"Believe this or not, old friend, but you are permitted to occasionally *leave* said home, also. Perhaps I'll bring some fun home with me next time, instead," Titus countered easily, and then he was gone, out the door and away.

Emir laid his book on his lap and let a low sigh escape him. He had no solution to this—other than to be *so* boring that Titus became tired of attempting to lure him out. But who knew how long that might take? And it was making things increasingly difficult between him and Jacob—the few times he'd been to the house since Titus's arrival, Emir had been purposely brusque with him. But he'd had no chance to talk with him alone, to explain. Titus was always there.

Shortly before dawn, Titus returned with a drunk woman slumped over his arm, who he dropped unceremoniously onto Emir's sofa while she laughed.

Emir came downstairs at the sound and didn't bother trying to hide his displeasure. "What is this?" he asked, and Titus slipped over to him and laid a too-familiar hand on his chest.

"A gift," he said. He leaned close to him, turning to look over his shoulder at the drowsy woman on the couch as he dropped his voice. "Do you want to share her?"

Emir looked past the other vampire. The young woman was dressed for a bar, which was doubtless where Titus had found her. She seemed barely able to gather herself, but she turned toward them and offered the pair of men a hazy smile.

"Is this your friend?" she asked, leaning her head back against the cushion as if she could no longer hold it upright. "He is cute."

"I wouldn't lie to you," Titus said with a smile, and he glanced back up at Emir. "I'll even let you go first, my friend," he whispered.

Emir swallowed and turned his head away from the girl. "I don't want another corpse in this house," he said under his breath. "You've brought enough attention here already."

"This is what we *are*, Emir," Titus pressed. "We aren't meant to drink cold blood from sterile bags. You are an *animal*, my friend. An animal that is meant to *eat*."

"I never was very good at being what you thought I was meant to be," he answered, looking back into the other man's eyes.

"Then don't kill her." Titus tilted his chin as he drew a breath away from Emir, his gaze on the darker man's lips. "Let her sleep, and when she wakes in the morning, she won't think anything more unusual happened than spending the night with a stranger. If you think you can stop. If you think you're so well matured beyond your base desires."

"You're trying to bait me," Emir whispered harshly. "I won't play your games. This is my home. Take her out of it."

Titus watched him steadily for a few lingering moments, then retreated, letting his hand drift over the back of the sofa and across the young woman's shoulders.

"I'm very sorry," he said with a smile on his face as he rounded the sofa to sit beside her. "You'll have to be satisfied with just me tonight, it seems."

Emir started to voice his objection, but Titus was already on top of the girl, pinning her to the cushions with his mouth fastened onto the side of her neck.

"Titus!" Emir hissed. He tried to pull the man away from her, but Titus was like stone—he held the girl fast while her arms pulled at him and then weakened, dropping limply to her sides.

When Titus lifted his head, he paused to lap at a dark rivulet still falling from the wounds he'd made in the girl's throat and looked back at Emir with faintly narrowed, fully black eyes and a look of smug satisfaction on his flushed face.

"I've left some for you, old friend," he murmured, and as he rose, he leaned close to Emir and ran his tongue briefly over the other man's mouth, leaving a heady stain that Emir licked his lips to taste despite himself. "Live however you like," Titus said as he brushed by his friend on his way toward the door, "but don't pretend to be something you're not."

Emir stood over the sofa in silence after Titus took his leave, looking down at the helpless woman breathing softly below him. The cuts on her neck still seeped red, and her eyebrows knit and she subtly shifted. The smell was overpowering, and Emir felt her pulse as closely as if he'd had his own lips on her skin.

When he caught himself reaching for her, he stopped, pulling his hand back to his chest as if it had betrayed him. He turned away and went back upstairs, then shut himself in the room with his sarcophagus and leaned against the door. She would sleep through the morning. She would wake up in a few hours, dazed but alive, and she would go back to her life. That was best.

No more bodies. He couldn't bear for Jacob to look at him the way he had that night ever again.

Emir waited, sitting on the floor beside his sarcophagus, until he heard the woman begin to move downstairs. He went down to meet her and easily caught her eyes, smiling as he apologized for his flirtatious friend's behavior. She seemed embarrassed for herself and touched the sore cuts on her neck, which Emir explained away by an unfortunate fall in the kitchen with some broken glass. He was just thankful no one was seriously injured, of course.

The woman didn't linger—she seemed eager to put distance between the herself of this morning and the one from the night before. Emir offered to drive her home, but she insisted on calling something called an Uber to take her instead. She waited outside for the car that came for her, and Emir let out a sigh of relief as her ride disappeared around the next corner.

It had been a long night.

———

Titus was at the house every evening now. He'd been showing up at the front door for three nights, and each evening, Emir had sent Jacob a text message that he needed privacy. It wasn't worth risking having them in the same room more than was absolutely necessary.

Emir was fast becoming exhausted—even before he'd settled into his routine alone, when he'd been more accustomed to the presence of another vampire in his life, he'd been drained by it. Now that he knew the peace that was possible in a solitary life and had been forced to deal with someone else—*especially* someone like Titus—it was almost unbearable.

But if he wasn't at least hospitable, then Titus would just become angry and be even more of a nuisance than he was now.

His phone rang early the next night, before Titus could begin his usual complaining and teasing, and Emir hesitated to answer it. Jacob. He didn't want to talk to Jacob where Titus could overhear—but to ignore the call would be a red flag, too. So he picked up, and answered in as blank a voice as he could manage.

"Yes?"

"Are you still needing all your private time?" the boy began snidely.

"I have a guest," Emir answered, refusing to show any response as long as Titus's eyes were on him from across the room. He'd taken one of Emir's bags from the fridge, and was now tearing it open and sniffing the contents as though it might be poison.

"I need to see you. It's been—it's been days." He sounded tired, and it made Emir's heart hurt.

"Very well," he said in his most placid voice. "Eleven. Be at the apartment."

"I don't want you in my place," Jacob spat. "But I—fuck. That's not true. I—"

"Eleven," Emir repeated. "I'll see you then." Then he hung up the call before Jacob could argue the matter further.

Titus took a sip from the bag, audibly gagged, and dropped it in Emir's lap. "Disgusting. I don't know how you can survive like this."

Emir picked up the bag by its top before it could spill itself all over his pants. "Quite happily, usually," he sighed as he brushed at a spot of red on his thigh.

"Was that your useless ghoul? What's happening at eleven?"

"I'm just feeding him," Emir answered blandly, leaning over to lay the bag on the coffee table to warm up slightly. "It won't take long."

"He doesn't come to you to be fed?"

Emir paused for a moment, then glanced up at Titus with a slow blink. "I thought you *wanted* me to leave the house more."

Titus scoffed and dropped onto the couch beside him. "What does that ghoul do, anyway? I haven't even seen him since I first arrived."

"I don't need much," Emir said, hoping he sounded off-handed enough. "I keep him on retainer mostly—for when I occasionally have him fetch me things from in town."

"What a waste of blood," Titus sneered. "He could at least be bringing people here, if you insist on hermiting yourself."

"He could, if that was at all what I wanted."

Titus groaned and let his head fall back against the cushion. "You know, you once called *me* insufferable."

Emir leaned across to the coffee table and picked up his book, opening it on his knee as he crossed his legs. "Only the once?"

Titus turned his head to smirk over at the other man, and Emir felt the slightest tug at the corner of his own lips.

15

When it got close to eleven, Jacob began to pace the length of his bedroom. He hadn't told Cordelia he'd asked Emir to drink again—there was no way he could, after spending the last few days doing nothing but bitching about him and his new houseguest. He had told her about dumping the body, simply because he had to tell *someone*. If she'd been put off by it, she'd hidden it well. But she had given him a bit more distance lately, and she seemed more pensive.

He wasn't concerned about it now. The only thing on his mind now was that it was now two minutes past eleven o'clock, and there had been no knock at his door or clouds coming through his window. Jacob sat down on his bed and dropped back onto the mattress with a huff of frustration—and as soon as his head hit the blanket, a sharp crack sounded from the window, and then something hit the wall and lodged into the drywall right beside his closet door.

"What the fuck!" he shouted, and he leaned over to peer at the hole in his wall. He hadn't heard a shot—but then he realized. It was a rock.

Jacob slid from his bed and hunkered low to the floor until he reached the window, but when he looked out through the cracked glass, the only thing he saw was Emir, standing in the complex's parking lot with eyes wide and both hands steepled in front of his mouth. Jacob tugged the window open, spilling a few shards of glass onto the carpet.

"I'm so sorry!" Emir called softly up at him, just as Jacob's door burst open, and Cordelia appeared in only a t-shirt and panties, brandishing a metal baseball bat.

She looked around briefly, then blinked over at Jacob. "What the hell was that?"

Jacob sighed and gestured out the window. "I think Emir tried to throw a pebble at my window." He started with a quiet cry as the vampire appeared in the window, and he backed out of the way as Emir clambered over the sill in a rush.

"I'm so sorry," he said again, glancing between them as Cordelia slowly lowered her weapon. "I only wanted to—" He frowned at Jacob with his brow wrinkled with regret. "You seemed upset the last time I just came in, so I—"

"So you tried to kill me with a fucking projectile rock?"

"I didn't think I'd—it didn't hit you, did it?"

"No, but we're damn sure not getting our deposit back now," Jacob said with a gesture toward the battered drywall.

"I'll pay for the repairs, of course. I'm so sorry to frighten you. Both of you," he added with an apologetic look at Cordelia.

"You fucking dweebs," she sighed. "I take it back," she said in Jacob's direction as she laid her bat on her shoulder. "You can have this one." Then she turned and left the room, pulling the door shut behind her.

Emir had his hands clasped in front of him, and he watched Jacob with a tentative frown. Even like this—even having just put a hole in Jacob's window and having mostly ignored him for almost a week, Jacob still wanted to go to him. He still wanted to pull him down, whisper in his ear, beg to be given a treat like a good little boy. That's what he'd called him for, wasn't it?

"I owe you an explanation," Emir began after a moment, and Jacob snorted.

"Do you even? Do you have to explain yourself to a servant?" he snapped back without thinking. "You didn't even let me talk on the phone. Just gave me directions and cut me off."

"Jacob," Emir gently pleaded, and Jacob turned his face away to hide the tinge of red in his cheeks. "You would have no way of knowing, but you must understand—among vampires, it's considered...impolite, I suppose—not done. To bother or harm another vampire's ghoul. As long as Titus believes that's all you are, he won't pay you any attention. And attention from him could be dangerous."

"*Isn't* that all I am?" Jacob snapped. "I'm someone you can just ask to get rid of a corpse for you. Clean your floor," he added with a sneer. "It's all just part of my service in exchange for your 'gifts,' right? That's what a ghoul is *for*."

"I'm sorry, Jacob," Emir sighed. "I didn't want things to be this way. I wanted—" he stopped himself, but before he could rephrase, Jacob was biting back.

"Wanted what? Wanted me to not be around when you started fucking your old vampire boyfriend again?"

Emir recoiled slightly in shock. "I'm not—that's not it at all," he insisted.

"I've seen the way he touches you. The way he looks at you. Don't try to tell me you guys didn't used to fuck."

Emir hesitated, and Jacob stared up at him with all the anger and bitterness in his heart. It shouldn't have hurt so much.

"It was three hundred years ago," he admitted. He sighed as he reached for the boy's shoulders, and Jacob allowed the touch but wouldn't look him in the face. "Please, listen. Titus and I...we were together for some time after he changed me. I suppose I didn't know it could be otherwise. But I left him because—we didn't...match. I didn't want the life he did. He...wasn't happy about it when I left."

"So now he's just going to hang around forever until you agree to go back to a world tour of murder with him?"

"I...don't know. I've been trying to talk to him, to convince him that I don't want to go back to living with him, but he's...persistent."

"He's a dick, you mean," Jacob corrected, and Emir allowed a faint smile to touch his lips.

"Yes," he agreed, then paused. "Do you...still want to continue? Knowing he may be here for some time?"

Panic squeezed Jacob's heart, and he looked back up at Emir's dark eyes. "Yes," he answered immediately. The thought of not having the blood again—of going back to the way he was, and severing this connection they had—he couldn't bear it, even when his more rational thoughts reminded him of the downsides. "But not—here," he went on, a little more quietly. He glanced over at his bed, where the vampire had pinned him down, kissed him, promised never to hurt him. He couldn't make more memories like that in this room. They'd been hard enough to ignore already.

"We can't go to my house," Emir pointed out. "Even if Titus isn't there now, he could return anytime. I'd rather keep you away from him as much as possible."

They both stood silent and pensive for a moment, but then Emir took his hand and led him from the apartment. Jacob looked at their laced hands as he followed the vampire down the stairs outside, trying to push aside the warm feeling in his chest and telling himself that it couldn't possibly be caused by the vampire's cold hands.

Emir led him to where he'd parked his car near the apartment and opened the back door. Jacob stared up at him.

"You're serious?"

"It's private," Emir said with a small shrug.

"Ish," Jacob grumbled, but he let himself down into the back seat anyway. This was somehow even more embarrassing than having Emir in his bedroom—this felt like some kind of illicit meeting. He sat near the far door as Emir climbed in beside him and shut them in, and he watched as the vampire undid a couple of the upper buttons of his shirt. His heart shouldn't be beating this way—but he was used to it by now. It was just the blood. He'd let himself become addicted—and Emir was his dealer. Maybe it was appropriate that they were meeting in a dark parking lot.

Emir wouldn't look at him, but he cut the skin near the base of his neck with one easy movement and opened his arm to Jacob just as he had before. Of course he wouldn't look at him. He wanted to act like he cared in person, so keep Jacob docile, but as soon as another vampire—someone who *mattered*—came around, he was just someone to be fed like a stray cat. Fine. Jacob could just take what he wanted, too.

He crawled across the seat to him and held himself up on the car door as he leaned across Emir's body and bent his lips to the bleeding cut. No matter how angry Jacob might be at the man himself, the blood was just as sweet. His chest warmed as he swallowed, and he let himself drop to his elbow against the door so that he could be closer. His head swam, his heart thudded against his ribs, and Emir's cool skin was perfect under his tongue. He expected any moment to feel Emir pull him away like always, but instead of the firm fingers in his hair, Jacob felt the vampire's hand on his back—pressing gently, palm flattened against his shoulder. Holding him.

How was that even better than the blood?

This time, Emir squeezed his shoulder to urge him away, and Jacob obeyed, breaking away from the wound in Emir's shoulder with one last, longing lick. He pulled back enough to look up into the other man's face, and Emir was watching him softly, hand still firm at Jacob's shoulder.

Jacob shifted, allowed himself to settle his weight on Emir's chest, and kissed him. Why was he kissing him? He pressed close to him and opened his mouth, allowing the vampire's tongue to brush over his with a chill that shot straight down Jacob's body to his groin. He touched Emir's side, tugging at his tucked in shirt until it came loose and he could push his hand against skin. Why was he doing this? He was angry at Emir. He'd been brushed aside. Talked down to. Made to commit felonies. But he still moaned softly when Emir cupped his cheek. He still fumbled with his shirt buttons, desperate to feel him under his hands.

Emir held him tight, thumb stroking Jacob's cheek with such tenderness that he shivered. This wasn't fair. Jacob could barely breathe, but he couldn't make himself break the kiss. He slid his fingers through the black hair on Emir's stomach and chest, and the vampire's hand moved down to press into the small of his back, urging him closer. Without really intending to, Jacob pulled himself more fully on top of the other man, causing Emir to slouch in the seat so that Jacob could lay his body on top of him. Emir's erection pressed against Jacob's hip, and Jacob rolled forward against him, sighing into the vampire's mouth as he got his first taste of sweet friction against Emir's thigh. This wasn't normal ghoul behavior—was it?

Jacob didn't care anymore. He let his dull fingernails scrape down Emir's firm stomach and fought against his belt buckle, whimpering as the older man's hand gave his ass a firm squeeze that hitched him up a little higher. Jacob finally had to break the kiss to look down between them when blindly fumbling with Emir's belt wasn't working, but he still could barely concentrate—Emir kissed his cheek, his temple, and his hair, and his hand slid under the hem of Jacob's shirt at his back to lift it up while the other trailed from his cheek to his chest, then his stomach.

"Fuck," Jacob whispered, ashamed of the desperation and need that swelled in him at even the suggestion that Emir might be doing what Jacob hoped he was doing. Jacob shifted to make just enough space between them as he finally freed the end of Emir's belt from its buckle and shoved it aside, pulling instead at the button and zipper of his pants. As soon as he got them undone, his hands stopped moving. Underneath the fashionable slacks and button-down Cordelia had chosen for him, Emir was wearing a bright green pair of briefs with a dark blue zig-zagging pattern across them. He leaned back with his knees on either side of Emir's hips and looked down at him.

"You didn't buy any new underwear, did you? This is twenty-year-old underwear."

Emir paused. If vampires could blush, the look on his face told Jacob it would be happening. "I—go out so rarely," he said softly, and Jacob snorted.

"I don't even care," he murmured, already leaning down again to press his lips against Emir's. He hesitated just a moment with his heart in his throat, and then he slid his fingers slowly over the cotton doing a poor job at restraining the vampire's erection. Emir shuddered underneath him, which put a powerful thrill in Jacob's belly—but then Emir's fingers were unbuttoning his jeans and pushing inside, and any sense of control Jacob had went immediately out the window. He melted under Emir's touch, whining and whimpering at the cool press of the vampire's palm against him. This was what he'd wanted that night in his room. What he'd wanted since the first time they kissed, if he was honest.

He tugged at Emir's horrifically ugly underwear and freed him from it, immediately wrapping his fingers around the vampire's cock and giving it a testing squeeze. It was cool to the touch, as he expected—it wasn't strange anymore. Emir groaned softly into Jacob's mouth and lifted him closer with the hand on his ass, allowing him to push Jacob's underwear down his hips along with his jeans. As soon as

Emir's hand closed around Jacob's dick, Jacob broke their kiss to look down. Emir's hand looked dark against Jacob's lighter skin, and the sight of him slowly stroking, his own stomach hitching under Jacob's tentative touch, was almost enough to send Jacob over the edge before they'd even begun.

Jacob laid his forehead on Emir's shoulder, allowing himself one more slow lap at the blood still staining his collarbone and smiling at the shiver it made in the man underneath him. Emir turned his head to him and lifted Jacob's chin with his free hand, drawing him into a slow, purposeful kiss. Neither of them breathed properly through it, both beginning the work of their hands in earnest and taking the time to fully explore each other's mouths. Jacob wasn't worried about cutting his tongue now—even if he did, he trusted Emir to control himself.

He paused just for an instant, then sighed and allowed himself to sink deeper into the kiss. He trusted him.

Emir ran the pad of his thumb over the damp slit of Jacob's cock and drew a quaking moan from him, so Jacob tried to focus on returning the attention. He wasn't going to last long—Emir's cool skin was oddly perfect around him. It might have almost felt strange to have a warm hand on him. And Emir felt cold under his hand, but the soft sighs and moans Jacob's every touch pulled from him had every sign of life.

When Emir kissed Jacob's cheek and bit his earlobe softly, whispering the boy's name in a moan, Jacob squeezed him tighter unintentionally.

"Fuck," he swore again, unable to keep his hips from pressing upward into Emir's hand. "I'm gonna—"

"Please," Emir murmured against his cheek, and he gently brushed Jacob's hand away from him, instead tugging him closer by his hip and taking them both into his hand. The cool, hard press of Emir's dick against his own made him cry out, and he clutched at the vampire's shoulders, bucking shamelessly into his grip until he snapped. He caught Emir in another kiss as his orgasm pulsed out of him, spilling over Emir's fingers and stomach and only making his caress slicker. Jacob's whole body quivered, and he moaned desperately into the other man's mouth, covering Emir's hand with his own to urge him to keep going.

"You too," he whispered, so close his lips still brushed the other man's. "I want to see you come."

The command made Emir suck in a sharp breath, and he clutched Jacob tight against him, stroking them both at a fervent pace until Jacob felt him tense beneath him and was lifted from the seat by the upward motion of Emir's hips. The vampire's moan almost made Jacob come again, it was so low and rumbling against his jaw. The fluid that touched Jacob's fingers was cool, just like Emir's skin—but that seemed right, too.

Jacob collapsed against him as soon as Emir's grip on him loosened, and he found himself encircled in the vampire's arms, held gently against Emir's chest with his head nestled in his shoulder. Emir's fingers brushed through the hair at the back of Jacob's head with a tenderness that made him ache.

"I'm still angry at you," Jacob muttered, muffled by the fabric of the other man's shirt.

"I understand," Emir answered softly.

They lay like that for a minute or two before Jacob peeled himself away, Emir releasing him as soon as he moved. Jacob awkwardly removed himself and sat back on the seat, trying to refasten his jeans as quickly and smoothly as possible. He averted his gaze as Emir did the same, not sure he could handle the sight of their mixed semen on the vampire's brown stomach.

"I hope I didn't take up too much of your time," Jacob said with his eyes on the parking lot beyond the window. He shouldn't have done this. For a hundred million reasons.

"Jacob," Emir said in a light scolding.

"I know you have a guest."

"I told you the reason that I—"

"Yeah, yeah." With his face hot and red, Jacob threw open the car door and let himself out. He couldn't stay in here—he couldn't handle Emir's dark, gentle eyes on him. "Just text me the next time you need something, boss," he added with venom in his voice before slamming the door.

He half expected the vampire to catch up with him on his way back to the apartment steps, or to try to stop him. But he didn't. Jacob made it back into the apartment and into his bedroom, where he shoved the door shut again and sighed at the hole in the glass. Why was he such a goddamn idiot?

He chewed his bottom lip to fight the anger and the aching feeling in his gut, then went into the kitchen to look for something he could tape over the window.

16

Titus had watched Emir curiously when he returned to the house, but asked him no questions about his feeding trip, so Emir offered no information. It wasn't any of his business, anyway—and the less Titus knew about Jacob at all, the better.

Emir spent another two nights entertaining him. It was, he suspected, not actually entertaining for either of them—Emir only wanted to read or practice his guitar, and Titus only wanted to go out on the town or regale Emir with stories about the places he'd been while they were apart. The only thing they'd agreed on was watching a television show that Titus informed him was related to Star Wars—which Emir hadn't particularly enjoyed in the first place, but found entertaining enough, if it meant relative quiet.

He wanted more than anything to be able to bring Jacob to the house again—he'd hardly been able to concentrate on anything, so fresh and clear were his memories of their breathless time in the back seat. But Emir didn't know how to force Titus to leave. He would have to just wait him out. Bore him to death.

So he did his best to hold a conversation when Titus initiated one, even though all he wanted to do was sit and read his book. To his credit, on the third night, Titus left him to his devices for almost an hour, just sitting beside him on the sofa with his phone in his hand. It still wasn't as good as being alone, but at least it was quiet.

It also didn't last for long.

"This can't be your entire evening, *every single evening*," Titus finally said with a great heaving sigh, as if he were the one put-upon by the situation. "I know this is a small town, but there must be something better to do than this. It's every night."

"If you're bored, you're more than welcome to find somewhere else to explore," Emir pointed out.

"Come on," Titus prodded, tossing his phone lightly onto the coffee table. "Come out. I'm your guest—you ought to show me what this city you've chosen has to offer me."

"You've sampled more than enough of this city, I think."

"When did you become this way? You never used to complain about feeding." He leaned on one hand and drew close to Emir's cheek, a smirk on his lips. "We had a good time in Florence, didn't we?"

Emir turned to look at him and retreated slightly upon realizing how close they were. "*You* had a lot of fun in Florence."

"Do you know what I think?" Titus shifted and dropped down into a seat beside Emir, then prodded him in the chest with one finger. "I think you're *lazy*."

"Is that so?" Emir said with a light sigh.

"It is. I think you've found a way to have blood delivered to your door so that you don't have to put the work in anymore. You're the vampire equivalent of an invalid, or an old man, waiting patiently to have your meals brought and spoon-fed to you. Maybe you don't even know how to hunt anymore."

"It just makes good sense. Why kill if we don't have to?"

"Spoken like a lamb, not a lion."

"I am *not* a lion," Emir pointed out.

"You were once."

Emir paused, then folded his book closed with his thumb holding his place. He kept his eyes lowered so he wouldn't see the derisive look he knew he'd find on Titus's face. "Times are different now, Titus," he said quietly. "I'm not ashamed of the way we lived. It's the nature of what we are. But wouldn't it be better for everyone if the lion *didn't* have to kill the gazelle?"

"No," Titus answered promptly. "Because then there would be too many gazelle. Just like there are too many humans now." He reached out to touch the back of Emir's head, threading his fingers through the other man's black hair with familiar ease. "Come out with me. Show me you still know how to hunt. Pick off the weakest of the herd, if you like—pretend you're the keeper of their little habitat here."

Emir didn't try to move his hand. He just frowned faintly over at him. "Do you remember what it was like? To be human? Or are you so separate from them now?"

Titus laughed and tilted his head, letting his fingers run over the back of Emir's neck. "Not at all. I try not to think about it, actually. What a pitiful existence I had before this one. Why? Do you?"

"I...try to."

"And do you know what would be an excellent reminder of that?" Titus turned Emir's head and leaned over to touch his forehead to the other man's. "Come out and be among them for a change."

Emir let his eyes shut briefly. If he continued to refuse, Titus would become more and more insistent. Was it better to go along with him, just this once, if only to prove him wrong?

"...All right," Emir agreed after a pause. "I'll go."

Titus let out a victorious laugh and released him as he stood. "I already know just the place."

———

The bar Titus led them to was more of a speakeasy, hidden behind a nondescript door on the street and up a dark flight of stairs. It was dim inside, and crowded with people, with music playing over speakers in the ceiling that was so loud Emir flinched when Titus first opened the door. Emir followed behind him as he walked up to the bar, weaving between bodies and trying unsuccessfully not to touch any of them.

The smell inside was overwhelming—everywhere the air was laden with sweat and alcohol and perfume. Emir wanted to turn right around and leave, but he knew that if he didn't at least appear to be trying, Titus wouldn't be satisfied, and he would have to have the same conversation again and again. He could nip this in the bud now—convince Titus that he wasn't interested in this life, show him that he was having a horrible time, and send him on his way.

Titus stopped at the bar and ordered two beers. Once he had them in hand, he moved to a quieter part of the bar and dumped a slosh out of each into the drain on the other side of the counter, then handed one off to Emir. It was a trick he'd seen Titus use many times. A half-empty drink was less suspicious than carrying around a full one, or none at all. They stood together near the bar, and Titus leaned close to him to speak under the music.

"Do you see anyone you like?"

Emir shook his head. "I said I would come out. I didn't say I would hunt."

Titus scoffed at him, offended. "What's the point, then? You just wanted to stand in a dark room and hold a beer until it gets warm?"

"I didn't want to come out at all," Emir reminded him.

"America has sapped every trace of fun you had in you," Titus sighed. He nudged Emir with his shoulder and smirked over at him. "Shall I choose someone for us, then?"

"The more people you kill, the more difficult you make my life here. You know that, don't you?"

"If your life here becomes *too* difficult, perhaps you should consider returning home with me."

"You don't have a home," Emir snorted.

"I'll have you know that I have a very nice villa in Marseilles as of about five years ago."

"It sounds lovely. You should get back to it."

"You're mouthy," Titus said with a frown. "If you keep on like this, you're going to hurt my feelings."

"Now *those* you don't have."

Titus shrugged. He glanced around the busy room and almost leaned his head on Emir's shoulder as he spoke. "I do know your type. Look there, near the corner table—he's young, tall. What type, do you think? Are you an expert on taste now that all your meals come in bags?"

"I'm going to go," Emir said, reaching back to set his beer down on the bar behind him, but Titus took him by the arm.

"Wait, wait. Listen—there's a reason I wanted to bring you here. I have a surprise."

"Titus, I don't want any more of your gifts or your surprises."

"You'll like this one. It's relevant to your interests. Trust me."

Emir hesitated, but Titus smiled broadly at him and pulled on his arm, so when he moved back toward the more densely-packed length of the bar, Emir followed.

"I was here a couple of nights ago," Titus began, and he forced his way up to the bartop and leaned an elbow on it. "And I met Ian, here." He waved over the bartender—a young man of maybe twenty-five, with ash blond hair and a freckled nose. "Ian, this is my very good friend, Emir. He's local." Titus smirked back over his shoulder at Emir and pulled him slightly closer. "Ian is from New York—moved back home with his parents to save some money."

Emir glanced hesitantly between the boy's face and Titus's. He didn't like where this conversation was going.

"Ian, if you have some time—I'd love for you to show my friend what you showed me the other night."

The young man smiled and tilted his head toward the end of the bar. Titus followed, guiding Emir with him by an arm looped around his elbow. The bartender led them into a quiet back office and threw the lock on the door once all three of them were inside.

"Titus, I told you I'm not—"

"Abup bup," Titus interrupted, and he gestured toward the young blond as though giving him the floor.

Emir watched in confusion as the bartender began to unbutton his white dress shirt, and, when it was loose to his stomach, he pulled it down past his shoulders, revealing pale skin marked by scars as numerous as leopard spots, tracked across his shoulders and down his arms. Emir knew these marks—knew what they meant. This sort of person was known by many names of varying degrees of disrespect among vampires. Donor. Follower. Feed bag.

"Isn't he beautiful?" Titus said, releasing Emir's arm to stand behind the boy and run his hands lightly down from his shoulders. He picked up Ian's hand by his wrist and turned it in his fingers, exposing his inner forearm, where the skin was pockmarked and thick with scars. "You must have been very popular in New York," he added with a tilt of his head toward the boy.

"I'm not doing this," Emir said, and Titus tutted at him.

"My friend, you'll never find a more guilt-free indulgence than this. It isn't even for free—Ian has bills to pay, don't you, Ian?"

"A lot of them," the young man admitted with a soft laugh.

"He only wants a hundred dollars," Titus went on. "It's very reasonable—you wouldn't believe some of the greedy bastards I've seen in Milan. As if their blood were liquid gold." He leaned close enough to brush his cheek over the boy's, but his eyes were on Emir. "It's my treat, old friend."

"I said no."

"Emir is shy," Titus said in a low, taunting voice, and he drew Ian's wrist up, brushing his lips over the scarred skin. He seemed to choose a spot and bit down, causing a flinching wince from the boy in front of him, who slouched back against Titus's chest with a soft, sighing moan as the blood began to flow. Titus supported him around the waist, the young man's head on his shoulder as he drank.

Emir turned his gaze away, focusing instead on the dusty health certificate framed on the wall. He shouldn't have agreed to come here. He should have known it would turn out this way.

Out of his view, Titus gave a hum of satisfaction, and when he called his friend's name in a soft voice, Emir reluctantly glanced back at him. Ian's arm was still bleeding as Titus held it out toward Emir like an offering, the seeping red running in thick rivers down his arm and dripping from his elbow onto the floor.

Wasted.

Emir shook his head and took a step backward. Don't think like that.

"He's ready and waiting for you, old friend," Titus said, watching him with eyes seeped full of black ink.

Ian's eyes were lidded, and he turned his head subtly toward Titus's neck as he watched Emir, calm and patient as if he wasn't in the arms of a killer. He wasn't afraid. He was willing. He was even being compensated. There really could be no pleasure more guiltless. But it was a slippery slope, and Emir knew it. He'd known he was on it when he'd tasted the blood of the woman on his living room floor and considered it a mercy. He'd already forgotten the name on her tag. If he did this—if he fed from this boy, who even seemed to want him to—then how long before Titus convinced him to take the next step?

He couldn't take this one.

He couldn't risk losing what he had.

"I'm going home," Emir said, and he unlocked the office door to let himself out.

"Damn it, Emir!" Titus called after him, but Emir didn't stop. He kept walking, through the crowded, sweating bodies and out the door onto the street.

He made it almost around the corner before he was pressed hard into the wall by Titus's arm across his chest. The other vampire stood with his face so close Emir could smell the blood on his mouth.

"Get off of me," Emir said evenly. If he escalated, Titus would never back down—and Emir likely wouldn't be the one to suffer.

"You would rather sit and rot inside that moth-eaten house than be what you are?"

"I *am* being what I am," he protested, fighting to keep his voice neutral.

"And this is how you choose to use the gift I gave you? I made you immortal—I granted you the strength of ten men and the power of their nightmares, and you use it to hoard books and hide from the world I handed you."

"I didn't ask you for it!" Emir snapped, and before he could stop himself, he shoved the other man away from him by the chest— though he only moved back a single step. For a few seconds, they stared at each other, Titus with anger in his eyes and Emir with pain in his chest. "I never asked for this," he said again, more softly now.

Titus snorted and looked down the street away from him for a moment, then dropped his head and nodded. "All right," he said calmly, but Emir didn't like the tone of his voice. Titus put his hands in his pockets and looked back up at him. "That's how you feel. So all right."

"...All right," Emir agreed, though he didn't quite relax.

"Go back to your books," Titus said with only a hint of a sneer. "I can see I've used up my hospitality."

He was gone then, and Emir took a moment to lean back against the wall and sigh. As nice as it would have been for Titus's dramatics to mean he was actually leaving, Emir knew him too well to believe that was the case.

17

Titus didn't come back to the house for the rest of the night—which was a sort of worrying relief. Once the sun had risen, Emir sat for a while longer on his bed upstairs, watching the sky brighten through the cracks in his bedroom curtains.

The night had been tiring, but the day was young. He needed to take the chance now, when Titus wouldn't interrupt him. He couldn't let another day pass without talking to Jacob. The boy hadn't been answering his texts unless they were direct questions, and even then he only got one-word responses. Things couldn't carry on this way.

Jacob didn't seem especially pleased to see Emir as he entered the music store—and Emir couldn't blame him. But that was precisely why he'd come now.

Jacob pretended he didn't notice Emir approach the front counter. He continued cutting open boxes and setting them aside for unpacking as if Emir wasn't standing a foot away from him on the other side of the glass.

"Can I talk to you?" Emir asked, and Jacob paused just long enough to make it clear he'd heard but still didn't look up.

"Can't stop you," he grumbled. "This is America. Oh," he added, straightening from his next strip of tape and gesturing toward Emir with his box cutter. "America is a free country, see. Democracy and everything. It probably wasn't like that the last time you left your fuckin' house, so just, you know. Update."

"Jacob, please," Emir sighed. "Can we be alone?"

The boy returned his attention to the box in front of him. "I can take a break in ten minutes. Meet me out back."

"Thank you."

Emir waited as he was told, standing near the back door of the store until it was shoved open by the push bar. Jacob approached him with a frown already set on his face and his hands in his jeans pockets, but Emir didn't mind. He deserved whatever bitterness Jacob had for him.

He looked over as the back door swung open with a thunk from the push bar and waited while Jacob approached him, hands stuffed into the pockets of his jeans.

"So, what do you need to talk about?" Jacob said, scuffing his heel against the pavement and looking down at it instead of at Emir's face.

"I wanted to see you," Emir answered simply. "I know that you're still angry, but...I really am doing what I can. To show Titus he's not welcome."

"Have you tried *telling* him he's not welcome, and to just get the fuck out of your house?"

Emir let out a light sigh. "You're underestimating how contrary he can be. If I do that, he might try to move in."

"Sure. And then you'd have no use for a ghoul at all, right?"

"Jacob, what would you have me do? You resent every task I've ever given you, but you get angry at me for giving you none?"

"Well I don't—fucking know," Jacob spat, his shoulders hunching slightly. "I feel fucked up. I'm mad because I can't see you, and I'm mad because I *want* to see you so bad, and I'm mad I let myself get so carried away the other night—"

"You regret it?" Emir interrupted him, but Jacob kept his eyes lowered.

"I...I guess I don't," he answered after a long pause. "I just...don't know where my head is at."

Emir wasn't much relieved by that response. Maybe he shouldn't have let it go so far. Jacob had just been fed, so his mind had surely been awash with any number of emotions—maybe he had been irresponsible. But holding the boy in his arms had been the most joy he'd felt in over a hundred years.

He only wish he knew how to tell him so.

Emir hesitated, then began again. "Could you perhaps...leave work early?"

Now Jacob looked up at him, one brow lifted. "Why?"

"Well, you've been neglecting your end of our arrangement. I haven't learned anything about the modern world in almost two weeks."

"Are you serious? What, dickhead doesn't watch Netflix? And anyway, pretty sure I *just* told you about America being a democracy now, so—"

"I've never been to a baseball game," Emir cut in. He released Jacob and straightened his shoulders slightly. "There's one this afternoon. I would like you to take me."

Jacob stared at him flatly for a few seconds. "...A baseball game."

"Yes. I've been in America for some time—though not long enough to know a time when it wasn't a democracy, thank you—and I should know the rules of its favorite pastime. Can you teach me?"

Jacob frowned, turning his head slightly to watch Emir out of the corner of his eye. "...I'll ask my boss."

Emir smiled and stepped aside to give Jacob space to go back into the store. He'd realized over the last few days how much he'd missed being able to simply sit with him—watching documentaries or talking about the books that either of them were reading. The prospect of spending the afternoon together, without Titus there to interject or deride him, made that longing all the more keen.

Jacob drove them to the stadium, but Emir paid for the tickets. The aisles and the stands were crowded, but refreshingly open—even through the dark tint of his sunglasses, Emir still enjoyed being awake under the daytime sky. Jacob wanted a hot dog, which Emir also gladly paid for, and then they took their seats high in the stands.

"So," Jacob began around a mouthful of hot dog, "you really don't know how to play baseball."

Emir shook his head. "I'm...tangentially aware of it. But I've never been very interested in sports."

"That's funny," Jacob snorted.

"Why?"

"Well see, there was this movie, and it had this whole vampire family in it, and they played baseball, and it was a whole thing. Like they were so fast, and the human girlfriend was so impressed, or whatever. I only saw it once."

Emir frowned faintly as he tried to piece together the words Jacob was saying to him. "The...vampire family?"

"I'll just show it to you. That'll be easier."

"All right."

Emir didn't quite understand the purpose of standing during the excessively long anthem before the game could start, and the sound of the cheering crowd was slightly painful to his ears, but once the players were on the field and the game began, he listened closely while Jacob explained the rules. The sun was oppressively hot—some of the seats in the stadium were underneath shade, but the ones they'd been assigned were, unfortunately, not.

Jacob glanced at him a number of times during the early part of the game, but when Emir turned to meet his gaze, he stared pointedly back out at the field, refusing to make eye contact. But after a while, he rose from his seat, told Emir to stay put, and began to hurry down the stairs. Emir frowned after him but obeyed, though he wasn't able to concentrate much on the game. Perhaps an afternoon together on a sunny day hadn't been the wisest choice.

When Jacob reappeared a few minutes later, he was carrying something. He dropped back into his seat next to Emir and presented the hat—a low and wide-brimmed canvas affair in beige and white, with dark blue claws scratching red lines across the surface. He pulled the tag off with his teeth and raised it up, so Emir dutifully ducked his head slightly and allowed the hat to be placed on him.

"There you go," Jacob said with a teasing smile. "Now your face is out of the sun, *and* you're an official fan of the New Hampshire Fisher Cats."

Emir hesitated to speak. Jacob had purchased many things for him over their weeks together, and not all of them with Emir's money— but this was the first thing that hadn't seemed like part of his job. This was...a souvenir. Bought because he'd noticed Emir was uncomfortable—he knew even if Jacob wouldn't admit it. Emir wanted to touch him, to draw him close and kiss him, to take him back to the house and hold him with what precious time they had left before Titus woke up. But he couldn't be sure that Jacob wanted those things—if he ever really had, or did any longer.

So instead, he touched the hat, smiled to himself, and asked, "What's a Fisher Cat?"

"Fuck if I know," Jacob laughed, and Emir found himself laughing, too.

No matter how much Emir enjoyed sitting beside Jacob at the game—and the game itself, too, he had to admit—the afternoon ran long, and the sun only got hotter. Eventually, Jacob had to rouse him from nodding off.

"Time to go, I think, boss," Jacob chuckled. He helped Emir to his feet and walked him drowsily down the stairs and out of the stadium again.

Even being in the shade the car provided was a relief; Emir settled back into the seat and tried to keep his eyes open, but he still needed Jacob's shoulder to make it into the house once they got back. Emir enjoyed leaning on him, grateful even for this allowed touch after what he'd put the boy through over the last few days.

Jacob took his hat off for him and left it on the couch on their way by, then supported him all the way up the stairs and down the hall.

"You've had a big day, little guy," he chuckled, but Emir didn't have the energy to respond to his teasing.

Emir moved the lid of his sarcophagus aside and sat on the edge of the stone container to kick off his shoes, but he didn't bother with any of his other clothes. Jacob was staring over Emir's shoulder at the dark earth inside but asked no questions.

"Thank you," Emir said softly. He looked up into Jacob's still faintly smiling face, and reached up for him, gently cupping his cheek to draw him closer. Since Jacob inched inward at his touch, Emir closed the gap and kissed him—but he wasn't devouring like before. He wasn't hungry. No part of Jacob seemed appetizing to him. He only wanted to kiss him. Emir forced himself to pull back after a moment and smiled as he let his hand slip from the boy's cheek. "It was a good date," he said, and he settled himself into the sarcophagus.

Before he slid the cover closed, he allowed himself to enjoy the stunned look on Jacob's face.

———

When Emir awoke that night, he barely had time to drink and settle himself before Titus was at the door. Emir allowed himself a faint sigh before he opened it to the other vampire's smile.

"Don't worry," Titus began on his way past him into the living room. "Tonight, I'm not here to pester you."

Emir followed him in, and came into the room just in time to see Titus tilt his head at the hat left casually on the corner of one back cushion. "What on Earth is this atrocious thing?" he asked with a soft laugh as he picked it up.

Emir instinctively strode over and snatched it from his hands. "It's nothing," he said, already turning away to tuck it aside in one of the side rooms. "Jacob...my ghoul brought it to me. As a joke."

Titus watched him curiously on his way back into the living room. "You see your ghoul during the day?"

"Occasionally. When the need calls for it," he added. "Not all of us are so unwilling to be awake with the sun."

"Here I am trying to be nice, and you're insulting me."

"This is trying to be nice?"

Titus spread his hands. "I came to apologize, actually. You welcomed me into your home, and I did nothing but question you."

Emir watched him with suspicious uncertainty and didn't answer.

"I can't say that I think you seem *happy* here, exactly, but you certainly seem to have...found a place. And if that suits you, then who am I to show up and disrupt you?"

"...Thank you," Emir offered, not sure what else there was to say. He didn't want to risk arguing with him and accidentally talking him out of what was starting to sound very much like a goodbye.

"In any case, I won't disturb you any further. Unless, of course," Titus went on, closing the distance between them with slow, easy steps, and looking up at Emir with a smirk playing on his lips, "you think we ought to bid each other farewell properly. Or have you taken a vow of chastity as well?"

"I never quite shared your...specific tastes."

"You never complained," Titus murmured, tilting his head slightly and looking down his nose at Emir's lips.

"You never let me believe I could."

Titus reached up and stroked his knuckles down Emir's cheek and along the soft line of his jaw. "Don't play coy," he said in a low voice. "I know how to be gentle."

"I don't think you do," Emir answered evenly. "Goodbye, Titus."

"You'll be a tease until the end of your days, my friend," Titus said with a resigned sigh. He let his hand come to rest on the side of Emir's neck and leaned in to press a kiss to his lips, but he released him after a moment and took a step back. "Enjoy yourself, Emir. I plan to."

Emir barely had time to let out his breath before Titus was gone. He stood still for a moment, fully believing Titus would be back in front of him with just one more "and another thing," but the house stayed silent. He really was leaving.

He walked to the front of the couch and sat down, enjoying the quiet for a long while. Things would be peaceful again. He could see Jacob again. He could talk to him—make him understand. Emir frowned faintly as he looked over at his phone, waiting on the arm of the sofa. He had to make Jacob understand—everything.

18

It had only been three days this time. Jacob had no excuse for feeling this way. His heel tapped the floor as he sat on the couch, fighting the anxious feeling in his belly that meant Emir was awake—and too far away for Jacob's liking. Only three days. It was too early for him to be this...hungry. He wanted more of Emir. More of his gift, more of his voice, more of his skin under Jacob's hands and tongue. He couldn't count the number of times he'd been hard at inconvenient times over the last few days because he let his mind wander back to the car. He'd never been this drunk on a person before—and it concerned him, when his mind was clear enough to let it.

But Emir had been so kind during their time at the stadium, and so exhausted even before he'd sat in the sun for hours—Jacob really could believe that he was just as bothered by Titus's presence as Jacob was. He had to trust him.

Cordelia left to have a drink with a friend despite Jacob's reminder that Emir thought it best if she stayed home—she just said, "Life is meaningless without the inevitability of death," and slung her purse over her shoulder on her way out.

Jacob tried to distract himself from his aching thirst by playing the newest *Resident Evil* Cordelia had brought home recently, but he had trouble focusing. He died a few times and got irritated, and just as he was about to toss the controller across the couch, a knock at the door startled him. He peered through the peephole, and his heart jumped at the sight of Emir's slightly distorted shape through the glass. He opened the door and tried not to smile too broadly as he backed up to let the vampire in.

"I came to tell you good news," Emir said once Jacob had shut the door. "Titus has gone."

"Gone? Gone...away?"

"I believe so. Or he will soon be, at least. He told me so earlier this evening."

"That does sound like good news."

"It's a relief," Emir admitted. "For many reasons." He stepped closer and cupped Jacob's face in his hands, causing a pleasant shiver down his spine. "I have something I want to talk to you about."

Jacob wet his lips and covered one of Emir's hands with his own as he looked up at him. "Can it wait?" he asked softly. "I was hoping..."

The vampire's expression changed; he frowned faintly and stroked Jacob's cheeks with his thumbs. "That's precisely what I wanted to talk about."

"Good," Jacob sighed. He tilted up his chin and leaned in to kiss him. Emir returned the kiss, but pulled back after only a brief moment.

Jacob reached to take hold of the front of Emir's shirt, meaning to pull him with him into the bedroom, but the other man stood still. He let his hands fall to Jacob's shoulders.

"I'm not going to feed you anymore," he said gently, and Jacob paused.

"What?"

"I'm not going to give you anymore blood."

Jacob frowned, then shoved Emir's hands from his shoulders. "Why? I thought...things were going well. Now you're dropping me?"

"Not at all."

"Then what the fuck?" Jacob demanded, louder than he'd meant to. "Is this because of Titus?"

Emir sighed softly. "Yes and no. Please—will you let me explain?"

"It better be fucking good," Jacob grumped, folding his arms to glare up at the other man.

Emir looked down at the floor for a moment or two, hands wringing in front of him, as if he needed to choose his words carefully. "While you're being fed—while you're a ghoul, you are, in essence..." He hesitated before looking up at him. "A thrall. As long as we continue, you'll always feel drawn to me. You'll always feel...well, like a servant. Whether you like it or not, and whether you admit it or not. I don't want that." He moved forward half a step as though he wanted to touch Jacob again but didn't want to overstep. "I want to know—how you really feel about me. Because I know how I feel about you."

Jacob couldn't do anything but stare for what he felt was an exceptionally long time. His cheeks were red, he knew it, and his mouth opened long before he was actually ready to speak. What, exactly, was it that Emir knew? And what was he expecting Jacob to tell him? How did he expect Jacob to have an answer like that at all? What kind of an answer did he want? What would make him happiest?

"I care for you, Jacob," Emir said, his voice gentle and hesitant. "I hope that you care for me, too, but...you can't tell me that until you're free of this bond."

Jacob moved closer to him without thinking, reaching for him and pulling at the hem of his shirt, pressing his palms against the vampire's stomach. "I'd feel a lot nicer about you if you'd give me what I want," he purred in a voice he hardly recognized as he leaned close to brush his nose over Emir's jaw.

Emir kept his hands at his sides, though Jacob could feel the tension in the skin under his fingers. "This hardly seems fair," he said.

"You really want me to have to be strapped down?" Jacob asked. He kissed the corner of Emir's mouth and let his hands drift to his sides and up over his ribs underneath his shirt. "Even with that dickhead showing up and everything that happened, I've felt...so good. I don't have to waste as much time sleeping. I hardly ever get hungry. I don't get tired lifting stuff at work. I've read *three* of my next course's books this week. I don't want to go back to the way I was before. I don't want to lose what you've given me."

Emir seemed to be holding in a sigh as he tilted his head to allow Jacob to kiss him again. "Jacob, please understand," he whispered against the boy's lips, then pulled back out of reach.

Anger flared in Jacob's chest for a moment, but then he slipped two fingers into Emir's belt and gave a teasing tug. "Maybe you're hoping I'll offer different kinds of services?"

The next instant, Emir had Jacob's wrists in his hands, and he forced Jacob away from him with such force that he flinched. Jacob looked up into the vampire's face with frustrated confusion. Emir seemed subdued, only holding Jacob firmly. Was he upset? Why was he upset? Jacob was only trying to do what he wanted—

"This is exactly what I was talking about," Emir said, a faint wrinkle in his brow. "Listen to yourself."

"Listen to—" Jacob huffed and snatched his hands away, but Emir didn't try to fight him. "Fine," he snapped. "You want to stop, so we stop. You're the *master*, after all."

"Jacob—"

"I'll just sit in the corner and not speak unless spoken to, right? Like a good boy? You fucking prick," he spat, struggling to keep his voice from shaking.

"Jacob, please."

"Have you learned enough about *the modern world* yet? Have I done my job to your *satisfaction*?"

Emir recoiled faintly with a look Jacob didn't recognize in his dark eyes. He hesitated just a moment before speaking, softly. "I...suppose so."

"Then pay me and...fucking leave me alone." Jacob turned away from him, holding his elbows tightly in his hands.

"...As you like," the vampire murmured. He stepped back and opened the front door, then paused at the threshold. "Good night, Jacob."

As soon as Emir was out the door, Jacob went to the window to watch him cross the parking lot below. He felt sick to his stomach as he slid down to the floor with his elbows on the sill. "Fucking asshole," he whispered, and he hid his face in his arms, ignoring the burning behind his eyes. What was he supposed to do now?

———

Cordelia returned to the apartment much earlier than Jacob expected—and she immediately hauled him to his feet and took him to bed when she found him still pouting on the living room floor.

"Just leave me alone," he grumbled as she shoved him into a seat

140

on the mattress.

"No can do," she answered cheerfully. "I have my orders."

"Your *what*?"

"Emir came and found me. He said that you were being de-ghoulified, and that it would probably take three or four days for you to get over it. So he asked me to keep you inside so you don't do anything stupid."

"Wh—no way. That's such bullshit!" Jacob stood to face her and scowled down into her blinking, unimpressed face. "He can't just cut me loose and then have you babysit me!"

"Well, that's what's happening. So do you want to behave yourself, or do you want me to actually strap you to the bed? 'Cause I won't even use the fuzzy handcuffs—you'll get the ones I stole off that campus cop last year."

"You're serious?"

She stood on tiptoe to stare directly into his eyes. "Do I look serious to you, Jacob?"

Jacob pressed his lips into a thin line and held her gaze for a few seconds, then relented. "Fine. But I have work in the morning."

"No you don't," Cordelia answered easily. "I texted Amy on the way home. You've got the flu. Gonna be out for days. You don't want to give it to anybody."

"You can't just—"

"Oh, I can. And I did."

Jacob tried to stare her down again, but she remained nonplussed in the face of his frustration, so he flopped back onto the bed with an irritated huff. "Fine," he said, already rolling away from her. "The fucking *vampire* knows what's best, I fucking guess. Just...let me get some sleep."

Cordelia gave his shoulder a squeeze that she probably meant to be comforting, but it only made Jacob feel worse. She was on Emir's side, too. They both thought they knew what was good for him better than he did—but where was Jacob's voice in this? Why didn't he get a say in the way he lived his own life? Why had Emir been making all his decisions for him for weeks now? That wasn't what he'd signed up for.

He never should have taken the blood from him in the first place.

All through the next day, Jacob felt twitchy. It wasn't so bad while the sun was out—he kept reading his books and drinking the water Cordelia forced on him, though he still had no appetite for food. But when the sun went down, he couldn't take it. He needed to leave. He needed to go to the house. Emir was there. Emir was waiting.

Cordelia planted herself in front of him when he tried to make for the front door, her hands on his chest as she leaned her full weight against him. He shoved her so hard that she hit the wall and cried out, which startled him enough to make him pause.

"Cords, I—"

"You win," she said, rubbing at the back of her head and grimacing. "But let me go get him, okay? You stay here. Just go lie down. I'll bring him."

"You will?"

She nodded and touched his arm, urging him back toward his bedroom. "You need to rest. Just wait here until I get back."

Jacob sighed with relief, and he settled against his headboard prepared to thank her—but the next thing he knew, his wrist was attached to the bed frame by a pair of silver handcuffs. He tugged hard against the restraint and thought he heard the wood begin to crack, so he pulled harder.

"Oh, no you don't," Cordelia grumbled, and she crawled up onto the bed alongside him, dropping down onto his middle and pinning him as she reached over the top of him. She grabbed his flailing arm and flung herself down to drag him with her, deftly fastening his other wrist to the other side of the frame with handcuffs covered in black fur.

Jacob's body twisted as he fought, but Cordelia sat down hard on his stomach and knocked the wind out of him.

"Hey. Hey. Hey," she said, smacking his cheek progressively harder with each word until he stopped thrashing and looked up at her.

"Let me go," he said, pleading desperation in his voice. "I need to go. He needs me. I need him. I have to go to him."

"Hey!" Cordelia said one last time as she gave him another firm slap. "If you don't settle down, I'm gonna pour NyQuil down your throat so you don't wake up 'til next week, you got it?"

Jacob turned his face away from her, blinking away the angry tears that slipped down his temples. "He needs me," he said again.

"He needs you to get well," Cordelia corrected gently. "Stay put."

Cordelia tried to leave him alone while she cooked dinner, but he pulled on his restraints so hard that the whole bed jostled away from the wall with his flailing, so she camped herself on his chest and ordered pizza instead. She offered him bites of pepperoni while she sat on him and chewed, but he only scowled at her.

Through the night, he tried begging and pleading. He threatened her. But all the while, she just kept her place on top of him, scrolling through her phone and largely ignoring him. When dawn broke, and light finally began to pour in through his poorly-taped bedroom window, Jacob's eyes began to droop. He fell asleep with Cordelia still firmly on his chest, and when he stirred hours later, he found her slumped over him with her full weight on his body, her head on his shoulder while she snored softly.

Jacob spent the next twelve hours significantly calmer, but also frequently vomiting. Cordelia had set him free the first time he began to heave over the edge of the bed, and he'd rushed to the toilet just in time. Even if he'd still felt the pull that had come over him the night before, he didn't have the strength to act on it.

He mostly stayed on the bathroom floor—Cordelia brought him some rice and broth and a few blankets to nest in between heaves. He didn't even really have anything to throw up; he'd eaten too little. He spent a lot of time coughing and spitting bloody foam into the toilet, as if his body was trying to remove every trace of the cursed fluid he'd swallowed over the past weeks.

By the end of the day, he was too exhausted to even try to get out of his room, let alone the apartment. He slept straight through the night and well into the next morning. He woke up with Cordelia curled up beside him and sat up slowly so as not to wake her. His whole body felt heavy and numb, like he'd had Novocain injected into every limb. He rubbed at his ears and stretched his jaw to pop them, but it didn't make them work any better.

He was starving.

He made his way to the kitchen and ate whatever he could easily reach—a couple slices of bread, the bottom half of a bag of Doritos, some cold leftover Chinese. When he was stuffed almost to the point of being sick, he sat down on the couch and leaned his head against the back cushion to stare at the wall.

He'd acted like an idiot. Like a spoiled, mean, spiteful idiot. Emir had deserved a little spite, for sure—but Jacob cringed at the memory of the way he'd begged, shouted—offered sexual favors. When had Jacob become a person like that?

Cordelia padded out of the bedroom after a few more minutes, and she watched him with caution in her eyes as she took a seat next to him.

"How're you feeling?" she asked quietly, and he managed a chagrined smile.

"I think I liked it better when I was too delirious to realize what an ass I was being."

"Hey—accepting you were an ass is the first step to recovery. But it wasn't your fault." She reached across to squeeze his hand. "Well. Not totally."

"Thanks heaps."

"Hey, but now you're better, right?"

"Then why don't I feel better?" Jacob sighed and freed his hand from her hold so he could rub at his eyes. "I treated him like garbage. I insulted him and—said things that I didn't mean. But he was right. He knew I was turning into a slave."

"He would know, I guess."

"Yeah." Jacob pulled one of his feet up under him on the couch so he could face his friend. "Thank you, Cords. I'm really sorry for the way I acted."

"It's no big," she said with an easy shrug. "We should all be lucky enough to have a hot vampire in love with us."

"In—no, no no no." Jacob laughed bitterly and shook his head.

"Be real, dude. Why else would he do what he did?"

"Because he was sick of my shit?"

Cordelia stared hard at him. "Is that what he said?"

Jacob frowned as the image of Emir's soft, sad frown reappeared in his mind. *I care for you, Jacob.* He sighed. "No. It's not," he admitted quietly.

"I didn't think so. You should have seen the look on his face when he came to ask me to take care of you. I think you really hurt his feelings. You *hurt* the *vampire's* feelings. Do you understand the kind of vampire you found, that you can actually hurt his feelings?"

"A...thoughtful one?"

"A *thoughtful* one!" Cordelia echoed, reaching out to shake his arm for effect. "This isn't some dramatic Dracula-type or a gross nosferatu hissing at you from a dark corner. This is an outrageously attractive, caring, donated-blood-only drinking, *thoughtful*, homebody vampire who just wants to hang out with you and talk about what books you read or documentaries you watched last week. Do you understand what I'm saying?"

"I mean, I understand the words, but I feel like you're getting at an underlying—"

"I'm saying you found probably the only dude on earth who is not only perfect for you, but who could also turn you into an immortal. You're living the dream, here, Jacob. Some of us train our whole lives to be chosen by a monster and swept off our feet, and it's happened to you. So you should think long and hard about how *you* feel about this vampire that's obviously in love with you. That's why he cut you loose—so you could make your decision."

Jacob took a deep breath and looked down at his hands as he laced them in his lap. "I get that," he said softly. Then he glanced back at her. "If I try to leave the apartment tonight, are you going to sit on me again?"

"You seem chill. I don't think that'll be necessary anymore."

He smiled. "Good."

Jacob took another nap in the afternoon, and when he opened his eyes, he found an envelope waiting for him on his nightstand. He sat up with a frown as he picked it up. He knew the neat, looping handwriting on the outside, but it somehow made him feel warm to see his own name written in it. He tore the back open and pulled out the contents—a single slip of paper, and a check written out to him for one hundred thousand dollars from the not-at-all-fake-sounding V.T. Bank of Wallachia. Signed by Emir Arzinjani.

He laid the check aside and hesitated with the folded paper in his hands. Was this a goodbye? Had he fucked everything up?

With a steeling breath, he unfolded the note and began to read.

Jacob,

As agreed. I don't want you to feel there are any more strings attached to my company. I wish only the very best for you. Please know that I've only ever tried to act in your best interest, and I deeply regret anything I've done that brought you pain. My house will always be open to you—should you ever want to visit.

All my love,

Emir

Jacob stared at the letter in stunned silence, then let his hands drop to his knees. This...fucking asshole.

19

Jacob let himself into Emir's house before the sun had even fully set, and he stalked across the living room and up the staircase, then down the hall and to the closed door at the end. He threw it open with a flourish just as the stone lid began to move, and he waited, hands on his hips with the letter in his hand, as Emir sat up. The vampire started at the sight of him and went still.

"Jacob," he said warily under the boy's glare, slowly pulling himself from the sarcophagus to put his bare feet on the floor. "Are you feeling well?"

"I feel fine. Seeing clearer than I have in weeks. What the fuck is this?" Jacob demanded. He shook the paper in Emir's face.

"I—don't know. Is it my—"

"What the hell makes you think you can do this?"

Emir frowned at him. "What have I done? You asked to be paid, so I—"

Jacob stepped closer to him and turned the page around, tapping the closing line with his finger scant inches from the vampire's face. "What the fuck does that say?"

Emir glanced between the letter and Jacob's face, visibly confused. "It says...all my love."

"Exactly!" Jacob huffed and shook the paper one more time before tossing it aside and letting it drift to the floor. "You think the first time you tell me you love me, you get to just slide it into a fucking notice of payment?"

"I—" Emir stopped, then softened as he took in the look on Jacob's face. "You're right. I'm sorry."

"Damn right you're sorry," Jacob scoffed. He stepped closer to Emir and straightened his shoulders as he stood in front of him. "Well?"

A warm smile touched Emir's lips, and he rose, stroking the boy's cheeks and letting his hands rest gently at the sides of his neck. "I love you, Jacob. I realized some time ago; I'm sorry it—"

Jacob cut him off by pulling on the front hem of his robe and tugging him into a long kiss. He slid his arm around the other man's neck and held him close, breathing in the faint smell of damp earth that clung to his skin. He pulled back slowly and let his fingers curl into the hair at the back of Emir's head as he looked up at him. "I accept your apology," he murmured with a teasing smile.

"Does...that mean that—"

"You're really gonna make me say it?"

"You made me say it," Emir pointed out, and he leaned down, his cheek brushing Jacob's as he drew close to his ear. "Just whisper it," he taunted.

Jacob clutched tighter to him, heat rushing up from his neck into his cheeks. "I...love you, too," he breathed. "And I'm sorry for every stupid thing I did."

"I did infinitely more stupid things." Emir leaned back to smile at him, then touched another soft, light kiss to his lips. "Will you stay? I've missed you."

"Are you gonna be all gooey all the time now? This is what I get now?"

"Perhaps not all the time."

Jacob smiled and pulled him down to kiss him again. "I'll take that, I guess."

Emir slipped his arms around Jacob's waist to keep him from escaping and held him tight, kissing his lips and cheeks with such reverence that Jacob squirmed. "I was worried," he murmured, cool lips leaving a pleasant tingle on Jacob's cheek. "I wondered if I'd been fooling myself." His hands pressed into the small of Jacob's back, almost lifting him onto his toes.

"Maybe into thinking I'm more than a salty piece of shit," Jacob chuckled as Emir nuzzled gently into his neck. He left kisses in a slow line back up to Jacob's lips, and Jacob leaned into him instinctively, opening his mouth to the other man's kiss and letting his fingers slide through his dark curls.

Emir ran his tongue slowly over Jacob's upper lip, smiling into the kiss as he murmured, "You taste fine to me."

Jacob didn't bother trying to hide his shudder. He sucked in a sharp breath and dug his nails into the back of Emir's shoulder, feeling like he might burn up under the other man's gaze. "So," he said, hoping but doubting that his voice sounded steadier than it felt, "you never told me why a guy who sleeps in a coffin needs a bed."

Emir hesitated, but then he kissed Jacob again, harder than before. Jacob whimpered softly and almost lost his footing under the force of the kiss, but Emir kept him upright until he got a grip on Jacob's thighs. Then he lifted him up as if he weighed nothing at all, and Jacob let out a stifled sound of surprise, clutching to the vampire with both arms and legs as he was carried from the room.

He didn't hear the steps Emir must have taken down the hallway to the bedroom, but he felt the soft blanket under his back and the dip of the mattress at his side from the weight of Emir's knee. Jacob didn't wait for Emir—he was already pulling the robe from his shoulders and prying apart the fastened toggle at his waist, eager to expose the soft brown skin underneath. As soon as Emir was free, he lifted Jacob's shoulders from the bed and pulled his shirt smoothly from him, abandoning it on the floor. He closed his mouth over Jacob's again, and Jacob let his hands explore the vampire's chest and stomach, enjoying the subtle arch he gave under the touch.

Emir laid slow, tentative kisses on Jacob's cheeks and chin, drifting over his neck and shoulder as his arm slid under the boy's waist to keep him close. Jacob reached down between them, running his fingers through coarse black hair on his way to wrap around Emir's erection. The man above him gave a soft gasp that flooded Jacob's head like a shot of whiskey, and his arm tightened around Jacob's waist. Emir worked on the button of Jacob's jeans and pulled carefully on his zipper, so Jacob lifted his hips obediently and allowed the other man to pull the denim down and off of him.

The vampire's body was cool against Jacob's, but he felt hot all over regardless. This was happening—this man was a vampire whose blood Jacob had tasted, and who had told Jacob two minutes ago that he was in love with him. He was briefly afraid for the physical safety of his body in the hands of a person capable of breaking his bones by holding him too tight, but Emir was being too gentle with him for it to last. Emir was, if he was honest, being actually a little *too* too gentle—even when he held Jacob's waist or stroked his cock, he used such a light touch that Jacob began to whimper for more. He bucked his hips up into the other man's hand and squeezed him harder as a hint, but Emir still seemed to be holding back.

"You won't hurt me," Jacob murmured against his lips between kisses. "I don't bruise easy."

Emir hesitated just a moment. "I'm sorry," he said uncertainly, and he shifted to kneel fully between Jacob's legs, running a ginger hand down his thigh to his knee to ease it toward the mattress.

Jacob frowned faintly at the crease in the vampire's brow, and he sat up on one elbow, then reached up to Emir and touched his jaw to draw his gaze. "Hey. I want this," he said. "This isn't a ghoul thing. I don't feel that anymore."

"I know," Emir answered quickly. "I...thank you. I'm sorry. It's...been some time. I don't want to—disappoint you."

Jacob's face grew so warm he was sure even his ears must have turned red. He paused, wet his lips, then pushed up onto his hands with a sly smile. "Then how about I show you what I like?"

Without waiting for an answer, he pushed on Emir's chest and turned him over so that he could straddle his hips. He kissed him, savoring the feeling of the other man's arms automatically circling him, but then he brushed them away. He moved down Emir's body, unable to keep from moaning as he ran his tongue over one of his dark nipples and caused a sudden sharp gasp. He kissed his chest and stomach, fingers already stroking him again, and when he settled between Emir's thighs, Jacob didn't hesitate to draw his cock into his mouth. Emir tensed beneath him and let out a slightly shaky sound of surprise. His hand reached for Jacob but hesitated just before touching him, so Jacob hummed his approval and placed the other man's hand in his hair for him.

Emir felt strangely cold on his tongue, but his skin was soft and smooth, and his uneven breathing was more than enough reward for Jacob's efforts. Emir didn't try to use the hand on the back of Jacob's head; he seemed more interested in simply touching him than trying to guide him. His fingers toyed with Jacob's hair as the boy's head moved, and he squirmed beautifully on the mattress when Jacob let him touch the back of his throat.

Jacob longed to taste the cool fluid he'd felt touch his stomach in the back of Emir's car, but just when he thought the vampire was getting close, Emir curled his fingers to grip Jacob by the hair and eased him away. He looked down at Jacob with dark eyes and parted lips and tipped his chin slightly to urge him upward.

"Come."

The single word, said so often and so casually over the last weeks, set a fresh fire in Jacob's belly now. He obeyed as Emir moved to gently grip the side of his neck, crawling up the other man's body and settling on top of him when Emir pulled him into a kiss. He jerked as Emir's other hand slid around his waist to grip his ass in a firm squeeze and rolled his hips back into the touch, whining softly at the friction of his cock against the other man's hip. Emir kissed him and licked his lips, and Jacob couldn't help the bucking movements he made, the hard press of Emir's dick so close to his making his breath catch in his throat.

Emir held him close and shifted to kiss his cheek and neck, tongue tasting the skin beneath Jacob's ear as they moved together. Jacob was desperate for Emir to touch him where he wanted him, and he almost reached back to move his hand for him, but then Emir's soft kisses ceased. He let out a husky breath against Jacob's neck and squeezed him so tightly that he winced.

He tried to pull back in the vampire's arms but was held fast. "Emir—" he managed to get out, but then he was shoved forcefully away, almost losing his balance and sliding straight off the mattress. He made an ungraceful sound as he caught himself on the blanket but moved immediately back to the other man. Emir was covering his face with both hands, so Jacob tugged on his forearms to pry them away and saw exactly what he expected—the solid black eyes that had stared up at him from the couch that night.

Emir sat up and pushed Jacob away from him more gently this

time, but he still forced him out of arm's reach while he took deep, steadying breaths. Jacob wouldn't be removed. He crawled back to him and wrapped his arms around him, holding the vampire's head against his chest and pressing his lips against his hair.

"You won't hurt me," he murmured. Emir touched his arm gently but kept still while he breathed. They stayed that way for at least a minute, until Emir relaxed in Jacob's arms and pulled slowly away from him.

"I'm...afraid that I will," Emir answered without raising his eyes from the blanket.

Jacob sat back on his heels and bent forward until he could look Emir in the face. "You don't scare me, tough guy. How can I take a vampire seriously who I once caught on the couch enraptured by the *Dark Crystal* prequel?"

Now Emir did look up, but it was to frown at him. "I—" He stopped, clearly deciding against defending himself, and gave a small sigh through his nose. "It's been...more difficult. Lately."

"What has?"

He hesitated. "Resisting," he said simply. He shook his head. "The entire time Titus was here, he did nothing but try to tempt me into killing again. After the woman you saw, it became...harder not to think about. When it was only me, alone in the house, it was easy to drink from my bags and put it out of my mind. But Titus kept pushing, and I almost..."

Jacob softened and inched a little closer to him. "You know, it's important that you even try. I mean, dark, insatiable hunger is sort of part of the whole vampire gig traditionally, right? It matters that you *want* to not kill people."

"I appreciate that," Emir murmured. "But it isn't a very helpful sentiment if I only *want* not to hurt you."

Jacob paused, then reached out to gently touch Emir's shoulder. He glanced away and shrugged when the vampire looked over at him. "I mean," he began, pausing to wet his lips before going on. "You never even asked."

Emir went still. "...What?"

"If you could...you know."

"I—no." He shook his head and leaned away as if to distance

himself from even the idea. "Jacob, I would never—"

"Even if I said it was fine?"

"I couldn't possibly—you'd—"

"I didn't say you could *kill me*, asshole. But, you know, if it's..." He frowned down at the blanket to keep the heat in his cheeks from showing, only peeking up at him. "If it's, like, a little bit, you know, if you get—caught up...I'd be okay with that."

Emir stared at him, wide-eyed, and opened his mouth to speak a second or two before any sound came out. "You mean if I...*during?*"

"What, like you and your fucking vampire ex never did weird blood shit?" Jacob said, shoving his arm.

"Well, that's—"

"I trust you," Jacob cut him off. "I know you won't really hurt me. I'm telling you it's okay."

"You don't understand," Emir countered softly. "If I bite you...this is awkward to explain. There's something *in* the bite, or...I don't know, exactly. But it has a...sedative effect. You wouldn't be able to move. So..." He shifted on the bed, and Jacob again got the distinct impression that he would be blushing if he could. "It wouldn't be...very enjoyable for you, I think."

Jacob sat with his hands on his thighs, considering. He would be putting himself completely at Emir's mercy, literally placing his life in the vampire's hands, and the best case scenario was that he would lose pints of blood and be incapacitated and helpless while the other man fucked him. "...Sounds hot," he said.

Emir's brow furrowed. "It...does?"

Jacob leaned in close and kissed him, then pulled back just enough to run his tongue lightly over Emir's upper lip. "I signed up for a vampire romance, here," he murmured. "Don't hold out on me."

Emir didn't quite relax as Jacob kissed him again, but he didn't resist, either—and it took no time at all for Jacob to stroke him back to readiness. He laid back down on the bed with Emir beside him, carefully caressing Jacob's side and reaching behind him to pull him close again with a hand at the small of his back.

"I don't suppose you have any lube somewhere," Jacob said as Emir kissed his chin.

"I...do," the vampire said with reluctance in his voice, and he released Jacob to lean across him to the nightstand. He took a full bottle of clear lubricant from the drawer and settled back on the mattress, and Jacob laughed.

"It's not twenty years old, is it?"

"No," Emir admitted. "I found it here on the table after Titus's first visit. I suppose he had...expectations."

Jacob sneered faintly, and Emir quickly unscrewed the cap to show him the sealed inner lid.

"It's unused," he promised, but Jacob shook his head.

"I just hate the idea of that asshole actually being helpful." He drew Emir close to him with an arm around his neck and kissed him, pulling the vampire's body over him and letting his weight distract him from thoughts of the other man.

Emir still seemed hesitant to lay more than the gentlest of hands on Jacob, but he at least finally lifted up one of his knees and slipped freshly-slicked fingers over him, moving slowly and gingerly until Jacob whined. Jacob breathed a deep sigh of pleasure and relief when Emir pushed a finger inside of him, and he tugged the larger man closer so he could better reach him. He stroked him as quickly as he wanted Emir himself to move but almost lost focus completely when the vampire crooked his finger inside him.

"Shit," Jacob swore through a tight jaw, one hand squeezing his partner's cock and the other tangled in his hair. He pushed back when the vampire eased another finger into him, back arching and head pressing into the pillow. His breath left him at the next light stroke of Emir's finger, and his erection twitched against his own stomach. "Fuck, just like that," he sighed, and Emir listened.

Soon Jacob was the one who was a mewling mess on the bed, panting into the vampire's shoulder and clinging to him with both arms around his neck now. He lifted his hips to try to get more of him, and when it didn't come, he whimpered in frustration.

"Come on," he breathed against Emir's cheek. "I'm ready."

A low sound formed in Emir's throat that lodged itself securely in Jacob's groin. Emir pulled his hand from him gently and pushed him fully onto his back, settling between his thighs and pressing them apart. He seemed to hesitate for just a moment, but then he ran his wet hand over himself and shifted Jacob down closer to him. He bent over him and kissed him, swallowing Jacob's moan as he eased into him. Jacob whimpered and raised his hips, hooking his legs around Emir's waist to urge him on. The chill of him washed over Jacob's whole body, a strange, shuddering feeling at odds with the burning the vampire's kiss made inside of him.

Emir didn't take much encouraging—he began to move as soon as Jacob nodded into his shoulder, and, almost as quickly, Jacob began to unravel. If he'd had more of his senses, he might have been embarrassed at the way he moaned as the vampire rocked against him at a steady, rolling pace. Emir's hands were firm on his hip and around his shoulder, and he seemed determined to let his lips touch every inch of Jacob's skin he could reach.

Jacob fit his hand between them so that he could stroke himself, but just as he was on the verge of losing himself completely, his arm went slack. Something tight and sharp fastened on his neck, and he sucked in a hissing breath as he flinched. His head swam, and he realized that Emir's mouth was on him. His heart made a rhythm of stinging throbs in his skin as his grip on the other man failed. But Emir didn't stop moving. He went faster, held him harder, and moaned deeper in his own chest. Jacob's body felt covered in pins and needles, and he had no chance of fighting the cries that fell from him as the vampire thrust perfectly against the bundle of nerves inside him. The tension built rapidly in his belly, but he couldn't even force his hips to move until his whole body jerked and shuddered, and he came onto his stomach in surges that seemed to match the beat of his heart.

Emir still kept going—he forced Jacob so far up against the headboard that when he finally broke away from the wound he'd made, he leaned back on his knees, jerked Jacob down against him, and fell on him again, this time laving his tongue over the fresh breaks in the skin. Jacob managed to force his hands back up to Emir's shoulders, at least, though his fingers felt thick and numb as if they'd fallen asleep. He jolted as Emir thrust hard into him and stilled, and he felt the cold pulse of the other man's orgasm deep inside of him, causing a shiver that ran through the whole of his body.

"Fuck," he breathed as Emir finally went still. His eyelids drooped, and he curled his fingers loosely against the vampire's bicep for just a moment before his hand dropped heavily back to the bed. He barely winced as Emir pulled out of him, only vaguely aware of the shift in the mattress until he felt a warm, damp cloth pressed gently against the side of his neck. Jacob's hand was lifted for him and made to hold the cloth in place, and his legs were carefully moved as he was wiped down with a second damp towel. He let it happen in a daze, but he finally focused on Emir's face as the vampire settled beside him again and took over holding the cloth to his neck.

"Are you all right?" Emir asked, and the worry in his voice put a bloom of heat in Jacob's chest that he wasn't entirely sure he had the blood for.

"I'm okay," he said, though he sounded a bit croaky. He smiled and reached up to brush away the crease in Emir's brow with his thumb. "Really."

Emir sighed with relief and let his forehead rest on Jacob's shoulder. He actually felt a little warm now. "I shouldn't have," he whispered.

"Hey," Jacob said, turning his head just slightly to nuzzle the other man's hair without causing too much of a sting in his neck. "I'd better be the only person you bite from now on, got it?"

He felt rather than saw Emir's smile against his skin. "I got it," he answered softly.

———

When he got home late the next morning, Cordelia came out of the bathroom from her shower, immediately zeroed in on the wound on Jacob's neck, and pursed her lips at him with narrowed eyes.

"The fuck is that?"

"The fuck is what?" he answered, not stopping on his way to his bedroom. It didn't matter—she followed him.

"He bit you?"

"I—*let him* bite me," he clarified. He tried to shut the door on her and she slammed her weight against it, forcing her way inside.

"Oh my god," she said, "can you two just not go a single day without exchanging bodily fluids?"

"Oh we exchanged fluids," Jacob snorted, then realized what he said and tried to shove her out with the door again.

"What fluids, Jacob? What fluids?" Cordelia bounced against the door as she fought, squeezing her head through the gap so he'd stop pushing. "What fluids?"

"You fuckin' know—"

"*You* fuckin'," she laughed. "What was that like? Was it good? How good?"

He finally relented and moved away from the door, sitting down on his bed and bouncing as she dropped down beside him. "A lady doesn't kiss and tell."

"Bitch, you just told me already. So tell me more." She scooted closer to him on her knees and put her face uncomfortably close to his as she whispered, "Does he come? Like, he's dead right, so does he...you know." She pushed her fingers through the thumb and forefinger of her other hand in a spurting motion.

"Cords, Jesus Christ." He shoved her face and turned away from her so she wouldn't see him blush.

"These are important scientific questions! Who else can I ask these things?"

"Yes, okay? Yes."

"Oh man—that changes everything. So I wonder if they're sterile, or if there are like...half-vampires wandering around. Do you think?"

"I have no idea."

"I guess he's not likely to impregnate *you*, so it doesn't super matter. But so what, you guys are a thing now?"

"I...guess? We didn't really talk about it."

"Too busy?" she teased, laughing at his huff.

"Here—that looks like it hurts." She pushed off the mattress and left the room, returning a few seconds later with their first aid kit. She gently cleaned the bite mark on his neck for him, tore some gauze out of its wrapper, and taped him up. "...Did it hurt?" she asked as she secured the last strip of tape.

"A little bit. But then it was...kind of nice? He said something about a sedative in his spit or something, so once he'd done it, I was a little...drowsy, I guess? Also because of blood loss, probably. But it was...good."

Cordelia sighed as she sat back on her heels and latched the kit shut again. "That's good to know."

"Why?" Jacob gingerly touched the bandage, checking that it was secure. "Are you planning on getting bitten by a vampire?"

"I mean, maybe! I just mean it's good to know that some of the more...romantic stuff is true. It would really suck if vampires turned out to be real and it was only Nosferatu types, you know? But the going out in the daytime, the mist and the bat, the sexy biting...you landed yourself a Bram Stoker variety. That's definitely a good one. Second only to Anne Rice, probably."

"Glad you...approve?"

She shoved him. "Man, you really don't know what you've got." She got up again with the kit in her hands but paused near the door. "Do you think he wants to turn you? Since you're not his ghoul anymore?"

Jacob frowned and leaned his hands on the edge of the bed. "He hasn't mentioned it. I mean, I guess he did—way back. He said he might if I wanted, after we were done with his...modern lessons, or whatever."

Cordelia leaned against the door frame. "But you guys *are* done now, right? He gave you a check."

"...Yeah. I guess with everything else, I just forgot about that part."

"Do you want him to?"

Jacob shook his head. "I don't know. That's...a huge decision, right?"

"Is it?" She shrugged. "I don't see any downsides, personally."

"Uh, besides an eternal monstrous hunger for living blood?"

She stared flatly at him. "That you can drink from a bag delivered to your house, apparently."

"I wonder if they can still eat real food. Like, do they throw it up if they try? I really like food. It was bad enough being a ghoul and barely being hungry. I mean, I got a lot more done, I guess, but..."

"Are you hearing what you're saying right now?"

"But then also," he went on without addressing her, "when I drank Emir's blood, it was amazing. So maybe, when you become a vampire, blood becomes the most delicious thing ever? So would I even miss food?"

"I do not even know what to do with you," Cordelia sighed. "You might have the opportunity to become an *immortal*, and you're worried about whether or not you'll be able to eat pizza again? Do you even understand what's on the table for you?"

"But...I like pizza."

"Oh my god," she groaned, waving him away and turning her back on him. "Tell Emir he can turn me instead, because I'm not stupid, and you can have all the pizza you want alone in your stupid human apartment."

Jacob smiled faintly as she disappeared around the corner, but then he laid down on his bed with one leg hanging off the mattress, frowning at the ceiling. Would that be something he wanted? To be changed into a vampire? Would Emir even do it? He didn't seem thrilled about being what he was. He had offered, it was true, but that was when Jacob was only an employee. Now he was...more.

If Jacob changed, that would mean that he and Emir would be together literally forever—and if he didn't, Jacob would get older, and Emir wouldn't. Jacob would get sick and die someday, and Emir wouldn't. He never would.

That made it an easy question, right?

20

Emir hadn't been so happy in a full century. Jacob had stayed with him the rest of the night, but they hadn't left the bed. Jacob had dozed off for a while, so Emir held him and kissed his hair while he rested. They'd talked and laid together until Jacob had assured him he felt well enough to go again—and Emir hadn't given much argument. They'd kissed in the doorway on Jacob's way out, and Jacob promised to be back the next night.

There was no way Emir deserved for things to turn out this well.

The following afternoon, he forced himself out of rest early and called Jacob.

"Not tired of me yet?" Jacob said instead of a greeting.

"Not yet," Emir agreed with a smile. "I wanted to ask if you would do something for me."

"I dunno," he said with mock uncertainly, "you know I'm not into any weird stuff."

"I want to have you over for dinner. You and Cordelia both. As a thank you."

Jacob laughed. "Like, at your house?"

"Yes, at my house. Is that strange?"

"I'm just saying, usually when a vampire invites you over for dinner, he's *inviting you for dinner*," he said in what he must have thought was a Transylvanian accent. "Also, do you even have anything to cook with over there?"

"That's why I'm asking you," Emir answered simply. "I'm going to need cookware, and some ingredients—"

"Woah, woah," Jacob interrupted. "We just did an entire thing about you not wanting me to be your servant anymore, didn't we? Now you're sending me on errands?"

"I—" Emir began, then hesitated. "I'm sorry. You're...completely right. I—phrased myself badly. I was only thinking I—" He pressed his lips together for a moment. "Will you...come with me?"

"...Sure," he said, far more warmly than a moment ago.

Within the hour, Jacob was at the house, and he let himself in to call for Emir. It felt comfortably like he was coming home, rather than visiting—he didn't hesitate to unlock the door himself now. Emir settled his guitar in its usual place beside the sofa and rose to meet him with a smile that faded slightly as soon as he actually saw him. He had a bandage taped over the curve of his neck.

He caught Emir looking at it right away and stepped up to him to press a long, successfully distracting kiss to his lips. "I'm good," he said without fully pulling back from the kiss. "Let's take you shopping."

"Yes. Thank you."

Jacob smirked faintly at him and turned to lead the way out of the house. It wasn't a very long drive to the apartment store, so they made it to the housewares section before it had even grown fully dark outside.

Emir had nothing, of course—no plates, bowls, or silverware, nothing to cook or serve food in. They had to stock his entire kitchen. Jacob picked out a few things Emir wouldn't have thought of and dropped them into their cart as they passed them, like a spatula and a few kinds of cooking spoons.

"Do you even know how to cook?" Jacob asked as he pulled a can opener from its hook and added it to the growing pile.

"It's been a while," Emir said, which drew a wary smile from Jacob. "But I'm not being ambitious. I remember a few simple things. Will you taste them for me as I go?"

"I don't have a super refined palate, but I'll give it a shot."

"Thank you."

It felt very normal, somehow—despite the complete abnormality of their situation—to be walking through a store together, finding things to make Emir's house slightly more livable. Emir feigned indifference when Jacob brought him to the aisle filled with flatware and silverware so that the boy would choose whichever he liked best. He enjoyed the idea of some part of his home having Jacob's touch on it.

"Oh, so," Jacob began as he scanned the sample plates on display, "is that offer still on the table?"

Emir tilted his head. "What offer?"

"The offer to turn me." He looked over his shoulder with eyebrows slightly lifted. "You said once that if I behaved myself, you'd do it if I wanted."

Emir glanced around them, but they were alone in the aisle. He spoke in a hushed voice anyway. "That's not something I expected you would want to discuss."

"Why?" Jacob leaned back so his head rested on the larger man's shoulder and looked up at him. "Haven't I behaved myself?"

"Not...particularly well, actually, now that you mention it. No."

"Fuck off," he laughed as he pulled away. He went a little farther down the aisle, checking plates as he went. "Does that mean you don't want to?"

"I...didn't think *you* would want me to. Your experience with...people like me hasn't been very positive."

"You gave me a pretty positive experience last night."

"Jacob," Emir scolded lightly, peeking up and down the lane again.

"Oh, I was going to ask, though." He made his choice and picked up a box of plates, setting them gently into the cart. "Before I commit, I'm gonna need to know if I'm missing any information. You know. Pros and cons."

"Pros and cons?"

"Yeah, like—live forever, pro. Be super strong and fast, pro. Have to sleep in the dirt, con. Have to drink blood—normally I'd call that a con, but with the delivery thing, I care less."

"Living forever isn't necessarily a pro," Emir pointed out as they moved on to the silverware. "Sometimes people end up thinking your house is haunted."

"Well not everybody forgets what time it is for twenty years, man."

"And the deliveries help, but you still feel...the pull. I told you how difficult it's been."

Jacob stopped walking and turned to face him. "Sounds a little bit like you're trying to talk me out of it," he said. "You hoping I'll stay human so you can keep me around like a nice, warm juice box?"

"No," Emir answered right away. "Of course not. I would never—think of you that way."

"So, then what else am I missing? Oh—Cordelia wanted me to ask about the, like, transformation thing. I've seen cloud—"

"Mist."

"I've seen cloud and bat, but are there more?"

"Yes. A wolf—though I can't remember the last time I had to use it."

"A wolf?" Jacob repeated, much louder than necessary, so Emir stepped closer to him and tried to softly shush him. "Man, I didn't know you could do a *wolf!* You've gotta show me."

"Jacob, we're in public—"

"As soon as we get home. You're showing me. Is it a wolf-wolf, or a monster-wolf?"

Emir sighed. "It's a wolf-wolf. Now please—"

"Oh, man. Cordelia's gonna shit," he said with a laugh as he returned his attention to shopping. "Well now I definitely want to do it. Is it like I think it is, like you drink from me, I drink from you sort of thing?"

"Yes. But you're very...cavalier about this."

Jacob put his chosen silverware into the cart with a shrug. "There aren't any downsides. And..." He finally went a bit quiet, and he picked at the plastic edge of the cart instead of looking at Emir's face. "If I do, it means we can stay together, right? Without...any issues."

Emir paused, and he found himself smiling as the boy glanced tentatively back up at him. "You're saying...that's something you want? To stay...together?"

"I mean, if we even are together," Jacob mumbled. "I'm not trying to say I need you to *commit* to anything or whatever, I'm just saying that I figured, you know, just based on yesterday, that..."

"Jacob," Emir said softly. He moved around the cart to stand beside him and touched Jacob's cheek, urging him to look up. "I don't tell someone that I love them lightly."

Red flushed the boy's cheeks, and it only seemed to grow deeper at Emir's tender smile.

"Do you?" he probed gently.

Jacob looked anywhere except Emir's eyes. "No," he muttered as if the answer should have been obvious.

"I want to stay together." Emir brushed Jacob's jaw with his thumb and leaned in to kiss him, which caused only a moment of tension in him before he relaxed into a soft sigh. "And I'm very glad that you do, too."

Jacob pulled back from him and turned his head into his elbow with an obviously fake cough, which he used as an excuse to turn away and continue down the aisle. "So, I guess that settles it, then."

"...Actually," Emir said as he pushed the cart after him, "I have...a concern."

"About what?"

"I'm sure you remember that I told you a ghoul is always bound to his master. Bound to have the desire to serve."

Jacob frowned back at him. "But I'm not a ghoul anymore."

"Yes, but—" He paused, trying to think of the words to explain. "While it isn't quite the same, a vampire and his maker...there is a bond there, like loyalty. A strong one. It's...difficult to ignore."

Jacob paused. "So that's why you didn't just kick Titus out on his ass?"

"Among other, more logical reasons I explained to you, but—yes. That's why. I will forever be tied to him. As you would be to me."

"That doesn't sound like a bad thing."

"Jacob, I would never want you to feel—beholden to me. For any reason. Especially if we intend to stay together...forever."

"So...what do we do?"

Emir shook his head. "I'll...think on it. And I'll give you an answer. But tonight, I don't want it to weigh on your mind. Can we just enjoy a dinner together?"

Jacob smiled and nodded. "Sure. Let's find you some pans."

Once they'd filled Jacob's trunk with a culinary housewarming package, they headed to the grocery store. This, Emir needed less help with—he may not have eaten real food for over three hundred years, but he remembered the smells and textures of the produce stacked high on the shelves. He chose the ingredients he would need and laid them in the cart Jacob pushed along behind him, trying to keep too much of his eager smile from showing.

When was the last time Emir had actually looked forward to having guests at his house? He couldn't remember. Mikaiel's wedding, perhaps. He paused for a moment mid-step, then carried on down the aisle. He ought to send David some sort of thank you, as well. Another time.

Before they returned to the house with their haul, Emir asked to drive Jacob's car so that they might make one last stop. He didn't argue—which made it easy for Emir to go alone into the small pastry shop Emir remembered, which, thankfully, was still in operation. He wrapped the plastic bag around the small carton a few times to hide its contents on his way back to the car, then tucked it into the back seat away from Jacob's curious eyes.

Once they'd gotten all of the groceries and pots and pans into the kitchen—and cleared away the various books and notes that littered the countertops and stove—Emir began to prep. Jacob thought to check the oven when Emir turned it on and managed to rescue five or six paperbacks that Emir honestly did not remember putting there, for which he thanked him with an embarrassed smile.

Jacob called Cordelia to invite her over, and she came straight away, long before the food was ready. Both of them lingering in the kitchen made Emir slightly anxious, like they were looking over his shoulder. It made him feel as if he couldn't have said how to open a jar if anyone had asked him. Perhaps this wasn't a good idea after all—Emir may have *thought* he remembered how to cook these things, but what if they were awful? Jacob could lie to him now. What if he lied about it not being horrible?

Jacob must have noticed his fidgeting and frowning, because he offered to take Cordelia on a tour of the house, which she immediately accepted, of course.

"Oh my god, can I see the coffin?" she asked, turning back to look at Emir from the kitchen doorway. "Please can I see the coffin."

"Yes," Emir agreed, offering Jacob a grateful smile as the boy led his friend toward the stairs.

After that, they stayed out of the kitchen to let Emir work, which was much better. The meal he made wasn't complex, but it did take some time. He tried to recreate what a family meal might have looked like when he was alive—chestnut soup, rice pilaf with lamb, pistachios, and black currants, chopped leeks in olive oil—and it made a nice-looking spread on the kitchen table by the time he was finished. It looked edible, at least, but Jacob had been too busy entertaining Cordelia to try any of it. Emir had tried to touch his tongue to the back of his spoon once or twice to test it himself, but it was pointless—everything tasted bland and revolting to him. It smelled right, at least. He only hoped it was appetizing to his human guests.

Cordelia gasped aloud as she dropped into her seat at the table, her hands pressed together at her chest. "This looks amazing!" She beamed up at Emir. "I can't believe I'm about to eat a vampire-cooked meal. This is incredible."

"Perhaps wait until you've tasted it to pass judgment," Emir suggested. He almost held Jacob's chair for him but caught the quick cutting glance the boy threw at him, so he removed his hand. He took the third and final seat and urged them to help themselves, but both of them hesitated, looking over at him with creased brows.

"It's...kind of weird that you're not eating," Cordelia said. "I feel a little guilty."

"Not at all—please. I couldn't even if I wanted to."

"Yeah, it's super weird," Jacob agreed. "Can't you at least have a drink or something?"

"I...wouldn't want to make anyone uncomfortable," Emir answered with a sidelong glance at Cordelia, who would obviously be unaccustomed to the sight of a blood bag, but the girl only gave another excited gasp and clapped her hands.

"Will you have it out of a wine glass? That would make my entire year if you drank blood out of a wine glass."

"...Oh," Emir said softly. Jacob offered him a knowing smirk and a small shrug, so Emir rose from his seat and went to the refrigerator to retrieve one of the sealed bags. "I don't...actually have any wine glasses, I'm afraid. But I'll—find something. Please, carry on." He returned to the table just while his guests spooned out their servings of soup, with his bag emptied into the only glass he had—an empty mason jar.

Cordelia snorted out a laugh when she saw it. "Well, that suits you better, anyway."

"You haven't seen real vampire high class until you've watched him just slurp it like a juice box," Jacob added, and Emir frowned at him, but it faded when Cordelia laughed again.

Humans who accepted him—who were comfortable enough to make jokes about his blood-drinking—would have seemed like an impossibility to him if he'd been asked a month ago. But here were two of them, eating a companionable dinner in Emir's own home. They even said the food was delicious, and Jacob smiled at him so warmly that he didn't doubt it for a moment.

When they were both leaned back in their chairs and holding their bellies, Emir presented them with the final course of coffee and his gift from the pastry shop—freshly made baklava. Both of his guests complained of already being overly full, but they also devoured the entire carton between them without much effort. Cordelia was licking the honey from her fingers and questioning Emir on differences in texture between warm blood and cold—when the front door swung open from the other side of the living room with a slow, steady creak.

Emir stood and moved to the kitchen doorway, a curious frown on his lips as he leaned to see into the entryway—and then he froze. Titus stood in the doorway, one hand still on the knob and an empty, deadly glare on his face.

"Titus," Emir said, instinctively shifting to place himself between the other vampire and his guests. "You...said that you were leaving."

"It seems we both told lies," Titus sneered. He stepped into the house, letting the door drift halfway shut behind him, and moved close to Emir to stare into his face. "Have I interrupted your happy little fucking family, old friend?" The term of affection dripped with poison as it fell from his lips.

"This isn't any of your business, Titus. I told you—"

"You *told me*," he interrupted bitterly, "that the boy was a ghoul. Just a ghoul. I should have guessed it was a lie right from the start. But I wanted to believe you. I wanted to prove to myself I was being too suspicious. But now—" He jerked his chin over Emir's shoulder.

"What's this I see, Emir?" In an instant, Titus had gotten by, and he gripped Jacob by his shoulders and leaned down from behind him to take a long inhale an inch away from the bandage on his neck. "You spend more than two weeks turning me down, pretending to be civilized beyond such base creatures as myself—and yet I smell you on this child's skin."

Jacob winced under the touch as Titus's fingers dug tight into his flesh, and Emir took a half step forward, then hesitated—he didn't want to give Titus any reason to act.

"Leave him out of it, Titus; if you're angry with me—"

"Angry with you? *Angry* with you?" Titus straightened, but his hands kept Jacob firmly in his seat. "You lied," he spat. "You hid this from me. Pretended. Did you think that I was blind?" He ripped the bandage from Jacob's neck with a single quick motion and dropped it to the floor, causing another flinch in the boy as the tape came loose from his skin. Then he took Jacob by the hair and stretched his head sideways, showing the unhealed cuts like the mark of guilt that they were. "You called me monstrous in one breath and fed from this boy in the next."

"Hey, take it easy," Cordelia said as Jacob hissed softly at the squeezing hand in his hair, but she recoiled slightly when Titus's glare turned on her.

"Titus," Emir cut in louder, "this doesn't have anything to do with them."

"This boy is the *source* of your hypocrisy," Titus growled. "He's so precious that you'd cast me aside? Me?"

"Titus—"

"You wanted someone breathing to warm your bed? Or perhaps his blood is laced with gold? Is it more satisfying than the gifts I offered you?" He tilted his head to look down at Jacob's exposed throat, and Emir tensed.

"Take your hands off him," he warned, but Titus only raised his eyes without pulling away from the boy in his grip.

"Perhaps he's worth trying for myself."

Emir didn't have time to warn him again. Titus's teeth were on Jacob's neck—so Emir moved. He rushed the other vampire and hit him with the full weight of his body, tearing him free from Jacob and crashing him back into the kitchen cabinets. A jagged crack ran up the countertop to the wall from the impact. Titus shoved him, but Emir kept hold of the front of his shirt, and before he knew what he was doing, he'd struck the other man in the face. Titus's head snapped to the side, and he turned it back slowly, a dangerous look in his eyes as they focused on Emir.

"Old friend," he said in a low voice. "You would raise a hand to me in violence?"

Emir's every fiber told him to release the man in front of him, to back away, apologize, perhaps run from him again—but he stayed, hand fisted in Titus's shirt. "I'll do more than that if you touch him again."

"For this?" Titus said, gesturing beyond Emir to where Jacob sat with his fingers pressed to his bleeding neck, Cordelia wiping away the blood with a cloth napkin and forcing it under his hand for him. "For this, you'd lay a hand on me?"

Emir swallowed and set his jaw, determined not to pull away. "For them—yes."

Titus watched him in tense silence for a few seconds, then brushed at Emir's hand so calmly that he released his grip without thinking. He stepped by Emir and paused by the table to scan the two humans with a faint scowl on his lips. Emir waited, ready to come between them if Titus made a move again—but he didn't. He slipped his hands into his pockets, glanced briefly back at Emir, and walked out of the house.

For a few seconds, they all stood in uncertain silence, but Cordelia broke it with a scoffing sigh.

"Well *that* was the hottest fucking thing I've ever seen."

"Are you serious?" Jacob snapped, wincing a bit and pressing the bloody cloth tighter against his neck. "That dude tried to kill me!"

"You just had a *vampire* get in a fight with his maker over you, you unappreciative dipshit," she shot back. She gestured to the damaged cabinets. "The counter is broken! He broke the counter because of you! Jesus," she added more softly, and she went quiet and leaned closer to him. "Is your asshole okay?"

"Cords, for fuck's sake." He looked up at Emir. "Are *you* okay?"

"Wh—me?" Emir bent to gently peel the napkin from Jacob's skin, frowning at the long tears Titus's teeth had left in him. "These are deep," he murmured. "You may need stitches. We should have a doctor look at you."

Jacob shook his head. "If I go to the doctor with this, they're gonna think I got away from the person who's been killing all the *other* people who showed up dead with bite marks."

"I mean, technically, you did," Cordelia pointed out.

"They'll ask questions," Jacob went on, frowning up at Emir. "And nobody here wants me to have to answer questions."

Emir sighed and opened his mouth to object, but Cordelia raised her hand to interrupt.

"I know how to do stitches." Both men turned to stare at her, and she shrugged. "What? That's a normal thing to know how to do. Just chill here. I'll go get my kit."

"Please be careful," Emir said as she picked up her purse. "It wouldn't be beyond Titus to take his anger out on you."

"A girl should be so lucky," she sighed on her way through the living room.

21

Cordelia had to dig in her dresser drawer a bit to find her suture kit, but once she had, she double-checked it still had supplies inside and tucked it into her purse. She knew she ought to hurry, but she couldn't help but take her time on the way back to the car. She wanted to give the two men she'd left behind some time alone—she could picture Emir comforting and tending to Jacob, all soft and remorseful, and the Jacob of her imagination was much more receptive to such attention than the real one was ever likely to be.

They definitely deserved each other.

When she parked the car on the street outside Emir's house and climbed out, she took long steps up the sidewalk toward the porch, but then paused. At the other end of the yard, a man stood underneath one of the large, shadowing trees, just outside the reach of the nearby streetlamp's ring of light. She couldn't make out his features, but his silhouette stood with folded arms, turned partly toward the house as if he was reluctant to let his own body face it. There was only one person it could be.

Cordelia went past the house and stood at the edge of the shadows, feeling more than seeing the man's gaze turn toward her. She clasped her hands behind her back and tilted her head up at him. "You're Titus, right?" He didn't answer, so she kept talking. "You're seriously out here *brooding*, aren't you?"

He gave a small tut of irritation, and she smiled. He *was* brooding.

"I'm Cordelia," she offered. She still got nothing. "You know, you shouldn't be too mad about what happened in there. Jacob is kind of a shit, but Emir is, like, by *far* the worst vampire I know, so they're a really good fit, actually."

He shifted just slightly to look at her head-on. "How many vampires do you know?"

"Two, now," she said with a smile. "You seem much more like it."

"Much more like what?"

"Like...you know. What a vampire is like."

Titus stepped from the darkness to look down at her, the streetlamp casting dramatic shadows on his features and seeming to warm the olive skin she knew would be cold to touch. She clenched her hands tighter together behind her so her shiver wouldn't show. This dramatic, gorgeous, moping asshole. This was *exactly* what a vampire should be like.

"Anyway," she forced herself to say, "I don't think you should be mad about it, is what I'm saying."

"I'm not *mad*," he muttered.

"Really? 'Cause you seemed pretty mad when Emir punched you."

"It isn't any of your—"

"Any of my business?" she finished for him. "Maybe not. But Jacob's my best friend, and I like Emir, so I don't want them to have a pissed off vampire after them. Plus I figure once you see a guy get his ass handed to him, it's the polite thing to do to try to comfort him."

She jerked backward and hit the tree at the edge of the yard, held tight in place by Titus's hand at her jaw. He looked down at her with dark, narrowed eyes, but before she could stop herself, she let out a small laugh.

"Buy a girl a drink first."

Titus paused, his grip on her loosening immediately. "...Aren't you afraid?"

She shrugged a little against the tree. "I can think of worse ways to go."

The vampire hesitated just a moment more, then released her and took a small step back. "You're a strange one."

"I've heard that before," she admitted as she dusted a bit of bark from the back of her dress. "So if you're not mad, what are you?"

Titus looked down at her with a tight frown, then let out a small sigh through his nose and turned his eyes back to the house. "Rejected, I suppose."

Cordelia had to bite her bottom lip to keep from saying something that *would* make him angry. This hot, temperamental vampire was out here brooding in the dark after an argument—because he was *lonely*? Emir was going to owe her a new pair of panties after this.

"Are you in love with him?" she asked, leaning just slightly to get a better look at his face.

"No. But he is...mine. And to be so...blatantly discarded—" He shook his head. "He's always been so malleable before this. A hundred years ago, I would never have dreamed he was capable of that kind of outburst."

"That sounds like a good thing to me," Cordelia shrugged. "Doesn't it to you? He stood up for himself."

Titus's expression seemed to soften just slightly in the dim light. "He did."

"He's a good guy. And Jacob will keep him on his toes; that's for sure. If you care about Emir, you ought to be happy for him—and not let wounded pride ruin the new kind of relationship you *could* have with him."

The vampire turned to her with just the faintest smirk pulling one corner of his lips. "Do you charge hourly for this sort of advice?"

"This one's on the house," she shrugged with a smile. "But if you want a weekly spot on my couch, it's gonna cost you."

"What's the going rate?"

Cordelia gave a pensive hum. "I'm sure we can work out the details."

Titus paused, glanced up the yard at the house, then back to her. "If I try to go back in, do you think he'll be angry at me?"

"Probably ought to wait until I finish stitching up Jacob's neck."

He tilted his head in thought. "Perhaps not."

22

Emir insisted that Jacob go lie down on the couch while they waited for Cordelia to get back, so he did as he was told. He lay staring up at the ceiling, listening to Emir clean up the kitchen and holding a progressively crustier napkin against his neck. Thankfully, the wound wasn't bleeding very much anymore—Titus really had only gotten a second's grip on him. He'd only briefly gotten woozy—it wasn't like when Emir had fed from him at all.

He rolled over on the couch when he heard the door open, but he scrambled up and over the arm in an ungraceful hurry as he spotted Titus, walking in through the front door behind Cordelia as if he belonged.

"What the fuck, Cords?" Jacob snapped, and Emir appeared in the kitchen doorway with a wary scowl already on his face.

"Everybody relax," Cordelia said. "He comes in peace. Don't you?" she added over her shoulder, and Titus spread his hands as if them being empty meant literally anything.

"I want to talk to you, Emir," the vampire said. "And offer you a gift."

"I've had enough of your gifts," Emir answered bitterly.

"You'll want this one." He stepped around Cordelia and approached Emir with steady steps.

Emir held his ground, though he cast a brief, uncertain look in Jacob's direction.

"I want to do something for you," Titus went on. ""As a...congratulations."

"What are you getting at?"

"You hit me in the face," Titus said simply. "*Me.*" He dropped his head for a moment to chuckle. "Upon...reflection," he said with a quick glance over his shoulder at Cordelia that Jacob didn't like one bit, "I realize that's something I ought to be proud of. *You* ought to be proud of. You love this boy?"

Emir frowned, obviously taken aback by the question. "I do," he answered softly.

"Let me turn him for you."

"What?" Jacob half shouted from across the room. "You're fucking joking, right?" Cordelia touched his arm to quiet him, but he kept his eyes on Emir. "No way! This prick's not laying teeth on me again!"

"You *want* him turned, don't you?" Titus continued without even a look toward Jacob. "But you're afraid that he'll feel about you the way you feel about me."

"I—" Emir paused, his brow furrowing even as he seemed to relax just slightly. "Yes."

"I see what's in your heart, old friend, whether you want me there or not," Titus said in a gentler voice. "Let me turn him for you."

Jacob was already vehemently shaking his head when Emir looked over at him.

"It is a solution, Jacob," he said, but Jacob scoffed at him.

"It's a fucked solution. So you want me to be bonded to *this* dickhead instead of you? How does that make any sense?"

Emir approached him, and Cordelia quietly stepped aside to make room. He took Jacob's free hand in both of his own and squeezed them gently. "I want us to be equals in all things. This would make that the case."

Jacob scowled at the floor, but he stopped himself from ripping his hand away. He didn't have any doubt that he wanted to be with Emir—even if it was hard to say out loud. But that meant he had to let Titus bite him on purpose and just *hope* that he kept his word and changed him instead of killing him. He chewed his lip and held tight to Emir's hand.

"Do you think it's the right choice?" he asked quietly, though he knew Titus could hear anyway.

"I might also point out," the vampire across the room spoke up, "that Emir has never done it before, and he's just as likely to succeed as to accidentally drain you."

Emir grimaced faintly as Jacob leaned back from him with a wary frown. "That's...also true," he murmured.

"And as Emir would probably throw himself into traffic if he killed you, which no one wants, best to leave it to the professionals."

"See?" Cordelia said, giving Jacob's arm a light squeeze. "All upsides."

Emir stepped a little closer to him and reached up to stroke his cheek, a too-public show of affection that brought a flush of embarrassment to Jacob's face. "If this is the life you want," he said, "then I think this is the best choice. I believe him—Titus may do a lot of things I don't like, but he wouldn't put on a show like this if he just meant to kill you."

"I am standing right here," Titus pointed out, but only Cordelia looked at him, a restrained smile on her face.

Jacob looked up into Emir's eyes for a long time, hoping to see something there that would make his decision for him one way or the other—but the vampire only watched him with an even stare, as if he was determined not to affect Jacob's conclusion. Jacob snorted and smiled faintly as he turned his head into Emir's touch. That made the decision for him in its own way. Emir would never force him to do anything he didn't want to do. He would never pressure him or talk down to him. He wanted an equal—a companion. And Jacob wanted to be that person for him.

"Okay," Jacob said. He nodded and blushed under the warmth of Emir's smile. "Let's do it."

"First of all," Titus said as Emir urged Jacob to settle on the sofa, "are you from here?"

"What?" Jacob frowned at him. "What does that have to do with anything?"

"The earth," Cordelia answered, speaking before the vampire could get out his own reply. "You need to have the earth of your homeland to rest in. Like Emir does upstairs."

"Oh. Uh. Then yeah. I'm from here."

"Good," Titus said. He approached the couch and put one knee on it, looming uncomfortably close over Jacob. He glanced up at Emir. "If we had an *actual* ghoul, the sleeping situation would be much easier to resolve."

"I know someone who will help, I think. Mikaiel has a grandson in town."

"Generational ghoulery; I like it," Titus chuckled.

Jacob looked between them in confusion. Who was Mikaiel? Emir knew someone else in town? Jacob didn't like the idea of Titus knowing something about Emir that he didn't—though he recognized what a ridiculous thought that was the second he had it. Just forget about it. Emir had chosen Jacob. That was what mattered.

"I'll see if I can have him find something tomorrow," Emir went on. "Do you have an aesthetic preference?" He asked with eyebrows slightly lifted in Jacob's direction.

"For...?"

"Your coffin, idiot," Cordelia sighed.

"Ohh," Jacob said with a nod. "Yeah, no, absolutely never thought about what kind of coffin I want before."

"We can sort the details out later," Emir said gently.

Titus plucked the bloody cloth away from Jacob's neck and tossed it to the coffee table, leaning down with one hand on the back of the couch. "Are you ready?"

"I...fucking guess," he said, taking a deep breath and letting it out in a huff. Cordelia crouched at the arm of the sofa and held his hand, but Emir stood back, holding his own elbows and watching with a subtle frown wrinkling his brow.

"This will hurt," Titus said, a little too cheerful for Jacob's liking, but he didn't get to answer.

The vampire locked onto Jacob's already-wounded neck in the blink of an eye, and Jacob was pressed into the couch beneath him. He barely had time to flinch before his body went slack, but it wasn't the same as before—he wanted to fight this hold, even though he knew he'd asked for it. His fingers only twitched slightly as he struggled to reach up and shove the other man away on instinct. His eyelids drooped, and the edges of his vision began to blur. A chill ran over him, a pulling, peeling sensation underneath his skin that seemed to draw the life from his extremities and up through his chest. It was a slow, drifting sort of death.

When the room faded around him, and he struggled to take even a shallow breath, Jacob was distantly aware of fingers cradling the back of his head. Something warm touched his lips, and his mouth opened automatically, accepting the press of cold skin that flooded his tongue with the taste of copper. He swallowed, and welcome heat flooded back into his body—but this wasn't the same as it had been with Emir, either. This blood was searing, painful as it poured down his throat, and he felt it leaving trails of fire through his veins, from his torso down to his fingertips. Even so, he couldn't pull away. He wanted more. He wanted all.

His heart beat for what felt like the first time in minutes, and the burning flow at his lips was jerked away, out of the fingers he hadn't even realized were gripping skin. He fell back a hundred miles into the sofa cushions, suddenly fighting to breathe. His body tensed and jerked, his skin feeling like it was fully on fire, and he heard himself cry out through ears that seemed stuffed with cotton. His heart was deafening, and every muscle in his body tightened—and then everything went silent.

The hand still holding the back of his head lowered him gently and slipped free, and Jacob lay still. His heart had stopped. He couldn't hear it. He couldn't feel it. He felt the fabric of the cushions under his fingertips, the overhead light stinging through his eyelids, the heat in his body quickly chilling.

Jacob finally opened his eyes in a few slow, squinting blinks, and raised his head. Cordelia was still at his side, Emir near to him with worry in his eyes, and Titus stood by with his own wrist in his mouth, pulling it away briefly to look down at it. Was that where he'd been fed from? Had it been Titus cradling him?

Gross.

Jacob pushed himself a little more upright on the couch and faltered slightly at how easy the movement was. He felt light, somehow—and alive despite the cold stillness in his chest.

"Congratulations," Titus said. "You're dead."

Emir moved to sit beside him and touched his hair and face, watching him with a soft frown. He didn't feel cold anymore—was

Jacob the same now?

"How do you feel?" Emir asked, and Jacob reached up tentative fingers to touch the back of the other man's hand. It was just as soft as always, but it definitely didn't have the same chill—or, at least, Jacob couldn't detect it.

"Kind of...dead," Jacob said with a smile that finally made Emir's shoulders relax. He touched the side of his neck and felt only the faintest imperfection where his bite marks had been. They must have closed up on their own. He felt around his mouth with his tongue, testing the sharpness of the newly grown teeth there.

This wasn't especially different from when he'd been a ghoul— more still, maybe. He noticed the lack of heartbeat more than anything. Jacob didn't know that he'd ever really paid attention to his heart unless he'd been exerting himself, and he certainly had never been able to feel the blood pumping through his body—but he noticed the lack of it now. He frowned and doubled over slightly as a gnawing pain twisted his stomach, and Emir fretted over him briefly before standing.

"You need to eat," he said, already moving into the kitchen.

"You're not serious," Titus called across the room. "You can't feed him dead blood on his first night."

Emir didn't answer; he came back with one of the matte plastic bags and pulled it open, offering it to Jacob as he sat beside him. Jacob took it in both hands and looked down at it. He was used to seeing Emir drink from these now, but having one given to him like a child being passed their dinner was different. He could smell it—dark and heavy and tempting—but something seemed off about it.

Jacob hesitated, bringing the tube straw closer to him but stopping short. Drinking from Emir had been pleasant, he reminded himself. This was what he was meant to have. He swallowed and then brought the tube to his mouth, slowly drawing up his first mouthful of the chilled fluid.

"This is the most depressing thing I've ever seen," Titus said dryly as he brushed at the last bit of blood on his wrist with the cloth from the coffee table.

The blood was thick in Jacob's mouth, and he had to swallow harder than he expected. It didn't have the pleasant burn Emir's blood

179

did, but it was rich and stung a bit like strong cinnamon. It wasn't bad at all. He drained the whole bag so quickly that Emir put a hand on his back as if warning him to slow down, but when it was empty, Jacob still felt a panging inside.

"Is that...all?" Jacob asked uncertainly, glancing sidelong at the man beside him. He hadn't thought to count before how many of these Emir had in a night. But one definitely wasn't going to be enough.

"Oh, shit," Cordelia whispered beside him, and she reached over and turned his face toward her with both hands, pulling down on his cheeks with her thumbs. "Your eyes! That's rad as shit."

Jacob swatted her away and leaned out of her reach.

"I told you," Titus said, but Emir didn't look at him. "A young vampire needs living blood. He'll waste away without it."

Jacob frowned over at Emir. "Is that true?"

"Take him hunting," Titus suggested. He approached the couch and gave Emir's shoulder a light shake. "Show him how."

"I don't want to go *hunting*," Jacob protested.

Titus looked down at him with a furrowed brow. "You really didn't think this whole idea through, did you?"

"I thought it would be fine, with the...you know, the bags! Emir does fine!"

"Emir is old; his body is settled into death. Yours is not. You need the strength fresh blood alone gives."

"Somebody maybe should have mentioned that," Jacob sighed.

"I'm sorry," Emir said. "As Titus said, I...haven't done this before. I didn't realize. Perhaps we could—the boy from the bar." He shot a questioning look up at Titus, who shrugged.

Cordelia stood from her place by the couch and moved to stand in front of them. "I'm full of living blood," she said, drawing three pairs of incredulous eyes. "What? I am. I'm right here. I'm willing."

"No way," Jacob said. "It's...that would be really weird."

"Why?" She put her fists on her hips. "My blood's not good enough for you?"

"But it's, like..." Jacob gestured vaguely toward Emir and himself, not entirely sure what he was trying to convey. "It's really...sexual? I don't want to do that to you. Super weird. And also I've literally never done it before, so what if I go too far, or..."

"Oh my god, you're such a baby." She gave a huff and gently urged Emir out of the way so that she could sit on the couch, then held out her arm to him. "It doesn't have to be *sexual*. Don't be a fuckin' weirdo."

"*You're* telling me not to be a weirdo?"

"No—you know what?" She pulled her arm back and held it to her chest as if he'd already tried to bite it. "I deserve better than this. And you *might* go too far. I like you, but I'd rather not die because you got greedy."

"Thank you," Jacob sighed, but instead of looking at him, Cordelia was on her feet now, tugging lightly at the front of Titus's shirt.

"Show him how," she said.

Titus paused. "...Pardon?"

"If I'm going to get bitten by a vampire, I want my first time to be good. So you go first. Show him how."

"Cords, be real," Jacob said, but she put out a blocking hand to shush him.

"You know what you're doing, don't you? You can stop him before it's too much?" She stared up into the vampire's curious face with much more composure than Jacob thought he'd had in his entire life, her chin jutted forward and one eyebrow slightly raised.

"...I can," Titus agreed after a moment.

Cordelia shook her head, spilling her black curls off of her shoulders and down her back. "So? Make it happen."

"Cordelia," Emir protested softly, but Titus cast him a brief glance that silenced him.

Titus pressed a stabilizing hand at the small of Cordelia's back and brushed the rest of her hair away from her neck as he drew close to her. Jacob wanted to get up and push him, or yell at him, or at least call him a rude name, but something stopped him. Titus wasn't going to hurt her. He felt it in his gut. More importantly—Titus didn't want him to interrupt. That somehow taking precedence over Jacob's own thoughts was not a comfortable feeling. Regardless, Jacob stayed in his place and watched while a vampire pulled his best friend against his body and bent low to her cheek. Was this the bond, the sensation Emir was talking about? What made it so hard for him to question this person?

Jacob saw the black ink seeping over Titus's eyes in the moment before he bit down on Cordelia's throat and tensed in his seat at the soft, hitching cry she gave.

Her arms hung heavy at her sides, and her knees seemed to give, but Titus kept her upright with one hand at her back and the other cupping her jaw to keep her head from falling too far backward. After only a moment or two, he pulled back from her with a trace of red on his lips and eased her carefully down onto the sofa beside Jacob. He turned her head to expose the small wound he'd made and let his hand drift down her arm from her jaw, holding her wrist lightly.

"Just there," he said in a low voice, and Jacob didn't even want to argue when Titus put his free hand in his hair and urged him closer. "Gently. Take what she's giving you."

Cordelia's blood seeped down her neck into the collar of her shirt. The smell was too much—without another thought in his head, Jacob leaned forward and licked away the spilled fluid, then closed his mouth over the wounds. He didn't have to do any work—Cordelia's heart pumped mouthfuls of blood onto his tongue, which he swallowed eagerly. It was even better than drinking from Emir—this was warming and sweet and flowed easily down his throat, like a cup of hot cider. He felt himself inch closer to her and begin to try to draw the blood more quickly into his mouth, but he was immediately forced away by a firm hand on his shoulder.

Jacob fell back against the far arm of the couch, where Emir put an arm around him to keep him still. Titus sat between them with his attention on Cordelia, his thumb running lightly over the inside of her wrist. He leaned in and ran his tongue over the cuts one last time, clearing away another small pooling of blood, then pulled back to look at her face. Jacob couldn't see much of her around Titus's shoulders, but he caught the low sigh she gave.

"I think I'm in love," she murmured with a smile in her voice, and Jacob did not at all like the low, quiet chuckle the words caused in Titus.

"How are you feeling?" Emir asked, touching Jacob's hair and stroking his cheeks like a worried mother.

"I'm...good." Jacob sat up a little straighter and glanced around the room. *This* was more like what he'd expected. Everything around him was just a bit sharper; he heard a car turning a corner outside, made out the water stains on one of Emir's books across the room. He could smell Cordelia's shampoo and even faintly hear her heartbeat—the only one in the room. "I'm really good."

Emir kissed him, and Jacob was, for that second at least, grateful that neither of the others were paying attention to them.

23

They left Cordelia resting in the bed upstairs with a fresh, clean bandage on her neck, and the three of them piled into Emir's car—with Jacob in the back seat like a child, of course. Emir drove them to a house near the edge of town that he seemed to know and parked along the side of the road. He led the way up the driveway to the door and knocked, and they waited an awkward amount of time before he knocked again, a little louder.

The door finally opened, and a skinny young guy in thick square glasses peered out at them. He didn't seem to want to come out from behind the door, so he just poked his face around the corner and scanned all three of them in turn.

"Mr. Arzinjani," he said with a small nod. "Are these. Uh. Friends...? Of yours?"

"Yes. Good evening, David. I'm hoping you can do another favor for me."

He cringed a little. "Look, I'm really grateful to you, for Papik and everything, but I don't think I can do that again."

Jacob leaned forward to frown around Emir's shoulder. "What did you make him do?"

"I—had to know whether the murders were happening because of another vampire or not, but the body had already been buried by the time I went to look, so—"

"You dug up a *body*?"

"Not personally. We can't enter sacred ground like cemeteries. So I asked David to do it."

"Jesus Christ, Emir. That's super illegal."

"That's what I said," David added.

"Well it's done now," Emir sighed. He looked back at David and pressed his hands together as if politely pleading. "There will be no bodies involved this time. You have my word."

He pushed his glasses up his nose and came out from behind the door, though he still glanced warily between Titus and Jacob. Jacob almost wanted to distance himself from the other two, tell this stranger that he wasn't like them, he didn't have to worry—but Jacob *was* like them. He could smell the heat from the man's body and see the subtle movement in the skin at his neck where his pulse beat underneath. Jacob was just as dangerous as the others were, now—well. Maybe not as dangerous as Titus, since Jacob at least still had a conscience, but even so. He was a vampire now. That thought was going to take some getting used to, for sure.

"Then what is it?" David asked.

"This is my friend Jacob," Emir said, reaching back to lay a light hand between his shoulder blades. "He needs a place to rest. But he has no earth, and no resting place."

The man frowned in confusion and glanced briefly at Jacob before returning his furrowed brow back to Emir. "I don't understand."

"He will need a coffin," Emir said simply. "And earth to rest in. From his home—not far from here at all," he clarified. "His childhood home would be best—Jacob's parents live in Hooksett, isn't that right?"

"Uh, yeah," Jacob answered, "but you didn't say anything about having to go to my parents' house. I already don't know how the hell I'm supposed to explain this to them, let alone ask to dig up the yard so I can sleep in their dirt."

"Hence David," Emir explained, gesturing toward the now exceptionally weary-looking young man. "He can go tonight, before dark, and get the earth we need. Tomorrow, he can purchase a coffin for you and bring it to the house. Then you'll be sorted."

"I'm going to get arrested," David sighed. "I'm definitely going to get arrested."

"You're hardly giving him incentive, old friend," Titus pointed out. He turned his gaze on David, who instinctively recoiled slightly. "Your grandfather was a ghoul, wasn't he? Don't you want the same gifts?"

"I don't want another ghoul, Titus," Emir interrupted.

"Not everything is about you." Titus shrugged one shoulder. "My last ghoul met with an unfortunate accident in Naples some time ago. I'm in the market, and this boy comes from good stock."

David crept another inch farther behind the door again. "What kind of accident?"

"It was my own fault, I suppose," Titus admitted. "I'd held onto him for too long. He was too old—brain had become addled. It happens. Poor idiot walked straight out into traffic. Shame—he always kept everything so tidy."

Jacob stared over at Titus with a mixture of disgust and disbelief. "You seem really broken up about it."

"Nothing to be done for it. Humans age—even ghouls." He looked back at David with a faint smirk. "But it doesn't have to be so quickly. Are you interested? I've had my eye on an apartment in London that will need furnishing soon."

"Hold on," David said, holding up a staying hand and taking a half step back from the door. "I don't even know what's happening right now."

Titus stepped forward, the toes of his shoes just shy of crossing the threshold of the house, and he tilted his head as he looked the man in the face. "Let's begin again. I am Titus Lanatus—for the time being, you may call me Sir. The newest member of my family needs a place to rest," he said simply, and Jacob sneered subtly at his word choice. "We will give you Mr. Arzinjani's address, and the address of young Jacob's parents, and you will bring us a crateful of earth from their property. How you do so is not our problem. I will provide you with money, and, in the morning, you will procure a suitable coffin for the boy to sleep in. He can let you know what sort when you bring the earth—which will be before tomorrow night at the very latest. If you perform these tasks well, then I will bind you to me as my ghoul, and you will enjoy all the benefits and convenience of such a state until such point as you wish to return to your human life. During your service to me, I will feed you, clothe you, and house you, and you will do whatever is required of you. I keep my ghouls in good comfort, but in return, I expect unequivocal obedience. Is all of this clear to you?"

"I...yes?" David answered. He hesitated. "So you mean...you'd take me with you? Like, back to Europe?"

"And wherever else I choose," Titus said. "I need someone to handle my day-to-day affairs. Human affairs. Can you do that?"

"I guess I can. Or I can...figure it out."

"Then you agree?"

"I—" He stopped, fidgeting with the door knob, and he looked up at Emir as if hoping for guidance.

"Titus treats his ghouls well," Emir assured him. "And I believe your grandfather had a good life in his time with me. But it's a decision only you can make."

"Will I have to...deal with bodies a lot?"

"Undoubtedly," Titus said. "But I can promise that digging *up* graves will be a rarity."

David stared at the floor for almost a full minute, but Titus just waited patiently, watching him with a placid expression. Finally, David raised his head to Titus and gave a small nod. "Okay."

"Good." Titus took out his phone and entered David's number as he gave it, then texted him both Emir's address and the one Jacob told him, as promised. "The earth will need to be left at Mr. Arzinjani's home until the coffin arrives, so make sure you have a suitable container for it. Here." He took a slim wallet from his pocket and handed David a credit card. "Use this for whatever you need. Do not lose it," he added in a more pointed voice, and the young man nodded quickly. "Text me when the earth has been delivered."

"Okay."

"Yes, sir," Titus corrected, and David frowned faintly up at him.

"Yes, sir."

"I'll hear from you soon, David." Without waiting for confirmation, Titus turned and stepped down from the porch, tilting his head to urge Emir and Jacob to follow. Even though Jacob was pretty sure he still hated Titus and would very happily never see him again, he had to admit that the older vampire knew how to get things done. He was a dick, but he wasn't an idiot.

Jacob turned to look back over his shoulder as he walked behind Titus, but David already had the door closed again. "Well that feels a lot like you just railroaded some guy into being your slave," he grumbled.

"I made the offer very clear, didn't I? He was already familiar with Emir—and his own grandfather was a ghoul. He understands. A ghoul isn't a slave, anyway," Titus added as he opened the passenger door of Emir's car.

"It felt a little like being a slave to me," Jacob said quietly, but he paused and reached out to give Emir's hand a quick squeeze when he caught the guilty look on the other man's face. When Emir softened, Jacob released him and climbed into the back seat again. "So what do I do in the morning, if I don't have anywhere to sleep?"

Emir's cringe was visible in the rearview mirror. That definitely meant Jacob wasn't going to like the answer. "Perhaps," Emir said, "we rushed a bit. We should have gotten this sorted before you turned him," he added with a glance toward Titus.

"In the absence of one's own home earth, that of one's maker will temporarily suffice," Titus said.

Jacob stared at the back of Titus's head, then whipped his gaze over to Emir, who had turned in his seat to frown apologetically at him. "You're saying I have to sleep *with him?*" he half shouted, pointing an accusing finger at Titus.

"It should only be for tonight," Emir said. "But you really should— when you've just been turned, these things are far more important."

"I'm staying at the DoubleTree downtown," Titus said, apparently completely unconcerned with Jacob's objections. "I'll bring him back tomorrow evening, and we can get him settled upstairs with you. I assume that's the plan?"

Emir smiled back at Jacob so warmly that his next protest died before it reached his lips. "I hope so," he said, and Jacob's stomach gave a small flip. It was good to know it could still do that.

"Yeah," he agreed. "With you...sounds good."

Emir stopped the car near the lobby of the hotel, but he turned back and stopped Jacob with a hand on his arm before he could get out the door.

"I'll take care of Cordelia," he promised. "Try not to let Titus...talk you into anything."

"Can't you stay too?" Jacob asked, all too aware of how pathetic he sounded.

"We all have to rest where we must," Emir answered. He pulled Jacob's arm gently to urge him closer and leaned over the back of the seat to kiss him. "I'll see you tomorrow night," he whispered against Jacob's lips. "And every night hereafter."

Jacob wasn't sure if he was imagining the warmth in his chest, or if he still had some left, but he smiled anyway. "Okay. Good night," he said as he scooted toward the door, then paused. "Good...morning, I guess? No, that's weird. Good night."

"Good night, Jacob."

He was reluctant to shut the door behind him, and he regretted it as soon as Emir pulled away and Jacob was left standing alone with Titus. The older vampire walked through the sliding glass doors, clearly trusting that Jacob would follow, and crossed the lobby to the elevators.

The room he opened on the top floor of the hotel was actually an entire suite—which Jacob guessed shouldn't have surprised him. It looked about as nice as any hotel in Jacob's small town could be expected to look, with a flatscreen TV, a leather sofa, and a sliding door open into a bedroom. The only thing that stood out was the fact that the oval ottoman had been shoved off to one side, and in its place, right in the center of the suite's living room, was a stone coffin. It was a tall, rounded rectangle of smooth white marble, each side marked with rows of waving lines expanding from a carving of a lantern. A snarling lion head holding a ring in its jaws jutted from both ends of the long side, each hair of their manes and crease of their noses carefully formed. The lid had been made into the shape of what looked like a lounging sofa, where a nude man draped in a cloth that only covered his most private parts lay peacefully sleeping, one arm folded delicately up over his chest to his shoulder.

Jacob stood and stared at it while Titus laid his wallet and cell phone on the displaced ottoman. He pointed at the statue lazing on the lid and shot Titus a skeptical look. "Is this supposed to be you?"

"Not a bad likeness, is it?"

"Jesus Christ," Jacob sighed. "This is some vampire bullshit."

Titus ticked an eyebrow at him. "Haven't you seen Emir's? Mine doesn't even have any gold on it. You're going to look like you're sleeping in a pine box, lying next to him." He gave a light sigh. "People just don't make coffins the way they used to."

"I'm fine with a pine box. Who cares what it looks like? I didn't have a gold-plated bed frame, either. How did you get this in here, anyway?"

"The porters brought it up."

Jacob frowned at him, then looked at the massive stone box and back to his face. "...Like, the guys who work at the hotel. They carried this in here for you. And nobody asked any questions, like 'why are you bringing a giant sarcophagus in here?'"

"You have a lot to learn," Titus said with a quiet chuckle. "Emir really hasn't been half the vampire he could have been when you were around, has he?"

"I *did* only find out tonight that he can turn into a wolf," Jacob admitted.

"Do you want to go out? We still have some time before dawn." Titus drew close to him and tilted his head to look down at him. "I can show you everything Emir would have you miss."

"He's not going to keep things from me," Jacob argued. "You just want me to go kill someone with you."

"I'm going to kill someone regardless. I need the blood, since I gave a good portion of mine to you."

"But you also took all of mine, so doesn't it...even out?"

Titus watched him, unamused, and blinked slowly at him. "No. It doesn't. You should feed more as well—get your strength up."

"I thought that was the whole point of Cordelia...doing what she did."

"Jacob, Emir would have you tethered—tied by this leash of human morality. He doesn't hunt because he can't be bothered, not because it makes him feel guilty. He's killed more people than you've ever met, in his time."

Jacob put his hands in his pockets and looked away, into the staring eyes of one of the marble lions. "I don't...think I can do that."

"You must," Titus pressed. "Did you think this life was going to be an easy one?"

"A little bit, yeah," he snapped. "Nothing about the way Emir lives seems hard."

"Emir is almost four hundred years old. You are not. You need fresh blood. You need to *feed*."

Jacob hesitated, rocking on his heels for a moment before looking back up into Titus's face. "Does that mean that I *have* to kill people? It doesn't, right?"

"In theory, no," Titus relented. "But how sustainable do you think it is, especially in a city of this size, to leave people half-eaten every night? You would surely draw a great deal of the attention Emir so hates." He leaned close and circled around behind Jacob, their cheeks almost touching as he spoke in a low voice. "But every now and then, a person goes missing. They die of mysterious causes. Such things happen. And you haven't truly been born as a vampire until you've felt a living heart fight for its last beat in your arms, and a once vibrant, breathing body give all of its warmth and life to satisfy your hunger."

Jacob's stomach tightened at the thought, and he felt a strange tug in his chest as he turned his head to meet Titus's dark eyes, so close to his own. "That sounds...good." He stopped himself and backed away in a rush, almost bumping into the sarcophagus behind him. "But I don't—" He shook his head. "I don't *want* to."

Titus straightened. "You can fight what you are, Jacob, but your nature will always win out in the end. Emir knows this, too. You chose this—to choose to only go halfway would do you no good."

"My choices have to mean something," he said. "I can choose to kill or not. I don't care about being strong, or whatever it is you think killing people will make me. I did this so that I can be with Emir. That's all."

"How noble," Titus said dryly. "As you wish. But I'm not leaving you alone tonight, and I need to feed. So you're coming."

Jacob tried to retreat farther from him and found his back against the stone coffin. "So I either kill someone, or I watch *you* kill someone?"

"Not everything is going to be within your control, little one. Let's go." Titus picked up his wallet and phone, plucked a set of keys from the dresser in the bedroom, and walked to the door, bidding Jacob to follow with a simple tilt of his head.

There wasn't any arguing with him.

Titus drove a black two-door sportscar, because of course he did, and he took them to the only bar in town that might have been mistaken for an actual club. Jacob watched curiously out the window as he rode in the passenger seat, squinting into the dark. Everything was so clear—it was like he'd been underwater his whole life, and someone finally handed him a pair of goggles. He made out each leaf in the trees through the darkness and spotted the scrambling of night animals in the underbrush as they passed by patches of woods. Even the movement of the car didn't seem to blur things. The scent of the car's air freshener, which Jacob couldn't see—it may have been thrown out already—was a bit sickening to him, it was so strong. It was like his senses, even compared to when he was a ghoul, had been turned up to eleven.

A small smile found its way onto his lips. He couldn't wait to get back to his books.

"So tell me about your friend," Titus said, snapping him out of his thoughts. "Cordelia, wasn't it?"

Jacob's smile withered into a scowl. "What about her?"

"She's interesting; I'd like to know more about her."

"You'd better not think she's fucking interesting," Jacob said.

"It's very rare to meet a human who isn't put off by what we are—even Emir didn't manage to find one," he added wryly as he glanced sidelong at Jacob. "And she tasted *very* good, didn't she?"

"You—don't even think about how she tastes! You'd better not go anywhere near her after tonight."

Titus parked the car, turned off the ignition, and leaned across the center console until his face was a breath away from Jacob's. "Watch me," he said plainly, and then pushed open the car door and let himself out.

"This fucking asshole," Jacob grumbled, climbing out and kicking the door shut so hard he left a dent in it.

Inside the bar, Titus had no difficulty picking out a target. He was handsome and *capable* of being charming, at least, so it didn't take him long to find a young man on his own who was willing to chat.

Jacob stood nearby at the hightop table, awkwardly holding a half-empty beer Titus had handed him. Jacob had always enjoyed the wheat smell of beer, but now it turned his stomach. He frowned and looked down at his beer, the floor, and around the room rather than watch Titus whisper in this stranger's ear. The music in here was too loud, and the smell of sweat and blood was everywhere. At least it was close enough to morning that the crowd had thinned somewhat, but it didn't help much. Jacob caught himself turning his head and leaning out to follow the passing of a waitress so he could breathe in more of her scent, and he forced his attention back to the table with one hand covering his nose and mouth.

Don't be a creep. Being a vampire doesn't give you permission to be a creep. Get a grip.

Titus had the man's hand under his on the table now, and the stranger was laughing, one finger lifting to brush against the side of the vampire's knuckles. Jacob grimaced and tried to hide it by taking a pretend drink of his beer. This was exactly what he'd thought Emir had been doing—flirting with him, teasing him, drawing him in. Jacob was lucky *his* flirting had been real, he guessed, since this one seemed likely to end in a murder.

There wasn't any point trying to stop it. Jacob didn't like his chances of physically restraining Titus, even if he'd had the desire. He couldn't go against what Titus said. Jacob scowled into another fake sip. Couldn't he? He could have just left—he could have told Titus to fuck himself and gone back to the hotel, or gone back to Emir's and done the best he could sleeping through the day there. But even Emir had said this was best. He might not have if he'd realized Titus was planning to take Jacob out on a murder field trip—but he was here now. And something inside him wouldn't let him fight Titus's wishes too strongly.

He was beginning to understand why Emir hadn't wanted this kind of relationship for the two of them—but having it with someone like this was almost as bad.

Titus's fingertips wrapped slowly around the stranger's wrist, and he brought his knuckles up to his lips with a smirk that made the other man's face go red. Titus pulled him from the table, abandoning their drinks, and led him to the exit, so Jacob set down his beer and followed.

Was he actually about to watch someone get eaten? Witness a murder? Seeing Emir with a dead body in his arms had been painful enough. But as they walked down the street, Titus with an arm around the young man's waist, Jacob didn't feel particularly ill at ease. For a vampire, this was the same thing as getting late night takeout. He cringed at the thought and wiped at his face with both hands. That was a human person—a living person, who was very soon to be not living. Someone who might have been in one of Jacob's classes. Who had a family, friends, probably a job and ambitions and hobbies. And Titus was about to kill him.

So why didn't Jacob care very much?

Once they were around the end of the block from the bar, Titus led the man across the street and into the park, walking at an idle pace through the paths underneath the trees.

Nobody had told this guy about all the murders happening in town lately, Jacob guessed.

Titus finally stopped when he reached a small cluster of trees that blocked out most of the light from the surrounding streets, and in a second, he had the young man pinned against one of the trunks and his mouth on his throat. Jacob stood back, glancing briefly around for passers-by, but his gaze was drawn back to the two men in the dark. The man didn't even seem to be suffering—he was held up against the tree by the press of Titus's body, his head fallen to the side, eyes half open and lips parted. Was this how Jacob had looked? Still, tranquil— almost blissful?

Jacob wet his lips as the drifting scent of spilling blood reached him, but he held his ground. Then Titus lifted his head and turned back to look at him with a smear of blood at the corner of his mouth, his hand moving down the man's arm to his wrist and lifting it in gentle fingers.

"Come share, little one," he whispered, but Jacob heard him as clearly as if he'd shouted.

Jacob's legs moved on their own. He stepped close to the slumping man and took his offered arm in both hands. He hesitated, but the hollow feeling in his stomach brought the still warm skin to his lips, and he sunk his new teeth into the inside of the man's wrist. He let the hot, spiced liquid flow down his throat with each heartbeat, unable to fight the small groan that slipped from him. He'd never tasted anything he wanted more.

The stranger's heart seemed to slow; Jacob could feel it pulsing more faintly underneath his skin. He fought the pull inside him telling him to finish it, to take every drop this man had and swallow it down—but even after he forced himself to pull back, dropped the man's arm reluctantly from his grip, and blinked away the haze in his vision, Titus remained. He still had his victim's throat under his teeth, and only when the man's knees seemed to give out completely did he break free, dropping the ragdoll body to the grass. He wiped at the edge of his mouth with the pad of his thumb and licked away the blood there, then turned his eyes on Jacob.

"Good boy."

Jacob stepped backward, holding his elbows in his hands. "I didn't...mean to—"

"I told you. Your nature will always win out. At least let me bear the weight of this death for you. But I'm glad you fed."

Titus started to walk away, back down the path and toward the street, so Jacob followed, though he glanced back over his shoulder at the abandoned corpse. Was Emir going to be angry at him? He'd warned Jacob not to let Titus talk him into anything, and now—

"Dawn is coming," Titus said. "We need to get you to rest." He put a light hand on Jacob's back and urged him to take quick steps back to the car, and Jacob followed in a daze.

He felt warm. And the man they'd left dead in the park didn't bother him nearly as much as it should have.

Back in the hotel room, Titus pushed the lid from his sarcophagus to the side and gestured to Jacob to come closer.

"We really gotta do this?" Jacob asked as he reluctantly moved closer. "It's...a tight fit in there."

"You will sleep too deeply to notice."

Jacob stood at the edge of the stone coffin and peered into the dark soil for a few seconds, then let out a sigh and lifted himself over the edge. He sat on the dirt, feeling it under the palms of his hands, and then laid down when Titus swatted at his shoulder. The other man climbed in after him, and Jacob scooted back against the side wall to put as much space between them as possible—but it wasn't much. Titus reached up to slide the lid closed again, sealing them in total darkness, and together they settled into the soil. It was more comfortable than Jacob expected; it seemed to give under him like it was accepting his weight. But Titus was still so close that he could feel the other man's body tight against him.

"Yeah, I definitely notice this," he muttered, voice echoing slightly in the enclosed space.

"Hush," Titus scolded, so Jacob gave one final grumping huff and shut his eyes.

24

Emir planned to stay awake until Cordelia rose. He stayed beside her, sitting up on the bed with his book and hoping it would distract him from the worry in his gut. He didn't like leaving Jacob alone with Titus. But it had already been very late when Emir had dropped them off—hopefully they'd just settled in and gone to sleep.

David arrived just past dawn, covered in dirt and with a large plastic storage bin filled to the brim with grassy earth. Emir took it from him and carried it upstairs, placing it carefully on the floor beside his own resting place.

"Jacob's parents didn't give you any trouble?" he asked, brushing a bit of soil from his hands as he came back downstairs.

"All the lights were out already when I got there. I think one of the neighbors might have seen me on the way out, but I had a hoodie on, so they probably didn't get a good look at me."

"Good," Emir said with a smile of relief. "With luck, they'll just think it was a strange act of vandalism."

"Here's the next problem, though." David wiped his hands on his jeans and took a second to breathe. "I...don't know where to get a coffin."

Emir paused, frowning. He didn't, either.

"I tried Googling it," David shrugged, "and I found a lot of websites, but I thought this might need to be quicker than that?"

"You can get them at Costco," Cordelia's voice drifted down from the stairs, and both men turned to look at her. She had one hand on the railing and the other rubbing at her eyes. "I wanna go. No offense, but I don't want a stranger picking out Jacob's casket. Hi," she added with a sleepy smile and a wave. "I'm Cordelia."

"David," the boy answered. He tilted his head slightly as if to get a better look at her bandage, then peeked back at Emir.

"She's human," he explained. "But a friend."

"Oh. Okay. Cool. Uh, yeah. I was gonna go home and change first, but if you want to—"

"I'll come now. I don't mind waiting." She started across the room and scooped her purse up from the floor by the couch, but paused when she reached Emir. "Thanks for sitting up with me. Get some rest; I'll help take care of the shopping." She put a hand on his shoulder to urge him down a bit and stood on tiptoe to kiss his cheek. Then she waved at him and flitted out the front door, leaving David to hurry after her.

Emir went back upstairs and sat at the edge of his sarcophagus, looking down through the transparent plastic at the soil that Jacob would rest in every night after this. Right here. Just beside him. He smiled as he turned to push open the lid of his own bed and climbed inside.

——

It was barely nightfall when Emir awoke. He bathed and dressed in a hurry, then returned to the room at the end of the hall. Jacob would need space. Emir took a moment to scan the size of the room, but he paused when he laid hands on his sarcophagus to move it. It was a bit like choosing which side of the bed to sleep on—he ought to let Jacob decide.

He went downstairs instead and circled the living room a few times, seeking an output for his anxious energy. Had Titus taken care of him? Had he been obnoxious? Had *Jacob* been obnoxious? Either seemed likely, or perhaps both.

Before long, Emir's phone chimed, and he checked the message from Jacob.

On our way to you. You owe me for making me share a coffin with this dick.

Emir smiled despite the anger in the text. At least he'd made it through the night in one piece.

Cordelia called soon after to let him know David had a casket in the back of his truck and promised they would bring it soon. Emir forced himself to sit on the sofa and wait, but he wasn't able to focus on his book. Jacob would be back soon—and he would stay. Maybe Titus would even leave soon. Then it could be just the two of them again. And Emir wouldn't have to worry about hurting Jacob anymore.

When Titus and Jacob arrived, it was difficult for Emir not to take the boy in his arms right away, but he knew it wouldn't be appreciated with company around. He settled for laying his hands on Jacob's shoulders instead.

"Are you well? How did your morning go? Did you sleep all right?"

Jacob faintly grimaced, and Emir smiled. He would miss how easily the boy used to blush—but it was a small price to pay for a new life together.

"I'm fine," Jacob promised. "Tight sleeping quarters, but it wasn't bad."

"Titus was kind to you?"

"I am *right here*," Titus cut in, but Emir ignored him.

"He was fine."

"Jacob did well for this first night," Titus continued. "But he could do with a bit less conscience. Congratulations, Emir," he said with a dismissive wave of one hand, "you've managed to find someone just as boring as you."

Emir looked back at Jacob with a furrowed brow. "Did something happen requiring little conscience?"

"We went out," Jacob admitted. "And Titus picked someone up. I...I didn't kill anybody," he added quietly, but he didn't have to finish the thought for Emir to fill in the blanks of his story. He knew how Titus could be—and he knew the influence he would have over a newly-turned vampire of his own.

"It's good for you to have fresh blood when you're young," Emir told him softly, smiling as Jacob looked up into his eyes. "And try not to let it worry you too much. It is what we are."

"It *didn't* worry me. It worried me how much it didn't worry me."

"A vampire is a predator," Titus said, approaching them to stand by

Emir. "And a predator must eat. It's a waste of time to concern yourself with the welfare of your food. You ate meat when you were human, yes?"

"...Yeah," Jacob said with a frown.

"This is no different. How many animals died for your meals before this?"

"I think there's a pretty big difference between eating a *person* and eating, like, a chicken."

"Even so," Emir interrupted with a pointed sidelong glance at Titus, "just as a human can decide to be a vegetarian, so we have the luxury of donated blood. You don't have to hurt anyone if you don't want to."

Jacob seemed hesitant, but he nodded. All three of them turned to look toward the door as the sound of a truck engine drew close to the house, but Emir moved first. Even in the short time it took him to open the front door, David and Cordelia had begun to haul a large box out of the bed of the pickup. Emir helped them to carry it inside and lay it down in the living room.

"Is this...?" Jacob asked, and Cordelia beamed at him.

"You're gonna love it." She and David pulled apart the box, and she brushed away the packaging inside to reveal a glossy black surface. The tapered hexagon was edge in silver, and its polished silver handles were carved into thick filigree at their base.

Jacob stood looking at it for a few seconds, then smiled and gave a soft laugh that warmed Emir's heart. "Yeah," he said, "this looks like something you picked out for me."

"But you love it, right?" she prodded, leaning close to him to nudge him with her shoulder.

He nodded. "It's great. Thanks, Cords."

Emir and Jacob carried the coffin upstairs, and Emir stopped him at the door at the end of the hall.

"I wasn't sure...which side you wanted," he said, and Jacob looked at him curiously. Then he smiled and stepped around the waiting coffin to pull Emir down into a kiss.

"You're ridiculous," he murmured. He tried to pull away, but Emir kept him close with an arm around his waist and kissed him again.

When Jacob finally pulled free, he and Emir pushed the stone sarcophagus to the left side of the room—after Jacob assured him he cared not even a little bit which side his coffin was on. They laid the sleek black coffin in its place next to Emir's and opened the lid, and together they filled the inside with the soil David had brought the night before. Then Jacob shut the lid and moved back a step to look down at the place he'd be sleeping for the rest of his days.

"Is it...all right?" Emir asked softly. "I know it's a big change, and the decision was made so quickly, it must seem very sudden—"

"I dig it," Jacob interrupted him. He reached over and laced his fingers between Emir's. "I'm just glad we have a bed, too."

"A—oh. Yes," Emir agreed, lowering his eyes as he laughed quietly.

"Can we go kick everyone else out now?"

"Yes," he answered in a sigh, and he let Jacob's hand slip from his own as they made their way back downstairs.

The box the coffin was packed in had been cleared away, and David sat awkwardly at one end of the sofa, as far as possible from where Cordelia was lounging against the opposite arm with Titus leaned over her, one arm half circling her along the back of the cushions. The girl had a sly smile on her face, and her fingers were twisting in her hair as she tilted her head back to look up at the vampire. Jacob bristled immediately and stalked across the room to them.

"So thanks bunches, Cords; we're all set up here," he said loudly. "I'm sure everybody has tons to do, so probably best to fuck off and go do those things, right? Far away from each other?"

"Yeah," Cordelia agreed without taking her eyes from Titus's face. "Busy night."

"It could be," the vampire agreed in a low voice, and David looked up over his shoulder at Emir as if asking for mercy.

"They've been like this the whole time," he whispered.

Emir sighed. "Titus," he called over the top of Jacob's imminent explosion, "you aren't planning to stay in town, are you? You must be getting bored of it by now."

"I made an agreement with David," Titus said, finally straightening and putting an acceptable distance between Cordelia and himself to look over at the young man. "We'll both be moving on." He glanced at

Emir. "I won't interfere with your honeymoon," he added dryly.

"Listen, you—" Jacob began, but Emir hurried over to him and wrapped an arm around him, placing a hand firmly over his mouth.

"What Jacob *means* is thank you, Titus," he said. He paused once Jacob gave up squirming, and he nodded to the other vampire with a faint, sincere smile. "Thank you."

"Who am I to stand in the way of the two dullest immortals on the planet being dull together for eternity?" Titus turned to face them and peeled Emir's hand away, then gave Jacob's cheek a soft pat. "Behave yourself, little one. I expect a good report the next time I visit."

"Yeah, see you never," Jacob spat, swatting angrily at the other man's touch.

"At least he has *some* bite. Come along, David—much to do." He tilted his head toward the door, and David obediently followed him out.

Cordelia lingered just long enough to gather up her purse, then took a step backward. "I'm gonna go too," she said, glancing briefly over her shoulder. "I'm sure you guys want to be alone. Have fun, and don't worry about the apartment; I'll tell my parents you found your own place and you can come get your stuff whenever, okay? Just not tonight. You wouldn't come over tonight anyway, right? Settle in. Have fun. I'll talk to you soon, okay?" She offered them a quick wave and hurried out of the house, leaving Jacob and Emir alone at last.

Jacob let out a long, heaving sigh. "She's gonna fuck him; I know she is."

Emir blinked down at him. "Pardon?"

"Titus. She's gonna fuck him."

"Oh. ...Oh dear." Emir put a hand on Jacob's back and leaned around him to look him in the face. "Well, she's...a grown woman."

"Sure," Jacob grumped.

Emir moved his hand up to the short hair at the back of Jacob's neck and urged him to lift his head. "I'm happy you're here," he said gently, and Jacob softened.

"Me too."

They spent some of the night cleaning up the house—Jacob didn't mind having a lot of books around, but he did object to having to dodge them just to get through a room. They set aside a number of them to donate to a used bookstore and organized the side room's piles, and Jacob vowed to arrange for more bookshelves.

He didn't seem bothered by drinking from one of Emir's bags tonight—that was a relief. It would be easier for him if he could carry on without the urge to hunt. They sat on the couch together, Jacob nestled snugly under Emir's arm, and watched a documentary about people who thought the Earth was flat. Emir felt warmer than his body should have allowed. He let his nose brush through Jacob's soft hair and inhaled the familiar scent of him. Jacob craned his neck to look up at him.

"Are you smelling me, you weirdo?"

"I love you," Emir said in place of an answer, and Jacob turned away from him again in embarrassment. He mumbled something incomprehensible, so Emir bent down and touched a kiss to the boy's cheek. "What was that?" he whispered.

Jacob shifted grumpily on the couch and wouldn't look at him. "Love you too," he forced out in a rush.

"Sorry—say again?" Emir teased. He brushed Jacob's cheek with his thumb and kissed the edge of his mouth. "I couldn't hear."

"You're an asshole."

Emir smiled and turned Jacob's head to place a single soft kiss on his lips. "I don't believe that's what you said."

"I said—that I love you," he half mumbled, so Emir kissed him again, shifting to urge him down onto the couch cushions and giving his upper lip a slow, purposeful lick.

"Still can't hear you."

Jacob shivered underneath him, and his hands clutched the front of Emir's shirt despite the frowning look on his face. He pulled Emir down into a long kiss, then forced him away an inch or two and looked up into his eyes. "I said I love you—asshole," he added,

but Emir was smiling.

"Do you feel at home here, Jacob?"

The boy paused. "...Sort of," he answered softly. "It's still weird to think about living here full time, but...I'm looking forward to it."

"Good." Emir cupped Jacob's cheek and leaned over him to kiss his forehead. "I'll do everything in my power to make sure you're happy here with me."

Jacob looked up at him with a warm smile, then glanced down at where his fingers fidgeted with Emir's shirt buttons. "Would you do something for me right now?"

"Of course, sevgilim."

"Would you show me how to turn into a wolf?"

Emir laughed and touched his forehead to Jacob's. "Yes. I will try."

EPILOGUE

They'd been meaning to get the headboard fixed. Jacob had accidentally knocked his hand into it too hard over a month ago and taken a chunk out of the top, and now he hissed in irritation as he grabbed hold of it in just the wrong place and the sharp edge dug into his hand.

"Are you all right?" Emir asked from underneath him, but Jacob shook his head.

"Fine," he said, shifting his grip so he could better steady himself where he straddled the other man's hips. Emir was happy to help keep him balanced with firm hands on his waist, and both men groaned in satisfaction as Jacob sunk down onto him. Jacob swore, his breath hitching as he gave himself a moment to adjust to the now-familiar sensation of the other man filling him. It didn't take long—he began to move, rocking his hips and keeping himself upright with one hand on the headboard and the other on Emir's chest.

Emir was always gentle with him; he always held him securely and kissed him softly and whispered in his ear—it was nice, but sometimes Jacob had to take matters into his own hands. Emir never complained.

Jacob was beginning to lose his composure from Emir's expert hand stroking him in time with his rocking thrusts, and he sucked in a breath as his stomach tightened—but then the front door downstairs swung open with a click and a high-pitched creak. Both of them froze, momentarily startled into doing nothing except looking at each other in panic, but then Jacob hauled himself off of the other man's lap, flinching slightly at the hasty exit. Jacob slid on his shorts and t-shirt as quickly as he could, tucking his hard dick up into his waistband and doing very little to hide it. Emir pulled on his robe and was already tying it around his waist on the way out of the bedroom.

Jacob was ready to frighten some burglars, but when he reached the bottom of the stairs with Emir, an even more unwelcome intruder was standing in the living room.

"Gentlemen," Titus said with a sly smile on his face as he opened his arms in greeting, "have I come at a bad time?"

"Yeah—I'm still alive," Jacob muttered, but Emir turned his head to gently shush him.

"I didn't know you were going to be in town," Emir offered, much more hospitably than Jacob liked.

"I wasn't planning to be. I was told to be."

Jacob frowned around Emir's shoulder in confusion, but then Titus reached a hand back toward the door. It was taken by slender fingers, and Cordelia appeared around the small entryway corner, smiling up at them as she allowed Titus to lift her knuckles to his lips for a brief kiss. Jacob's eyes narrowed, then widened as realization hit him—she wasn't human anymore. The smell was all wrong. There were no heartbeats in this room.

"What. The fuck." Jacob half pushed Emir out of the way so he could cross the room. "Cords—you told me you were taking the year off from school to go backpacking."

"I did!" she protested with mock offense, then laughed. "I never said who I was traveling *with*."

"Are you for fucking real? *This guy?*"

"Yeah, *this guy*," she agreed, smiling and leaning her head back against Titus's shoulder as he drew her hand around his neck and bent to kiss her cheek.

"And you're not worried about the being bound to him thing. Having to do whatever he tells you?"

Cordelia flicked a teasing glance over at the smirking vampire beside her. "I like it when he bosses me around."

"Fuck, I'm gonna throw up," Jacob mumbled, turning away from them and throwing Emir a pleading look. "Can vampires throw up?"

"I...wouldn't recommend it," Emir said gently.

"Are you done?" Cordelia asked. She pulled away from Titus to prod Jacob in the back of his shoulder until he turned around. "If you actually ever looked at any social media, this wouldn't be such a shock, you know."

"What are you doing back here then, if you're having so much fun?"

"Uh, I missed you, you piece of shit?" She laughed as Jacob finally cracked a smile. "You should come with us—Titus's apartment in London is the absolute tits."

"Summer's ending soon," Jacob protested, though the slight purse in Cordelia's lips told him his temptation was showing. He couldn't say he didn't want to see Europe. But doing it with Titus would be the worst. "I have a couple of potential positions lined up at the university for fall semester."

"You're still getting a job? Does the university hire vampires?"

"Well obviously I'm not going to tell them that part, Cords."

She laughed. "Just be the creepy TA in the ballcap and sunglasses every day? Or do you only teach night classes?"

"I wouldn't have bothered finishing school if I didn't like the subject. I don't want to just quit."

"Jacob was very dedicated to his classes," Emir added, and Jacob frowned a little in embarrassment.

"Yeah, well—I'd gone through a lot to pay for the tuition," he grumbled, not looking at Emir's gentle smile. "I can at least work there until it starts to get suspicious that I still look twenty-five."

"Well, I guess I admire your work ethic," Cordelia said with a sigh. "But you've talked before about wanting to see London. Prague. They were both great—you'll love them. And you can get a job whenever, right? It's not like you have to worry about being unemployed, with your infinite-money boyfriend."

Jacob gave a noncommittal grunt and scratched his fingers through his hair. Emir touched a light hand to his back to draw his attention.

"I'll go," Emir said, "if you want to go."

"But *you* don't want to go," Jacob countered. "Weren't you always complaining about all the traveling and partying you did before?"

Emir's faint smile softened. "I...don't want you to come to resent the life I've chosen. I'm happy to live here in solitude because I've *done* my traveling. You haven't. You ought to see all of the world that you wish to see. We have the time," he added warmly.

Jacob frowned up at him, glad once again that he wasn't able to visibly blush anymore. "...Okay," he agreed, keeping his eyes on Emir through Cordelia's cheer of victory. "But—I want to go to Istanbul. I want you to...show me your home. Then I want to come back to our new one."

Emir smiled at him and pulled him close by the back of the neck to kiss his lover's hair, and Jacob didn't even squirm. "Of course."

"Now *I'm* going to throw up," Titus sighed.

ABOUT THE AUTHOR

T.S. Barnett is the author of The Beast of Birmingham werewolf thriller series, steampunk horror romance A Soul's Worth, dark urban fantasy series The Left-Hand Path, and a number of m/m paranormal romances.

Tess likes to write about what makes people tick, whether that's deeply-rooted emotional issues, childhood trauma, or just plain hedonism. Throw in a heaping helping of action and violence, a sprinkling of steamy bits, and a whisper of wit (with alliteration optional but preferred), and you have her idea of a perfect novel. She believes in telling stories about real people who live in less-real worlds full of werewolves, witches, demons, vampires, and the occasional alien.

Born and bred in the South, Tess started writing young, but began writing real novels while working full time as a legal secretary. When she's not writing, she reads other people's books, plays video games, watches movies, and spends time with her husband and daughter. She hopes her daughter grows into a woman who knows what she wants, grabs it, and gets into significantly less trouble than the women in her mother's novels.

www.hisprincelydelicates.com

www.ingramcontent.com/pod-product-compliance
Lightning Source LLC
Chambersburg PA
CBHW031409250626
47155CB00004B/1477